*The Lur*

# The Lure of Satyria

## CHERYL MILDENHALL

Black Lace novels are sexual fantasies.
In real life, make sure you practise safe sex.

First published in 1995 by
Black Lace
332 Ladbroke Grove
London
W10 5AH

Copyright © Cheryl Mildenhall 1995

Typeset by CentraCet Limited, Cambridge
Printed and bound by Cox & Wyman Ltd, Reading,
Berks

ISBN 0 352 32994 7

# Chapter One

The protuberance that thrust upwards from the flat-topped rock was smooth and thick and just the right size. Hedra gave a frustrated groan and ground her pelvis even harder upon it; her movements becoming frantic as the heat between her thighs spread and grew. Her breath was coming in short, sharp gasps.

She was nearly there. Very, nearly, there . . .

'Yes!' she screamed out, the cry of release bursting from her lips and echoing in ebbing waves around the thick walls of the grotto as her muscles spasmed in harmony. The violent exclamation was of no consequence; there was no one to hear her pleasure. Nobody ever came near enough to this enchanted place. Indeed, she doubted that anyone else knew of its existence but herself.

It was just as well. The majority of Parsimonia's inhabitants would be shocked to the very core to learn that Princess Hedra – daughter of their beloved King Hector, the purest of all men – habitually visited a deserted cave so that she could sit astride a rock and assuage her undiminishing desire on a long, fat, phallus-shaped stone. Her Pleasure Stone.

The last tremors of her zenith were abating and now she smiled to herself and luxuriated in the afterglow.

The tender flesh that still gripped the protuberance cooled and calmed down to a simmer as she kicked her feet backwards and forwards in the sparkling water that surrounded the rock. The agitation of her limbs cast a fine spray over her, the diamond droplets clinging to her naked body.

The grotto really was a beautiful place. Not dank and cloistered like any of the hundreds of normal caverns that occupied her land but capacious and airy, with a high ceiling. She glanced around at the glittering chips of semi-precious stones and valuable gemstones embedded in the surrounding rock, delighting, as always, at the way they cast a rainbow of colour around her each time a ray of sunlight permeated the shadowy interior.

And everywhere she looked she could see her reflection, the vision repeated over and over again in the smooth, glassy walls.

Turning her head this way and that she eyed her own image with pleasure. Without the benefit of false modesty, she saw herself as others saw her: tall, proud, strong and straight-backed as always as she sat on the rock. A satisfied smile spread across her heart-shaped face and, as she flicked her finely toned limbs backwards and forwards again, she concentrated on staring straight ahead into her own dove-grey eyes.

Due rather more to her innate self-confidence than to her royal ancestry, her head was habitually held erect and her shoulders down – the assertive stance forcing her proud, full breasts to jut out in front of her like an offering, their succulent rosy tips tilted upward. She glanced down at herself and sighed with an erotic frisson of pleasure as she brought her delicate, long-fingered hands slowly and lingeringly up the sides of her body to cup the luscious globes – a generous handful in anybody's estimation. They gave her immense pleasure, her breasts. The nipples were large and particularly sensitive, full teats surrounded by perfect circles of pink-brown skin that contrasted so nicely with the milky white flesh of the rest of her body. Ah, yes, the rest of her body.

With a definite smile once again curving her full, red lips, she glanced over her shoulder like a coquette, entrancing herself. What a shape she had. So perfectly sinuous, like a sandglass, her tiny waist having a span no greater than the length of a young salamander, her hips flaring tantalisingly outward then tapering to strong, slender thighs.

She turned her head further, looking behind with difficulty. It did not matter. She already knew from the appreciative comments of others that the long, smooth sweep of her slender back was deliciously curtailed by the twin moons of her buttocks.

Now there was a banquet to behold.

Her smile became more pronounced as she relished the pleasure her own bottom gave her. Its dimensions and resilience were perfect. High, rounded buttocks that quivered tantalisingly under the erotic caress of a smacking palm. Mmm. She shivered inside, then wrapped her arms around her body and hugged herself with delight. It had been a long time since anyone had shown the temerity to spank her. What a shame. There was nothing quite like it.

She closed her huge, thickly lashed eyes momentarily, relishing the memory. Then she opened them wide and stared at her image once again. She hadn't yet congratulated herself on her crowning glory, the sight that made people stop in their tracks and stare as she went past. Throwing her head right forward and then back, she glowed with self-approval as she watched her dusky violet hair fall around her shoulders in continuous silky waves that rippled down her naked body, the ends trailing the rock on which she sat.

There was no doubt about it, she thought to herself, I am every inch a fairy princess.

Unfortunately, the place where she was forced to reside was no fairytale land.

Parsimonia, as its very name suggests, was the most

3

dull and boring of all the Fantastic Lands. And there were indeed many. With its over-zealous attention to a frugal, almost saintly way of life, it was not the place for a spirited and lubricious girl like Hedra. How could she indulge her many lusty desires in a country where sin was reviled and purity revered?

By the mystics, if she had not had the occasional luck to chance upon the odd traveller from another land her licentious heart would still be residing in the body of an innocent! Now there would be a sorry state of affairs. It was bad enough that visitors to Parsimonia were few and far between and she was thus forced to resort to daily visits to the grotto to avail herself of her Pleasure Stone. But to have never experienced the body of another . . . now that would be the greatest horror of all.

Outside the grotto, she could see that the great trio of moons had risen in the sky and a blanket of grey evenfall had already started to descend over the distant mountains, telling her that the darkness would soon catch up with her. And around the mouth of the cave, a flock of great crested sharls wheeled and cried. They were hungry, their eyes protruding on stalks to enable them to perceive their prey as it scurried across the red earth. Hedra nodded sagely to herself at all these indications. There was no doubt in her mind it was time to return to the castle.

Easing herself reluctantly from the stone, she rose to her feet and stretched her stiff body. Her pleasure bud had ceased to pulse and now she was left with a feeling of great languor. She would like to sleep for a little while but the late hour and her location made that impossible. Instead she waded through the calf-deep water which had been warmed to bathing temperature by many hours under the first and second suns, exited the mouth of the grotto and stepped up onto the mossy bank. To the sensitive soles of her feet it was like treading on the most luxurious green velvet and she smiled yet again at this added pleasure. The

4

sensuous experience was an apt finale to her visit to the grotto.

As she bent to pick up her discarded robe she disturbed a young stubby, its tiny green feet carrying its round furry body away from her at great speed, its tail slithering from side to side behind it like an earthworm. Seeing it, she jumped in surprise then laughed aloud at the sight. Hedra loved nature with a passion. In her view, living things were metamorphosised in the Fantastic Lands for only one purpose, to give each other pleasure. If that was not the reason, then what was the point of anything?

At this philosophical thought she frowned. And, as she tied her pale blue silken robe around herself with a plaited belt of larvie hair, the delicate fabric clinging like a lover's embrace to the damp, naked flesh beneath, she considered her father's kingdom and its subjects. The average Parsimonian wouldn't know pleasure if it bit him, or her, or it. By all the deeds of her forefathers, she had to get out of there while she was still young enough to appreciate the physical delights of others.

It wasn't the first time she had allowed her mind to dwell on such thoughts and as she advanced toward the age of twenty she thought of little else.

All at once her musings were disturbed by the insistent whinnying of her unicorn, Vanora. Glancing up in surprise at the urgent sounds, Hedra turned and began to walk toward the anxious beast, her mouth emitting encouraging words as she drew nearer to the most precious friend, apart from her father, she had. 'There, now, my beauty. Your mistress is coming. There now, what a pretty girl you are . . .'

Vanora was tethered to a low, gnarled branch of a barbol tree. A white leather bridle and rein encrusted with emeralds and rubies were the only adornment to her natural beauty and, as the young princess reached the unicorn's side, she smiled fondly and began to stroke her hand rhythmically along the warm, undulating body. Underneath her palm, Hedra fancied she

5

could detect the creature's rapid heartbeat, the pace quickening as Hedra moved her other hand to slide over the unicorn's brow and along the hard, ridged cone of her horn.

'You like that don't you, my beauty – you love your mistress Hedra?' As Hedra spoke, the great white beast whickered softly in response, her long, pink-lashed eyelids almost closing under the blissful sensation of her mistress's caress.

Climbing onto a low stone and gripping Vanora's glossy blond mane in her left hand, Hedra mounted her steed, hitching up her long skirt so that she could sit astride her and ride bareback as usual. The sensation of Vanora's warm body beneath her naked pleasure parts and buttocks gave Hedra a glow of her own and, as she rode across the flat red plain that separated the grotto from the castle, she delighted in the way her sore, slightly abused flesh was stimulated and punished by the rolling friction of the ride.

She arrived back at the castle looking more than a little dishevelled and feeling decidedly aroused once again. The grotto always seemed much closer during the journey there, before the onset of pleasure, than on her return. And yet the glory of reaching her zenith was already little more than a distant memory.

As soon as she reached the other side of the wide drawbridge, its ancient boards crumbling at the edges and slippery with moss, and rode into the castle's inner compound, she realised something was amiss. Straight-away her eyes took in the familiar scene, whilst her sixth sense fought to adjust to the strange overtones that appeared to pervade her home.

The high grey stone walls of the four round towers usually cast their shade down upon the cobble-stones below like long grey-sleeved arms reaching down to her. Every other evenfall she had felt the arms were there to enfold her, to protect her. But at that moment they appeared threatening, as though they intended to rain down blows upon her and drive the breath from her body.

This is not right, she found herself thinking with growing panic, things are not right here at all.

She glanced around, her eyes wary, her whole body alert to the atmosphere that encircled her. Being the hub of the castle, the central courtyard normally teemed with life and spectacle, yet right at that moment it was deserted and eerily silent.

Where were the worker-women in their coarse sack-cloth dresses and aprons, the simple garments dusty and stained to a patchwork of dirty hues, who normally swept the stones with brooms of twigs, or plucked at chickens, some of which still struggled upon their laps? And what had happened to the vendors? Again mostly hardy country women whose thick, fleshy arms were tanned dark brown like well-roasted hams. And who had muscles strong enough to support the heavy wicker baskets and creels laden with fruit and vegetables, or the delicious, sugared sweetmeats that Hedra could never resist.

Most disturbing of all, she realised, there were no children at play. No scruffy, cheerful village urchins with their impish grins that shone out from grubby faces. No tiny bodies, full of life, skipping or dancing around the ornate, lichen-covered fountain, or running to and fro in frenzied games of tag. No laughter. No squeals of delight. No fun.

The innocent scenes which, on every other day of her adult life, had either irked her or gone unnoticed entirely, were now acutely missed. She glanced around, her stomach knotting tighter and tighter with increasing distress. She hadn't been particularly fond of the old Parsimonia but she cared for this desolate version even less.

Just as she dismounted from Vanora a young female courtier came running up to greet her, the front of her full-skirted brown silk dress caught up in her fists and her slippered feet sending up small clouds of dust as

7

she sprinted across the cobbles. By her whole demeanour, Hedra could tell she was obviously agitated about something and her own heart pounded as an echo of the girl's distress.

'Mistress. Oh, mistress!' the girl cried. 'Thank goodness you have returned at long last. Your father awaits you with terrible news.'

'Calm down and come to your senses, Rosie,' Hedra said, her voice deliberately stern as her eyes searched the girl's flushed countenance. 'Can't you tell me?'

The girl's chestnut curls bounced and bobbed as she shook her head. 'No, Princess, I cannot,' she said, almost crying with insistence, 'it is not my place. You must speak to your father with all haste.'

Feeling even more worried than before, Hedra left Vanora in a groom's safe keeping and allowed the young girl to take her arm and lead her across the courtyard to a black metal door that led into the castle's great hall.

Again, Hedra glanced around swiftly, her eyes taking in the familiar stone walls, their coldness warmed by home-worked tapestries and other more exotic wall hangings which had been brought by visitors and knights returning from far-flung places. Almost against her will, her gaze travelled in the direction of the high ceiling draped with pennants and standards of all descriptions to the point where, just beneath their dangling tassels and fringes, the minstrels' gallery was eerily deserted. Usually, at this time, it was packed with extravagantly dressed musicians, tuning their instruments and practising their repertoire in preparation for the coming evening's entertainment.

Her stomach clenched with real trepidation as she marched through the empty hall, onward through the throne room, which was equally devoid of people, until she finally emerged into a small ante-chamber housed at the base of one of the towers.

She called out to her father the instant she entered the round, bare-walled room. It contained no furniture

8

other than a high-backed wooden chair where her father now sat and a rough wooden table, about three feet square.

'Sire, what is it – I was told you have dreadful news?' she asked when she reached his side. Her strident tone dropped slightly with relief now that she could see at close quarters he was not injured or ill in any way. She sank to her knees beside him and gazed up at him beseechingly.

For a minute or two King Hector simply stared at her in silence, his pale blue eyes looking sad and rheumy. She noticed with a pang that the grey-hued skin that stretched tightly across his noble skull looked as thin and as dry as parchment.

'It is a disaster, my daughter, truly a disaster,' he said at long last, running a hand distractedly over his thinning white locks.

She was about to harangue him, to insist on more details and to tell him to stop being so dramatic about something that was probably no more than a minor problem but she stopped in her tracks. This time her father did indeed look distressed. In fact she had never seen him look as old or as weary as he did at that moment.

He held out his hand to her and she allowed him to stroke her soft, violet tresses as she pressed her pale cheek against the midnight blue velvet of his sleeve. Her nostrils twitched. His gown had a musty smell, overlaid with the distinctive, almost appetising scent of sage moss. It was a combination that would never leave her memory.

'Tell me, Father,' she said, her lips moving against his sleeve, 'please tell me what is so bad that it banishes what little life and warmth Parsimonia has known.'

Even in her distress she couldn't resist a jibe at their kingdom. It had held her prisoner far too long and she couldn't imagine the problem being *that* awful, nothing that wouldn't look much better in the fresh light of the coming day.

9

King Hector looked down at his Hedra with kindly eyes and thanked the mystics, as he did every day, that he had been blessed with such a beautiful daughter. It hardly mattered that she was wilful and a little too spirited for the moral constraints of Parsimonia; he always believed that she would grow out of it in time. Now he could no longer be certain that time was on their side.

'Our kingdom is being threatened by invasion, my princess,' he said, making his explanation deliberately blunt, as he had never been predisposed to sweetening the bitter pill. 'They taunt us with the plague and expect us just to concede defeat. Well, they shall never take us alive. Never!'

He leapt to his feet, his sudden movement uncharacteristically agile, and Hedra stared up at him in alarm.

'Who – what plague?' she demanded. 'How dare they?'

'That's my girl,' he said, looking down upon her with obvious pride. 'Unfortunately the threat is of Monomania. The worst blight of all. The only one from which breathless repose is no option, not even by one's own hand. And the man who threatens us is King Randolph.'

The gold-trimmed hem of his long, flowing robe swished quietly across the yellow sandstone floor as he began to pace agitatedly up and down and Hedra had to fight to control her breathing as she watched him in horrified silence. The Monomanian plague was indeed the worst of all infamies – a condition that not only ensured obsessive madness in its victims but cruelly withheld the ultimate release. And, if that were not bad enough, word had it that King Randolph was the worst of all rulers, a tyrant who was truly power-mad.

'What shall we do?' Hedra asked as she joined her father in his pacing, their paths crossing every star-twinkle. 'We can't just let him do as he wishes.' There was no doubt in her mind that it was just as much her responsibility to find a solution to the dreadful situation that faced them and threatened their entire land.

'We cannot fight it,' King Hector said.

'Then what – ' interrupted Hedra immediately but her father put up his hand to silence her.

'I am doing everything in my power to seek a peaceful solution,' he said, 'but only time will tell if I am successful. Unfortunately, as you have probably noticed, many Parsimonians have already fled this kingdom for safer lands.'

Hedra nodded. 'I had noticed,' she said. 'It is awful. Everywhere is so deserted and still.' She paused then resumed her pacing. 'If . . . well . . . just suppose you are not successful in averting this disaster, what will become of us then?'

'Escape is the only option,' he said calmly, having thought about nothing else throughout the period of the second sun. 'You, my dear girl, will flee with the others. I want no arguments,' he added, his forcible tone stopping her in her tracks as his hands reached out to grip her tightly by the shoulders. He knew she would protest most vehemently and she did. 'It is no good. My mind is set. You will travel with my most trusted section of Chivalrous Knights and until it is time to leave I shall appoint a knight to guard you at all times.'

'But what about you?' she said, unable to mask her distress.

He put out a consoling hand and touched her shoulder far more gently than before.

'I cannot desert my throne even if there is no one left to rule,' he said, 'but my alchemists have promised me a potion which they are almost certain will counteract the effects of the plague.' Knowing that his daughter's safe world was about to be turned upon its head, he wanted to do his best to reassure her and felt a powerful anger at himself for not being more prepared for such an eventuality. 'Unfortunately,' King Hector continued, 'the ingredients are very scarce and the alchemists cannot promise to produce more than a few drops of the potion at a time. If only there were enough for everyone, there would be no need for exodus.'

Hedra nodded, wondering, if the the worst came to the worst, how long it would be before it would be safe for everyone to return. But despite her fear and sadness at the turn of events, she couldn't help feeling a little flicker of anticipation at the thought of finally having the opportunity to leave Parsimonia.

'Where shall our bold little troop be headed, Father?' she asked, fighting hard not to show her true feelings and to make light of the situation for his sake. 'Where will our new kingdom be?'

'You will travel to Piosia,' King Hector said, bracing himself for her response and trying to placate her a little in advance. 'The king has already promised you will be well cared for as part of the royal court.'

Just as he feared, her reply shot from her lips with full force.

'Oh no, sire!' she exclaimed passionately. 'I cannot bear the thought of going to Piosia. I would rather stay here and catch the plague!'

Piosia was the most boring of all lands, even more pure and sedate that her own place of metamorphosis. There the people were not even allowed to wear fine clothes or jewels and were expected to spend their entire time doing good works; idleness or personal indulgence of any kind was frowned upon most severely.

King Hector looked pleadingly at her as he spoke. 'I knew you would resist, Hedra,' he said, his voice barely more than a sigh, 'but you must go, for your own sake and for mine.'

Hedra glanced at him and softened immediately. She could see he was distraught and her own stubbornness was not helping him, so for the time being she would go along with his plans.

'Very well, Father,' she said, desperately trying to convey sincerity with her eyes, 'if that is what you decree, so be it. And it won't be for long, we'll soon be back together.'

The king stared at her for a long moment, concerns crowding his mind and jostling for importance. Oh my darling daughter, he thought to himself sorrowfully, if only you were plain and unquestioningly dutiful like the other girls your age, then I could rest easily for once and for all. He wanted to warn her. To tell her of all the evils that might befall her outside Parsimonia. But he loved her dearly the way she was and instead he took her sweet, resolute face in his hands and planted a gentle kiss on the smooth skin of her forehead. There was still the hope that he could persuade King Randolph that Parsimonia was of no value to him. With luck, Hedra would never have to leave the boundaries of their kingdom at all.

Hedra and her father took their meal in the great banqueting hall as they did every other darkfall. King Hector wore his customary gown of midnight-blue velvet with matching ermine-trimmed cape. And she had changed into a long flowing gown of rose-pink silk. It was one of her favourite dresses. The hem, cuffs and neckline were trimmed with a thick band of white moleskin and the bodice was stiffened and boned so that the upper part of her breasts swelled enticingly, her skin even whiter than the fur. On her feet she wore a pair of soft white kid slippers but she had discounted any other adornment save a thin collar – only three rows – of perfect, pink-hued pearls.

The king and princess were a splendid sight as they made their customary grand entrance into the banqueting hall. And, miraculously it seemed, a huge crowd of courtiers had appeared. All of them were magnificently clad in elaborate costumes. Their bodies were a rainbow of silk and velvet – the women's throats, ears and hands heavily bejewelled. And, along with a hastily gathered band of minstrels, a troupe of acrobats led by a jester

13

had also been pressed into service to amuse the falsely cheerful gathering.

Hedra and her father took their seats at the head of a long, highly polished table. Covered only by a thin cloth of white muslin it groaned under a hundred place settings of the finest gold and crystal. Huge bowls and platters heaped with a lavish assortment of fruits, tiny bread rolls, cheeses and sweetmeats filled the centre of the table and took up every square inch of an equally long wrought-iron dresser at the side of the room.

Although she often enjoyed the banquet's sense of occasion, Hedra found lute-playing and the singing of madrigals an insult to her eardrums at the best of times and on this particular evening she was sorely tempted to scream out at the musicians to shut up, to tell them that they sounded like strangled cats and ask them if they didn't all have homes to go to. And the jester irritated her even more. His brightly coloured costume gave her a headache, his jokes made her wince and if he shook his stick of bells in her face one more time she felt sure she would rip it from his hands and snap it in two.

Of course, being the polite, well-brought-up princess that she was, she did none of those things. Instead, as she picked at her food and plucked at the gauzy white hem of the tablecloth, she kept her temper reined in and brought her own, more interesting thoughts to the foreground to amuse herself.

Fortunately, the Chivalrous Knight assigned to guard her appeared quite charming and handsome, although she hadn't had the opportunity to say more than a half-dozen words to him. Even now as she, King Hector and their retinue dined, the knight sat beside her – too conscious of his new responsibility to eat all that much, his body held stiffly upright, like a big cat poised to spring upon its unsuspecting prey.

If he had the instincts of an animal, she thought, glancing at him surreptitiously, his ears would be cocked, listening for any unusual sound, however small

14

or slight; and his hair would spring to attention on his skin each time a door opened and closed, or someone disturbed the harmony of the air around them by walking past their backs.

To her disappointment, the light downy hair on the wrist nearest to her did not even twitch.

At that moment, the acrobats began to tumble around the perimeter of the long, wide room and she stole the opportunity their diversion created to appraise properly the young man beside her. His appearance was drenched in clarity from the dozens of candles that burned brightly above their heads in one of several large chandeliers that graced the room. And, in truth, she could see nothing in his brilliant countenance that offended her.

He was aged about nineteen like herself, or perhaps twenty at the most, with hair the colour of ripe corn that curled almost girlishly around the nape of his neck and perfectly shaped, flat ears. His face was nicely shaped, not too round, not too square, with evenly spaced features. And his eyes, like those of most Parsimonians, were thickly lashed, the irises coloured a very pale blue. As the windows to his soul, they displayed quite clearly that he harboured no guile, nor bad sentiment of any kind.

But it was his lips that enticed her the most. Soft, pink and fleshy like ripe fruit, she fancied they would taste sweet and juicy like plums or pomegranates, or perhaps even a little tart, like a blood orange. With a deep sense of longing that was almost pain, she stared at those lips, desperate to press her own mouth against them, to taste him for herself. Below the cover of her dress she was naked and beneath the heavy damask napkin that lay across her lap she felt her lower body awaken from its light slumber and grow warm, the pleasure parts of her stirring and swelling.

Touch me . . . she urged silently. Want me . . .

'Hedra . . . Hedra!'

Frantically trying to clear the mist that seemed to

have descended around her, Hedra turned her head to look at her father.

'I am so sorry, sire, I was miles away,' she said respectfully. 'You can imagine why.' She bit her lower lip and twisted her hands together in her lap, detesting herself at that moment for using a terrible situation to her advantage, although it wouldn't be the first time she had done such a thing and it certainly wouldn't be the last.

King Hector put out his hand and covered hers. 'I understand,' he said softly, his smile indulgent. 'I wanted to know if you were still hungry. You have hardly touched the food on your plate and there is still a whole forest boar to come.'

She followed his gaze to the large fireplace that took up almost the whole of the end wall. High enough for a good-sized man to walk into without brushing his hair on the sooty stones and wide enough to accommodate a whole army of cooks, the fireplace contained a roaring fire above which a spit had been rotating for the best part of evenfall – the skewered beast browning and dripping its juices into a long metal pan on the hearth below. Either side of the spit two hearty women sat on three-legged stools, their round faces red and glistening with the heat as they continuously turned the spit with one hand and dipped long-handled ladles into the metal pan and basted the meat with the other.

They need pans to catch their juices too, Hedra found herself thinking as she watched each woman in turn wipe a weary arm across her perspiring brow. Whether it was this thought, or the sudden realisation that her safe world was about to be shattered, she didn't know for sure but her stomach suddenly clenched tightly and the thought of ingesting any food at all became a nauseating prospect.

'I couldn't eat another thing, sire,' she said, shaking her head in horror. 'In fact, if you will excuse me, I think I shall retire for the night.'

King Hector was both alarmed and contrite. 'Of

course, my princess,' he said, rising slowly to his feet to offer her a helping hand. 'Sir Derwent here will take you to your quarters and guard you as you sleep.'

The young knight nodded and also rose to his feet, a few crumbs falling from his lap and scattering like snowflakes on the polished flagstones. 'Please, take my arm,' he said to her solicitously.

With an inward smile of satisfaction, Hedra reached out and placed her hand on his forearm, her palm and fingers reacting delightedly to the soft white leather of his uniform.

'I love leather,' she said in a low murmur, as soon as they were out of earshot, 'it is so warm and supple, like a living, breathing animal.'

The knight glanced down at the princess whose full, rosy-red lips had curved into a foxy smile. As she was almost as tall as he his gaze did not need to travel far but he couldn't help noticing the provocative appearance of her garb: how the neckline of her dress was cut a mite too low for modesty, the bodice a little too tight and the delicate fabric of her skirt seeming almost transparent in the odd half-light cast down by the torches that flickered on the walls. All of a sudden he became very aware of her nearness, his nostrils filling with the light floral scent she wore as his arm burned under her touch. He felt himself becoming slightly dazed and a strange stirring in his loins disquieted him.

'Leather is merely a practical covering for the body,' he said, forcing himself to keep his tone even. 'Without it we Chivalrous Knights would all perish.'

17

# Chapter Two

Hedra breathed a sigh of relief as she reached the top of the narrow winding staircase and entered her own private part of the castle which was located at the very top of one of the four towers. Placing herself as far away as possible from the rest of the court, she had deliberately chosen to make her private rooms reflect her true personality: decadent and luxurious, the rooms displayed a wealthy profusion of mainly pink-and red-hued silks and velvets. Now, safe in the womb-like familiarity of her bedchamber, she allowed herself the luxury of a proper appraisal of her knight.

Upon entering the room, he had immediately elected to stand erect by the carefully bolted door, his hands clasped behind his back. And now he tried not to tremble with inexplicable anxiety as the lovely vision of his princess approached him on purposeful, softly slippered feet.

As she reached out and touched him he flinched but Hedra quietened him with a soft shushing sound, such as one might use to calm a frightened animal. Using one slender finger, she traced a slowly meandering path across his wide brow, over the prominent hardness of his right cheekbone into the soft valley of flesh below and across the rough terrain of his harshly bristled jaw.

In the centre of his chin her fingertip became lodged in the slight dimple there. Using only the pressure of her fingertip and the respect her royal birthright earned her, she turned his head until he faced her properly and she caught his gaze with her own, trapping him in the deep grey pools of her irises.

'Look at me properly, my fine knight,' she said with an air of command, 'look at me and tell me what you see.'

'I see my Princess Hedra,' he replied immediately, his tone clearly displaying his confusion although his expression remained stony and impassive.

'That is not enough,' Hedra said with more insistence. 'I know who I am. I want to know what it is you see when you look at me.'

Realising what she meant, he hesitated for a moment. 'I see a girl,' he said cautiously, about my age and very pretty.'

'That's better,' Hedra said approvingly, 'but I want to know more. What do you think of my face, Sir Derwent, and my body; do they please you?'

His eyes glanced over her face. 'It is not my place to be either pleased or displeased by you, Princess,' the knight said quickly.

Hedra fought down her natural inclination to impatience. By all the gods, she wanted to shake this young man and slap him repeatedly about the face. Where was his spirit and his individuality – didn't he possess any opinions of his own?

When she spoke again her words emerged calmly but through slightly clenched teeth.

'I give you permission to speak freely and to admit to your true feelings,' she said. 'Now tell me, my fine knight, do you find me attractive?'

'I . . . I do indeed find your countenance most pleasing, Princess,' he said carefully.

'And . . .' she urged.

'And your body is very . . . very . . .' The knight broke off suddenly to cast his eyes down the length of

19

her, his gaze travelling up again more slowly. 'Your body is very womanly,' he said at long last.

'Womanly!' Hedra cried, taking a step back from him and removing her finger from his dimpled chin which now quivered slightly. 'Of course it is womanly. I am a woman. Look!'

Whether from anger or frustration, or a mixture of both, she began to tear wildly at the thin silk of her gown, ripping it into tatters so that it eventually fell away from her body and she was left entirely naked before him. Ignoring his shocked gaze, she stepped forward once again, the very tips of her breasts brushing against the soft leather that covered his chest.

'I am a woman,' she said more softly, her breathing coming in short, irregular gasps. Reaching behind him she forced his clenched hands apart and clasped them around her straining breasts instead. 'Tell me how I feel.' Her voice was husky with passion and she prayed he would not tell her that she felt like a woman.

'Oh, by the mystics, you feel good,' he said, his voice little more than an anguished moan, 'you feel so soft and warm.'

'Yes,' Hedra urged, pleased by his response, 'yes, tell me more.' In her anticipation of his downfall she felt the moisture gathering inside her, the first drops poised on the inside of her sex, ready to flow around her gently swelling pleasure parts.

'I cannot,' he said, releasing her breasts instantly as though they had suddenly stung him. His arms dropped limply by his sides and he spoke in desperation, the words emerging from his lips like a strangled sob. 'Please do not tempt me any more, Princess, please.'

Hedra stared at him in mute amazement. For once words deserted her and she felt the undeniable anger and frustration that had gripped her on and off for the past five years welling up inside her once again. It wasn't her royal stature that stopped him from touching her and it certainly was not due to a lack of physical response on his part – a brief glance at the front of his breeches told her that: the way the supple leather was forced to stretch to accommodate the large bulge of his phallus was confirmation enough.

His problem was the Parsimonian creed, the allegiance to purity and chastity. Now his problem was her problem too.

'You disappoint me, Sir Derwent,' she said, hoping her voice would not betray her. Tears pricked at her eyelids and she was afraid that she might break down in front of him. That would never do: she bore her royal status with pride and therefore to show such weakness to an underling would be unforgivable. However, it wasn't in her nature to give up, so in a quietly beguiling voice she added, 'You do realise these could be our last days – that this could even be our last night. Do you not wish to make the most of the time we have left?'

He dropped his gaze. It was not his wish to make Princess Hedra unhappy; he admired her greatly and thought her truly beautiful. But his first allegiance was, and always would be, to King Hector.

'I cannot break the trust your father has placed in me,' he said, finally admitting his dilemma. 'As much as I would like to hold you and to touch you – ' He broke off and gazed longingly at her naked breasts, the tips capped by rosy little buds that almost beckoned to him. He licked his lips and squeezed his eyes tightly shut. 'I cannot succumb to you, Princess.'

Hedra listened to him and felt her renewed hopes plummet. Violent emotions raged within her but she was not prepared to beg him, or order him, to make love to her.

'Do not be concerned,' she said finally, with a small shrug of her smooth, white shoulders. 'I feel tired. I am going to bed.'

Attending to her toilette as quickly as possible, she slipped her unsatisfied body between smooth silken sheets and clamped her thighs tightly together to try and assuage the passion that burned between them.

21

Not even she was shameless enough to slip her fingers between the swollen lips of her sex and pinch the hard little bud until her pleasure peaked. Not with Sir Derwent watching her every move.

Hedra hardly slept at all that night, dozing only fitfully from time to time then awakening suddenly in the grip of panic. The air around her was clammy, saturated with the threat that hung over the land. And despite the warmth that the thick stone walls and heavy floor and wall coverings afforded her bedchamber, she shivered and pulled the silken sheet and heavy red velvet counterpane around her shoulders. It made no difference. She was afraid, and fear was not an emotion that touched her lightly.

In the end, she conceded defeat to the night-time terrors and rose from her bed. Wrapping a thick cloak of pure-white fur around her naked body, she wandered barefoot across the carpet with its dog-rose pattern and settled comfortably upon the richly upholstered seat in front of the high, narrow window.

Remembering Sir Derwent, she glanced towards the door where she had left him standing on guard. He had obviously succumbed to tiredness at some point during the night as he now sprawled on a low stool, his legs splayed out in front of him, his head fallen limply to one side. As she watched him he emitted a light snore and suddenly she felt overwhelmed by contempt for this man who had first shunned her and then deserted his post.

Tensing her shoulders angrily she turned away from the sight of him and drew her knees up to her chin. A chill waft of air stroked her, encouraging her to pull the cloak even tighter around her hunched-up body and she rested her chin on her left shoulder as she stared morosely out of the window. Her bedchamber was at the top of one of the four towers, giving her a high vantage point. As she looked down, her gaze travelled restlessly over the black-hued landscape searching for any unusual sign of activity until the familiar elliptical shape of the day's first sun began to appear, like a huge red dragon's egg, behind the distant range of mountains that bordered their land to the North.

When the first pink rays of morning light eventually began to permeate the room, bathing it in a comforting rosy glow, she sighed in despair. It was not that she wanted to spend the rest of her days in Parsimonia, far from it. But she didn't like being forced to leave her kingdom. If there were no other reason, it was enough that it went against her natural inclination to stand firm and repel invaders. And to make matters worse, it bothered her greatly that her father would not be joining her. She shook her head from side to side in frustration. Sometimes she wished he were not such an honourable man. Why couldn't he just desert their threatened land like everyone else?

Slipping from the window seat she moved quietly to a mother-of-pearl dressing console, picked up a silver-backed comb and mirror and began to dress her hair in readiness for the coming day. There was no need to rouse her lady-in-waiting; it was a task she was quite happy to perform for herself. Working deftly, she pinned up the long tendrils at the sides so that they didn't fall about her face and then she set about securing further stray curls with elaborately worked combs of gold and silver inlaid with precious jewels, of which Parsimonia possessed an abundance.

A glance towards the corner of the room reminded her that her other maidservants had already sorted out the best of her belongings and packed a bag in readiness for instant flight if necessary. Only one bag! She had protested strongly at first but her lady-in-waiting had been adamant that the Chivalrous Knights would not allow more than one piece of luggage per person. No exception would be made for her. She was to be treated just like anyone else. Now that would be a novelty.

Despite her concerns, she allowed a flicker of a smile to cross her face. During the past couple of hours her churning fear had been gradually overlaid by another, more poignant sensation. One of excitement.

Her situation was a tragedy, yet it was also an adventure – perhaps the only chance she would ever get to live the sort of life she had always desired.

When she had finished attending to her hair, she bathed quickly and sparingly, pouring fresh spring water from a crystal jug into a delicate matching basin. The water refreshed her and she used a little bar of orchid soap to cleanse her skin properly. Finally she dried herself with a soft, fleecy towel and then stepped into a gown of oyster-pink satin, pulling the simple unadorned garment up her body and easing her arms carefully into the tight sleeves, each of which fastened at the wrist with a single pearl as large and as flawless as a teardrop.

Just as she slipped her highly arched feet into a pair of soft kid slippers that perfectly matched her gown, the knight awoke and Hedra raised her head to greet his awakening with the sweetest smile.

'I trust you slept well, sir?' she said.

Unaware that the princess's pleasant demeanour concealed contemptuous thoughts, he stretched lazily and smiled back at her, looking for all the world like a sleek, white cat.

'Yes, thank you, Princess,' he said in reply.

When she did not speak again but merely nodded, he placed his palms on his thighs, pushed against them and rose stiffly to his feet. Pulling down his tunic and smoothing back his hair, he moved to the window and looked out.

'As you can see,' Hedra said, sarcasm now dripping freely from her tongue, 'the castle has not yet been beseiged. Although I hesitate to think what might have become of me if our enemies had attempted a raid during darkfall. I am sure I would have perished right here in my bed.' She hitched herself onto the piece of furniture to which she referred, wriggled slightly upon the rumpled counterpane and kicked her legs back and

24

forth with a nonchalance that quickly gave way to her barely contained anger. 'How dare you fall asleep at your post, sir? Be certain my father shall hear of this.'

The Chivalrous Knight whirled around in surprise. The princess looked deadly serious. Her normally sweet countenance had darkened considerably and there was a dangerous glint in her eye. Suddenly he felt himself in the grip of real trepidation. A simmering fear such as he had never experienced during a quest, or even in the bloodiest battle, or whenever he had been forced to pit himself against the most ferocious dragon.

'Forgive me, Princess,' he began but she stopped his words with a single warning look.

Slipping from the high bed, Hedra crossed the room with ominously silent steps until she stood directly in front of the hapless knight. In his misery his posture seemed to have deserted him somewhat, whilst Hedra had assumed an even prouder stance and now her eyes were directly level with his.

'Would you permit leniency to another knight under the same circumstances?' she asked in a voice so deceptively calm and soft that it chilled him to the bone.

He shook his head. 'No, of course not.'

A tiny smile snaked around Hedra's lips. 'If that is so, pray tell me what his punishment would be.'

Unaware of the trap he was laying for himself, the knight answered immediately and with conviction.

'A flogging certainly,' he said, 'or perhaps worse. There is every possibility he could be stripped of his rank and banished from the Chivalrous Order for eternity.'

Hedra was not interested in banishment. 'A flogging you say?' she said in a low voice.

Now the knight looked truly frightened and he began to renew his pleas with even more passion than before but Hedra placed a soothing hand upon his chest, her palm flat against the soft white leather.

'There is no reason why I should not show you some clemency, Sir Derwent,' she said, raising her chin imperiously. 'You are, after all, steeped in the best of intentions, are you not?'

'Oh, yes, Princess,' he said with an anxious gasp, 'indeed I am.'

'Then be reassured that I shall not inform my father or your captain of this misdeed,' she said, taking a step backward to acknowledge properly the relief that spread across his face. He opened his mouth to speak but Hedra put up her hand to silence him. 'Do not be so free with your gratitude, sir. I have merely stated that I shall not broadcast your failings. That does not mean I shall allow you to go unpunished entirely.'

The knight looked confused, as well he might. What could this slip of a girl possibly do to him that could be worse than the threat of the king's displeasure?

'What would you have me do to make amends, Princess?' he asked.

Hedra appeared to consider his question carefully, although she already knew well enough what his punishment would be.

'I would have you chastised by my own fair hand,' she said in a low, controlled voice, the fleshy lips of her secret parts tingling and thickening with anticipation. 'Lower your breeches, sir. Bend forward with your legs apart and your palms flat upon the seat of the stool.'

As she expected, the knight looked aghast at her suggestion and began to shake his head.

'Do it!' Hedra said sternly. 'Do as I say, or you'll regret the day you ever set eyes upon me.'

The knight was almost beside himself at the prospect of submitting to her command.

'I cannot. Please, Princess, I cannot,' he said, his eyes beseeching her now as he recognised her immutability, the obstinate set of her jaw, the hard unflinching stare. Oh, how could he have ever thought her kindly – how could he have ever allowed himself to fall into this dishonourable state?

Enjoying his discomfort already, Hedra blatantly ignored his pleas and moved decisively across the room to open a cupboard set in a niche. It was a simply constructed cabinet of polished wood and in there she kept all sorts of things that mostly went unconsidered from one day to the next. Amongst them were a selection of riding crops that she had never been able to bring herself to use on Vanora's delicate rump, although she had always harboured the feeling that they might come in useful one day.

Reaching out she selected a long, thin crop, its length flexible and braided with dark brown leather. She slapped it against her palm a couple of times and felt the sting of it across her tender flesh. Yes, this one would serve her very nicely.

When she turned it pleased her to see that the young knight, resigned to the hopelessness of his situation, was facing the stool and fumbling with his belt. A moment later he unbuttoned his breeches and slid them down his hips until they pooled around his knees in soft, white waves.

'Now bend over and place your palms upon the stool as I instructed,' Hedra commanded.

When the knight was properly poisitioned she crossed the room and regarded him carefully. His thighs were lean and muscular, the skin white and covered with the finest blond down; his heavy scrotum was similarly covered, although the hair around his testicles was just a little darker and more coarse. She could not see his phallus from where she stood, which indicated to her that it must be at least partially erect. Good, she mused, with an inner glow of satisfaction.

'Good,' she said aloud, 'but move your legs wider apart. I want to be able to see *all* of you.'

The knight cringed, knowing that she meant she wanted to see the tight little nether mouth that hid between his tightly clenched buttocks. He thought momentarily about protesting but already realised the pointlessness of such effort. Using one hand, he pulled his breeches down to his ankles and spread his legs wider. Now no amount of clenching could disguise the

27

tight, puckered ring and his face flamed with mortification.

When he had obeyed her order, Hedra released a long sigh of satisfaction. She realised she would probably be forced to relieve her own physical ache afterwards. No doubt her virtuous knight would rather fling himself from the window of her bedchamber than risk touching the flesh that now throbbed remorselessly between her thighs. Even thinking of it sent a sharp dart of desire shooting through her and her sex suddenly spasmed, encouraging her body to give freely of its nectar.

'Very well, Sir Derwent,' she said, swallowing deeply to contain her mounting excitement, 'now you are properly positioned, let me see how well you take your punishment.'

Standing to the side of him, she raised her hand up to shoulder level and, cutting the air with a sharp whistling sound, brought the crop down hard – first striping one buttock and then the other in a continuous motion until she quickly found a rhythm that suited her.

For his part the knight moaned and bowed his head further and further as his tight, white bottom wagged from side to side trying to flinch away from the blows. But of course, in Hedra's charge, the crop shadowed his movements relentlessly, never once missing its target and all in all he bore his punishment with good grace.

Eventually, Hedra felt her arm begin to tire. She stopped beating him and instead stroked the tip of the crop down the cleft between his buttocks and prodded it into the tiny hole that resided there. At that the knight protested but Hedra commanded his silence.

'Your punishment is not over yet. You may not speak unless I give you permission,' she said, twitching the end of the crop to and fro across the bulging sac between his legs.

The knight groaned as she tormented him with the

crop. Princess Hedra had surprised him time and time again that morning. It was not the first time he had been given corporal punishment but usually it was the captain of the knights who administered such discipline, or one of the lords.

Never had he been beaten by a woman. Indeed he had not considered the possibility of such an ignominy. And he had certainly never imagined that one of noble birth would carry out such a deed. Nor had any knight ever been flogged across the naked buttocks; it was normally the back or chest that took the punishment.

He clenched his teeth as the crop probed and tickled him. It hardly mattered what he thought or expected, or what went on in the outside world. Within the seclusion of her bedchamber Princess Hedra was mistress and his only concern should be to obey.

Unaware of the turmoil that she created within the submissive knight, Hedra continued to work the crop. Although she used it more tenderly now, taking the tip between his legs to slide along the length of his erect phallus. She could feel his hardness via the crop and the length of his erection was indeed impressive. Of the few sexual encounters that she had managed to enjoy, the men involved had only sported members of a more modest size.

'Stand up,' she said, deciding that she no longer wanted to beat him. 'Turn around to face me.'

With flaming cheeks he did so, knowing that her gaze would immediately drop to the shamefully engorged length of his phallus.

'Please, Princess . . .' he began again but she silenced him, slapping the crop smartly across the front of his thighs.

'I commanded silence,' she said, in case he was in any doubt, and she tapped the crop lightly against his erection for good measure.

Immediately, he let out a groan of anguish. The pain and the pleasure her handling of the crop afforded him were unbearably exquisite in equal measure. Biting the

29

soft flesh inside his cheeks, he turned his eyes up to the ceiling.

'Look at me, sir,' she said softly. 'Watch my face as I deal with you. I do not give you permission to look away.'

The knight lowered his gaze reluctantly and fell into the trap of her grey eyes, soft again now that her anger had been assuaged somewhat. To his consternation, the princess began to stroke the tip of the crop along the length of his phallus, every so often circling the swollen glans and occasionally tapping the stem lightly. In response, that part of his body twitched and jumped and grew ever harder and more painful.

'Your private parts look desperate,' she said at long last.

The knight nodded but did not trust himself to speak. Then he remembered the princess had not given him permission to do so and breathed a sigh of relief that he had not inadvertently disgraced himself yet again.

'My body is also reacting with pleasure,' she told him candidly. 'Would you like to see for yourself?'

Before the knight had time to respond one way or the other, Hedra gathered up her long gown and raised it to her waist. Parting her legs slightly and placing one foot on a stool, she shamelessly displayed her swollen nether lips and the trickles of nectar running down her inner thighs.

'I would be prepared to relieve your discomfort, if you would afford me the same courtesy,' she said, hoping her voice did not display the urgent need she felt for him to agree.

The knight stared at her wordlessly for some time. Inside him a battle raged. Oh, how he longed to touch her, to spread open those puffy, reddened lips with his fingers and stroke the soft inner flesh. Through the wispy, violet hair that strived for concealment he had no difficulty making out the enticing folds of her pleasure parts, nor the wetness that glistened around the opening to her sex. His fingers itched to plunder her, yet he reined himself in.

Women's bodies were there to be practical or looked upon as things of beauty. They could be vessels for the growth of a child put there at the woman's request by a sorcerer, or they could cook and clean and sew, or simply appear decorative. But they were not intended to be defiled – that was what he had been raised to believe and thus he would adhere to it until his final day.

'I pray that you will forgive me for this, Princess,' he said at long last, his erection wilting slightly as proof of his misery. 'You may beat me and torture me from dawn until dusk but I shall not break the code of purity and honour to which I have sworn allegiance.'

As though a bucket of iced water had just been thrown over her, Hedra knew then that she was beaten. Once again Parsimonia had taunted her with promise and then been found wanting. She dropped the hem of her gown and the crop simultaneously.

'It is of no account,' she said bravely, her voice betraying no emotion whatsoever. 'Please, Sir Derwent, cover yourself and let this be an end to the matter.'

Without giving him a second glance she turned abruptly on her heel and walked to the window, where she stared out in silence until the knight's discreet cough told her that he had repaired his modesty.

Recovered slightly from her disappointment, Hedra broke the night-time fast with her father – dining in his private chambers at a small round wooden table covered only by a simple linen cloth. In the hearth a small fire was dying, its heat being replaced by the strong rays of sunlight permeating the window. Feeling more than a little wistful, she found her eyes following each one of the long golden paths that the sun made along the bare walls and stone-flagged floor, as though she believed they could somehow lead her to a better place.

Despite the fact that she had hardly touched her meal

the night before, her stomach was only able to cope with a few bites of zayan fruit and she glanced apologetically at King Hector, who merely patted her hand and nodded his understanding.

After their meal she spent some hours wandering aimlessly through the castle grounds, picking wild flowers and stripping them savagely of their petals, or simply sitting on a rough stone wall or grassy knoll and staring pensively up at the deep orange sky.

Throughout this virtual inactivity she was shadowed by a different knight, Sir Derwent having been given leave by her father to get some well-earned rest. The the young blond knight had flashed her a look of shame, overlaid with regret, but Hedra had simply shrugged her shoulders and hardly bothered to acknowledge his departure nor the existence of his replacement. What was the point? The Chivalrous Knights were all the same and, therefore, of no interest to her.

In the afternoon she took to her bed for a little rest, then got up and read for a while before dropping the book in disgust and taking up her tapestry. She cared not what she sewed, or how large, or how even her stitches were. Nothing amused her. Nothing diverted her mind from the threat that hung over the kingdom. And nothing she managed to do during hastily snatched moments of solitude seemed enough to pacify the craving for physical release that burned within her.

For days the intolerable situation continued. The torpor was relentless, made worse by the fact that she was instructed by her father to remain within the confines of the castle. Without the escapist luxury of her grotto and the inanimate rigidity of her Pleasure Stone, she thought she may as well give up breathing. If she had thought life grey and dismal before, now it was a hundred times worse. Nay, a thousand times. What little pleasure and respite she had enjoyed was now being denied her. This was not living. This was already nothingness.

'Daughter, what is it?' her father asked her that darkfall as they sat in cloistered silence together, Hedra having refused yet another meal. 'You will be ill if you do not eat.'

'What is the point of eating, Father?' Hedra said, knowing all the time that she was behaving thoughtlessly, yet unable to stop herself. 'What is the point of doing anything that will just prolong life when we shall all be thrust into madness, or slain by marauders from another land anyway?'

King Hector was shocked. It was not like Hedra to give up under any circumstances.

'How can you talk of defeat. My efforts have been rewarded so far have they not?' he said, gripping her hands as they lay limply in her lap. 'We have not been invaded yet, therefore there is still hope of a peaceful solution.'

Hedra looked up at him. 'I am not criticising your efforts, Father,' she said, 'but I cannot feel hope when all around there is despondency. And I feel so bored and so utterly helpless.'

'I know, Hedra, I know,' the king said. He had no other words to comfort her. Indeed, he had heard rumours that the invasion was imminent and he felt tempted to send her away there and then, for her own safety. If he had known how badly she yearned for action of some kind, then he might have considered it. As it was, he pulled her to her feet and kissed her gently on both cheeks. 'Why don't you go to bed? Things will doubtless look different in the morning.'

Little did King Hector know then how prophetic his words would turn out to be.

# Chapter Three

*F*or the first time in many nights, Hedra did actually manage to sleep, although as she was so exhausted and so thoroughly depleted through lack of appetite it was hardly surprising. Of course, she would sleep soundly on the one night that danger came knocking at the castle door.

The knight on guard in her bedchamber at the time the messenger came galloping up to the castle with news that it was about to be besieged, awoke her by shaking her shoulder roughly. There was little time for pleasantries or subtle coaxing.

'What is it, whatever is going on?' Hedra said, rubbing the sleep from her eyes as she sat up hastily and looked around her.

'There is no time for discussion, Princess,' he said grimly. 'The news we have all been dreading has finally come. Now it is time to flee the castle.'

Hedra watched, wide-eyed, as the knight moved to gather up the few things that lay upon her dressing console – including her silver-backed brush, comb and mirror and a bottle of scented oil, the delicate glass blown and cut to resemble a diamond beetle. As he quickly stuffed the items inside the bag that was already packed and waiting, the reality suddenly hit her. It was not a case of if, but or maybe any more. All hope of a reprieve was lost. It was time to leave Parsimonia.

Throwing back the covers, she jumped down from the bed. Without bothering to change from her thin muslin nightgown she wrapped the thick fur cloak around her shoulders, tying the ribbons securely around her neck. Then she slipped her feet into a pair of stout, black leather shoes with golden buckles. There was no need to waste time on changing her clothes now. The nights were warm enough at this time of year, she would hardly perish and they could always stop at the first inn they came to so that she could wash and dress herself properly.

The knight carried her bag and led her in silence from the bedchamber, down the narrow passageways and staircases to the castle's rear exit. Then, turning the heavy iron door handle with his free hand, he ushered her out of the familiar confines of the castle.

Outside, in the small rear compound, a crowd of about thirty courtiers had assembled, most of them lords and ladies. And a small group of servants also stood by, their arms and backs laden with bags and food sacks and an assortment of cooking pots.

Hedra spotted King Hector easily amongst the others and she ran to him.

'Is this it, Father?' she said. 'Am I to leave?'

Even as the king nodded and a tear rolled down one cheek, the attention of father and daughter was stolen by the arrival of the Chivalrous Knights.

Hedra felt her breath catch in her throat. The knights truly were a magnificent sight. All were fully decked out in their customary white leather tunics, breeches and boots, over which they wore various pieces of armour – a breastplate, knee and shoulder-pads – fashioned from silver. On his head, each knight wore a silver helmet crested by a tall plume of white horsehair, upon his left wrist a large round silver shield and in a scabbard around his waist, each carried a finely honed

35

sword, with a jewel-encrusted and silver-filigree handle.

Despite her disappointment with the knights in general, Hedra couldn't help gazing at the spectacle with something approaching awe. The knights had trotted two abreast into the small compound, each seated astride a proud white charger, his leather-booted feet thrust into silver stirrups encrusted with semi-precious gemstones. And behind the lofty troop a band of minstrels followed in their colourful garb, every one of them prepared to march and play their lutes and whistles and tambourines for the duration of the journey if necessary. But this was not the end of the noble procession, for bringing up the rear was a young page, no more than a boy, who had been honoured with the task of bearing Parsimonia's distinctive blue and white royal standard.

Hedra smiled to herself at the sight of the boy's obvious pride in his elected station, then glanced away from him as another flurry of dust heralded the arrival of the grooms. They led ordinary horses for the courtiers and a few of the luckier servants and all at once Hedra was relieved to cast her eyes upon the familiar beauty of Vanora as she too was led into the compound.

On this occasion the fabulous unicorn sported Hedra's bag and a thick, white leather side-saddle to match the bridle she usually wore. Hedra glanced at the saddle and then at the groom but the young, red-faced groom hurriedly explained to her that she would be travelling a great distance and to do so bareback would not be a comfortable experience. Silently, Hedra nodded her assent and turned to mount her steed.

'Take all good care, my princess,' King Hector said, pulling her against him in one final embrace that almost crushed the breath from her body. 'As soon as it is safe, I will send for you again.'

'I know, Father, I know,' Hedra said, swallowing deeply. She had not intended to cry but now as she returned her father's kiss they both wept. 'I love you, my liege.'

She knew he would consider it the finest of tributes and, having given him a final, tearful kiss goodbye, she gathered up the hem of her delicate nightgown and allowed the groom to assist her as she mounted Vanora.

Landing in the saddle she hurriedly straightened herself so that she sat in her usual erect position. There is no doubt about it, she thought to herself with an inward smile, if I am forced to flee, I am certainly going to do it with dignity.

At that moment, a knight walked his horse alongside her. Unlike all the other horses his steed wore a plume of feathers plucked from an unlucky bird of paradise and was panting and snorting loudly with the effort and frustration of being restrained.

'I am the captain of the knights and your assigned protector for the journey, Princess,' the knight said, introducing himself with a gentle, yet undeniably masculine voice.

She glanced into his honest face and despite the certain knowledge that the captain was as uncorruptible as all the other knights, she shivered with uncontrolled delight at the sight of him, so close to her and yet so far removed. He looked strong beneath his armour. The sleeves of his tunic were supple enough and the cut of his breeches tight enough for her just to be able to make out the definition of his musculature.

A fierce surge of desire clenched at her belly and she inhaled deeply, desperate to assuage another of her senses. Yet she should have anticipated disappointment. Unlike the travellers from other lands, men of Parsimonia did not have their own scent but smelled of soap and violets and other pure, unmasculine things.

Resisting the urge to touch him, as she already knew such an overt advance would be ignored, or even unacknowledged, she merely nodded, assured him that she was as ready to leave as she would ever be and

37

turned to stare straight ahead in the direction of their departure.

Only when they were well and truly across the moat did she allow herself the luxury of looking back at the familiar grey walls of the castle. Already, her father was too far away for her to make him out properly but she could tell by his stance that he harboured a fierce pride as he watched them leave.

Brushing a stray tear from her cheek she forced herself to hold her emotions in check and instead turned her head to look forward once again. It was not an encouraging sight. All she could see was a wide expanse of flat red Parsimonian earth extending to meet the indistinct boundary of the forest and mountains, their ghostly forms cloaked in a light pink mist.

It was then she received the first surprise of the day.

Speaking in a low voice – as though he truly believed they could be overheard above the harmonious sound of trotting hooves and the playing of the minstrels – the captain told her that he had deliberately chosen a different, more indirect route out of the kingdom; one that bypassed every single village and all but the roughest of tracks.

'Also, we shall not be travelling directly from Parsimonia into Piosia,' he explained, leaning across the gap that divided them to speak directly into her ear, 'but shall firstly cut across the south-western corner of Satyria.'

Hedra was confused by his disclosure. 'Why the change of plan?' she asked. 'Do you believe King Randolph and his men will come after us?'

To her consternation he nodded readily in reply to her question. 'There is every possibility of that, so what I am attempting to do is try and outwit him by taking none of the routes he would expect,' he said. 'Even King Hector is not aware of my true plans. Therefore he cannot be forced to disclose them if – ' At this point he broke off, looking embarrassed.

'If what?' Hedra persisted. 'If he is tortured? Is that what you were going to say?'

'It is very unlikely, Princess,' the captain said, anxious to reassure her. 'I am merely taking every possible precaution.'

Hedra was silent for a moment, listening to the music and the faint murmur of voices coming from the procession behind her.

'We should not be making so much noise,' she said at long last.

Once again the captain nodded in agreement. 'There is method in my madness,' he said with the faintest glimmer of a smile. 'When we come to the next fork a small band of us shall turn left and take the route I just mentioned to you whilst my lieutenant leads the others more directly into Piosia so – '

'So if King Randolph does attempt to halt our escape, it is more likely to be the others that he follows,' Hedra said excitedly, finishing his explanation for him. 'That's a damn fine plan, sir!' She always admired a cunning mind and had no compunction about showing her feelings. Yet again she felt herself wishing that this man were not a Chivalrous Knight. She could find it just as easy to admire his mind as well as his body.

For a fleeting moment, as they reached the fork and she and just a handful of knights broke away from the main party as the captain had planned, she felt a flicker of remorse, wondering if the others would ever get to Piosia safely. And yet now that their much smaller band was unencumbered they were able to ride much faster, Vanora's swift hooves keeping up easily with the knights' white chargers.

Consequently it seemed they had been riding for no time at all when the landscape began to change hue and form. Instead of being flat it became rocky and then increasingly mountainous, signalling to her that they had reached the boundary of her land. Now they were about to enter the unknown. Territory that was, at least as far as she was concerned, uncharted.

As soon as they had crossed the mountains they slowed their pace once more and began to follow a clearly defined path which cut through the brightly hued forest, the trees forming a fringe around the base of the rocks like a colourful beard.

After they had been travelling along this path for some time, Hedra gradually allowed boredom and the soporific rhythm of Vanora's movements to lull her into a light trance. The drowsiness that had eluded her the past few days now overtook her body and she found herself deep in reverie – her idle fantasy mainly that of a wonderful new life in which she enjoyed untold riches and luxury and a huge comfortable bed that was never devoid of a handsome, virile male.

She didn't know it but the thoughts had caused her lips to curve into a dreamy smile and her nipples to harden visibly beneath the thin muslin nightgown.

This was the sight that met King Randolph's eyes when he and his men launched a silent raid on the unsuspecting group, picking off two of the Chivalrous Knights and slaying them and frightening the remainder so much that they scattered to the four winds. Only the captain and a few of the bravest knights remained, unharmed but observing keenly and from close quarters as the king rode up to Hedra.

Unlike so many others who had attained his lofty station in life, King Randolph was, with all thanks due to carefully executed patricide, still in his thirties. Undoubtably, he was a fiercely handsome man and startling to look at: with prematurely white hair worn long to the shoulders, a square, brutally chiselled face – partially concealed by a moustache and closely cropped beard – and a thin red mouth that was as cruel as the glint in his coal-black eyes. Feared and revered by everyone who knew his name, he ruled his land with a rod of iron and his women with a whip of the harshest, parmerian leather.

As soon as his phalanx of knights had swooped upon the innocent group, his assessing gaze had caught sight of Hedra and held her captive. Removing his battle helmet, a fearsome-looking death mask of purest gold, he galloped up alongside her, his steed a proud stallion whose powerful muscles rippled under a satin sheath of chestnut brown and whose lustrous mane was plaited into more than a hundred braids, each one entwined with leather thongs. Although King Randolph did not attempt to halt her progress at all, neither did he allow the beautiful young woman her freedom.

Eventually, realisation dawned upon Hedra that it was no longer the captain who rode beside her. Her subconscious began to realise that the familiar, faint swishing sound of the plume upon his helmet had been replaced by the strident clank of metal. And, almost in a daze, she turned her head and gazed sleepily at the gold-suited man beside her, her expression beatific.

At once she found herself looking into the eyes of a stranger, the irises glinting like chips of black marble in his tanned and weathered face. Surprise rather than fear gripped her at the sight and she found her eyes travelling rapidly over the skin that stretched across his noble cheeks and brow. It appeared as tough as rhino hide and the even rows of strong teeth exposed by his grinning lips seemed all the brighter against the swarthy canvas.

Death and destruction were reflected in his gaze and intruded on her curious stare, bringing her swiftly to her senses. And she hastened to dig her heels into Vanora's sides, anxious only to flee the cruel eyes that bored into hers. It shocked her to realise that ahead of her the path was clear and a quick glance around told her that while she had been daydreaming her small group had been attacked.

There was no time to think about her situation; in her mind only escape was imperative. But even as she rode hard, Vanora's hooves kicking up the red dust so that it settled over them both in little speckles, she could hear the snorting of the stranger's own steed as he caught up with her. And she could almost feel the harsh

41

warmth of his breath upon her cheek as he drew alongside. Realising she could not outride him she gave a light tug on Vanora's reins and the unicorn obediently slowed her pace.

After a brief, stomach-clenching moment Hedra found the courage to turn her head, look him full in the eye and speak out.

'Who are you, infidel – what is your business?' she said, her demanding tone of voice displaying far more bravery than she felt.

To her consternation, the rider laughed harshly. Without dislodging his seat for a second, he reached out with his whip and allowed the end of it to trace an insolent path down the proud length of her bared throat and across the milky white flesh of her upper breast.

Immediately, her nipples grew harder still and to her shame she felt the familiar swelling of her lovelips and a telltale wetness soaking through her thin nightgown. Almost unconsciously, she tensed her thigh muscles and raised her buttocks slightly from its seat but it was already too late to halt the pulsating proof of her arousal.

'I declare,' he said with a devilish glint in his eye, having noted the effect he was having on her, 'you're a pretty one and spirited too. I'll wager the golden blood of royalty runs through your delicate veins?'

By this time they had both slowed to a brisk trot and now his steed fairly pranced beside Vanora. Hedra stole a glance at him, surprise rippling through her as it had the first time she had set eyes upon the shocking whiteness of his hair. He was young and yet the colour of his hair and an indisputable air of nobility made him seem much older. And, despite the harsh authority his every word and action displayed, she sensed a voluptuousness about him that both beguiled and terrified her.

The grip of his stare was so intense that she found her eyes begin to ache and she was forced to look away, lowering her gaze instead to stare at her hands, the white bones of her knuckles showing clearly through the delicate skin as her fingers gripped Vanora's reins.

It took her the utmost effort to nod her head in reply to his question.

'Your assumption is correct,' she said, turning her grey eyes upon him once more. 'You address Princess Hedra of Parsimonia . . . sire.'

She afforded him the respectful title after glancing at the third finger of his left hand which bore a heavy gold ring displaying the combined seal of all the kingdoms of the Fantastic Lands. Her father had a ring just like it, she remembered. And suddenly she felt overcome by a surge of homesickness and desperation at her plight. It was the first time she had ever felt truly unprotected.

'And who are you, pray?' she added.

However worried or afraid she felt, Hedra would never allow her true feelings to betray her. And even under these trying circumstances she spoke haughtily and raised an imperious eyebrow as she desperately tried to ignore the fact that his exploring whip had delved slightly lower and now stroked the deep valley between her breasts.

Just as he opened his mouth to reply and the split second before his questing whip ventured to actually torment her swollen nipples, a loud cry of panic rang out behind them and he turned his head sharply to see what had alarmed his men.

Seizing the opportunity, Hedra pulled firmly on Vanora's rein with her right hand and urged Vanora away from the stranger at a rapid gallop, the route quickly plunging them into the depths of a deeply forested area. Despite the loud snapping of twigs as they ventured deeper and deeper into the eerie darkness of the forest, Hedra could hear no other sounds and her keen senses told her that no other person was in the vicinity.

Endless minutes passed without the renewed threat of capture and as they continued to pick their way through the dense, dry bracken, her rapid breathing slowly returned to normal. Eventually she halted

Vanora in a clearing, straightened up in the saddle and let out a long, cleansing breath that hovered in front of her in the chill early morning air.

Part of her felt relief at having evaded the clutches of the scurrilous king and yet another part felt disappointment in herself for choosing to curtail such an interesting encounter. But her overriding emotion at that moment was excitement and the certainty that the adventure which she had always craved was about to unfold.

If it was an adventure, it had got off to an extremely tedious start, she reflected two moon casts later as she prepared to spend yet another day alone in the forest. At first, she had been buoyed by her excitement and by the novelty of riding across yellow earth rather than red. And she had found intense delight in the strange beauty of the surrounding flora: tall, majestic trees cloaked in velvety leaves of deep moss green, wine red and even a rich variegated blue-mauve; and weirdly shaped bushes and exotic flowering plants of all types and hues. Really, the strangeness of this land, which she assumed to be Satyria, had proved sometimes to be almost too wondrous to behold.

But now she just felt disgruntled. Nay, disgruntled and dishevelled, she thought, fingering the ripped and grubby skirt of her dress. It had started out as pale blue silk, stitched with gold and decorated with a girdle of gold and sapphires, now it was just a rag, like all the other clothes that had been packed for her. And this was the very last dress of her meagre wardrobe.

To make matters worse she had not even been able to find a stream in which she could bathe properly, just the odd small trickle of fresh water that served only to slake her thirst. If there was one thing she hated it was to feel dirty and unscented. She laughed then. Oh, she was scented all right, enough to frighten off the fiercest predator in the forest!

Thinking of forest animals made her think of food

and her own, gnawing hunger. The small amount of sweetmeats that she had secreted in her bag had long since disappeared in a single gluttonous binge on the first day and since then she had enjoyed nothing more than a few berries. Now she thought wistfully of the banquets she had attended at the castle, of the roast boar she had refused, the dishes of stewed venison, the jugged hares. Her mouth watered and her stomach groaned in sympathy. Even if she was cunning enough to catch her own prey, she could never bring herself to prepare it. Why, she didn't even know how to make a proper fire. Thank goodness the darkfall was warm here in this land and she still had her fur cloak to protect her.

For someone like Hedra who had spent her whole life being idle and pampered, life in the Satyrian forest was a dreadful state of affairs. The only thing that kept her going during the long days was the memory of the warrior king. She couldn't help remembering, with a delighted shiver, the way he had looked at her with those disrespectful eyes and the knowing manner in which he had explored her body with the end of his whip. It was his image she held in her head last thing at darkfall and which greeted her eager memory at first light.

One of the other problems she faced, one of the most difficult to deal with, was the absence of her Pleasure Stone. It had been all right on the first day, she had not even missed it as she rode through the forest determined that she would find adventure before the second sun started to drop. But halfway through the following day she began to feel the familiar, insistent pulsing inside her, the knotting of her nerves and the disturbance to the clarity of her thought patterns that could only be assuaged by the filling of her body cavity and rhythmic friction around her pleasure bud. Now, she awoke on day three feeling as though she would explode.

Her memory of the licentious king filled her mind

and fuelled her fantasies as she continued her trek that morning. Even her hunger for food was forgotten, buried temporarily under a much greater physical need. Then, just as she began to despair of anything going right for her ever again, she came to the edge of the forest, rounded an outcrop of dark purple rocks and found herself confronting a sight so welcome she wondered straight away if it was a mirage.

To her right, from a cleft in the rocks way, way up above her head, tumbled an unending flow of water. The cascade was so tumultuous that it roared as it fell, seemingly from the tops of the highest fir trees in the forest that surrounded it; the sparkling water exploding on impact as it hit the surface of the pool below. Hedra stood some way off yet she still felt lightly drenched by the spray as she dismounted from Vanora and started to lead her around the rocks to the edge of the pool where her beloved unicorn could drink the clear, pure water.

As they reached the pool, she dropped the rein and Vanora bent her head obediently. While the unicorn drank, Hedra looked around her. The water looked so inviting, so clean and clear as it shimmered under the sun which glowed most strongly from its apex point. Gazing into the pool she realised she could see right to the very depths, where small glittering stones were scattered over a soft yellow sandy base and shoals of minnows darted here and there, their narrow rainbow bodies flicking from side to side. And on the surface of the pool small insects landed: tiny beetles with shimmering wings and hard purple bodies and dragonflies, their gossamer wings of many regal hues sweeping gracefully down to hover over the water.

Watching the antics of two such dragonflies as they lunged and parried like two swords without their knights, she laughed aloud and clapped her hands together with unrestrained delight. The sounds obviously startled the insects because they quivered then darted away and she turned her head regretfully and watched the cascade take yet another plunge instead.

The pool sparkled like a huge multi-hued gem-stone under the reflection of the forest and she felt as grubby as the lowliest peasant. The wish she had held for the past three days had now come true and this was no time for false modesty. Without further hesitation, she quickly stepped out of her shoes, stripped off her gown and took two long-limbed steps into the water, her toes immediately curling into the soft sand at the bottom of the pool. Further and further she waded, shivering with delight as the cool water inched up her legs, covering her knees and thighs, then up over the curve of her buttocks to touch the small of her back with tiny icy fingers.

It felt so good that she moaned with unbridled pleasure and in a moment seized the courage to bend her knees and sink herself quickly into the refreshing pool, immersing herself up to the chin. For a while she simply floated in the water, enjoying the feeling of weightlessness. Then she began to swim, using smooth controlled strokes to glide across the pool towards the cascade. As she reached it, she hesitated. She had never dared to enter one before, to stand beneath its mighty flow. Yet there was something undeniably beguiling about the prospect that she dared herself to do just that. In moments she stood proud and naked, allowing the water to rush down upon her and flow over the curves of her body.

She needed the cooling, restorative effect of the water, although she hadn't realised how much. Turning this way and that she simply revelled in the cascade for a moment, allowing the water to cleanse her body thoroughly and turn her hair into thick ropes that hung down her back and over her shoulders. Moving forward a couple of paces into the full force of the flow she cupped her breasts in her hands, holding them under the powerful jets and delighting in the way her nipples swelled and hardened of their own accord.

47

Sharp darts of arousal shot through her, bringing her whole body to life and yet all the time she stood like this she pressed her thighs tightly together, trying desperately to ignore the way the pulsing sensation between her legs had turned to a slow, insistent throb.

With a sigh, almost of defeat, she released her captive breasts and dropped her hands to her upper thighs. Easing her feet apart carefully so that she didn't lose her footing, she reached between her open thighs. Straightaway she could feel how swollen her clitoris had become. How the outer lips had puffed open slightly, like a rosebud coming into flower, to display the finer layers of flesh beneath and lay open the entrance to her sex. Her body was ready for a man but, as usual, she had no one at her disposal.

Instead she caressed herself carefully, knowing how to give herself pleasure. And, after a few moments of blissful stroking, her fingertips automatically sought to spread open the fleshy lips that concealed her pleasure bud and to pull back the little hood of skin, exposing the centre of her arousal to the full force of the flow.

The moment she did so her mind and body were lost. The water hit the swollen morsel of flesh and in no time her body began to spasm, her legs and buttocks quivering as she fought to maintain her stance under the erotic onslaught of the cascade. Tensing her jaw, she allowed her head to drop back and offered her face to the full force of the water's flow. It beat down upon her mercilessly, attacking her eyelids, her cheeks, her tightly compressed mouth as she wavered under the ebbing flow of her zenith and waited for the water to clear her mind.

She stood like that for a seemingly endless length of time, waiting, waiting for her thoughts to realign themselves and her body to cease its demand for release. Neither gift was bestowed upon her by the force of nature and so she was compelled to touch herself again, to bring about a second zenith that left her feeling no more fulfilled than the first.

Just as she cried out with desperation and plunged her fingers inside her own throbbing body, she heard a low, almost bestial noise. The sound was unmistakable and she opened her eyes quickly, expecting a wild forest animal to emerge from the trees.

Releasing her body, she whirled around to scan the surroundings and felt her eyes widen with shock. The sight that met her eyes was not that of a beast, although the male creature who stood on the bank – strong muscular legs set wide apart and similarly developed arms held akimbo – was not of any heritage that she had come to recognise. Covered only by a brief loin-cloth, his whole body was stocky and powerfully built, like that of a bull, yet his head was distinctly leonine.

Hedra stared at him and tried to make sense of his appearance.

It wasn't simply the broad prominent brow, long wide nose and firm jaw that made him look like the king of the beasts. Oh, if only it were that simple, she thought, feeling real fear welling up inside her all at once. Nay, what had surprised her most of all and set the terror hammering in her chest was the long central mane of white hair that grew from the very front of his skull and fell in a long straight sweep to the base of his spine.

Hedra caught her breath and held it, her eyes wide and staring in awe. The creature on the bank did the same, his gaze travelling with undisguised curiosity over her naked body. It was obvious from the way he nodded and continued to eye her blatantly that he was not the least bit afraid of her.

As the wordless gap between them widened, Hedra realised she couldn't continue to stand under the water indefinitely. The second sun was starting to drop in the sky and before long it would be evenfall and after that the dark night would come bringing all its usual terrors to add to the ones she already felt. Unless she acted now, she would perish for certain.

Hovering uncertainly under the cascade for just a

little while longer, she stepped purposefully into the deeper water and began to swim to the bank where the creature stood. She had no option, the bag holding all her belongings sat there on the ground next to him.

As she drew nearer she realised that he was, to all intents and purposes, a man, despite his distinctly odd appearance.

She didn't feel brave enough to stop swimming directly in front of him but carried on to a point along the bank a little to his left. Taking a deep breath for courage, she clutched at thick tufts of silky yellow grass and climbed out of the pool. With her face turned away from him she stood on the bank, apparently oblivious to his interested stare and the way his eyes swept unashamedly over her naked body, his unseen gaze warming her skin which still glistened under a diamond robe of water droplets.

'If you ever find the courage, or indeed the good manners, to turn around and face me I would be only too happy to go through the usual introductions,' the creature said at long last, his tone heavy with amusement.

His voice broke the silence that had surrounded her for almost three whole days and at first she didn't even notice his sarcasm. She was far too surprised that he could speak at all; for some reason she had expected grunts. Bending down slowly, and with as much decorum as she could muster, she retrieved the discarded tatters of her gown. Then, clutching the grubby fabric to the front of her so that it concealed her breasts and pubis, she turned to face the strange interloper.

Their eyes clashed warmly and for a brief, heart-clenching moment Hedra felt the breath dashed from her body, as though he had lunged at her with a physical attack.

'I . . . er . . .' she said, stammering badly in her confusion.

'My name is Gideon,' he said, reaching out to take

her hand. 'I live not far from here at the edge of the forest.'

Hedra studied the proffered hand. As she expected, the huge palm and thick fingers were distinctly paw-like but there the similarity ended. The backs of his hands were smooth, almost hairless and his fingernails were not fierce talons but cut quite, quite short. She breathed a sigh of relief and smiled, although she didn't dare to offer her own hand in return; that would mean letting go of her gown.

'Please excuse me for not shaking your hand,' she said, her smile continuing for his benefit as his nod showed her he understood. 'My name is Hedra, Princess of Parsimonia. I am on my way to Piosia but as you can see I have become a little lost.'

At this the creature who called himself Gideon threw back his head and laughed. It was a loud roar that almost seemed to shake the forest. At the very least it startled the birds from their nests so that they fluttered upwards in brightly coloured flocks of confusion.

'I would say you have strayed more than a little,' he said, putting his great arm around her shoulders and walking them both forward so that he could pick up her bag. Hedra felt uncomfortable in his embrace and started to resist but he silenced her, although he did remove his arm. 'I shall turn my back and give you a moment to dress. Then we shall return to my cottage. Please do not argue,' he added as Hedra opened her mouth to protest yet again. 'You need food and somewhere comfortable to rest and I have both. After a good night's sleep I shall deliver you to Piosia myself.'

As he turned his broad muscular back to her Hedra realised she would be foolish not to let him take charge for now. 'You're very kind,' she said, her lips curving into a smile as she stepped into her dress and glanced up at the solid wall of his torso once again. 'I don't know how I shall ever repay you.'

# Chapter Four

$A$lthough Hedra hadn't heard the sound of hooves while she stood under the rushing water of the cascade, Gideon had obviously arrived on horseback because he left her side to walk over to a dark grey mare grazing close by.

'She's beautiful, isn't she?' he said fondly, ruffling the thick tuft of white mane between the horse's ears, so reminiscent of his own hair.

Hedra, nodding her agreement, walked over to him and put out her hand to stroke the mare's silky neck. 'What is she called?' she asked.

'Rowan.'

'Like the tree,' she said, her voice a low murmur.

'Yes, like the tree.'

Gideon turned to glance at Vanora who had finished drinking long before and was now standing under the sprawling purple shade of a lady's lustre – a tall thin tree with a high parasol of shimmering branches. Under his breath he emitted a low, trilling whistle that immediately attracted the unicorn's attention.

To Hedra's amazement, she came trotting obediently over to them and stood patiently by Gideon's side as though awaiting his next instruction.

'You certainly have a way with animals,' Hedra said,

observing the way Vanora whickered blissfully and nuzzled at him as he stroked her and spoke in a soft, crooning voice.

'Not just animals, or so I've been told,' he replied with a confident smile. 'Women, too, are not averse to soft words and caresses.'

Hedra felt a shiver run through her at the promise in his words.

'Shall we make our way to your home?' she said, taking up Vanora's rein, 'evenfall will be upon us before we know it.'

They rode side by side, the short journey taking them around the perimeter of the forest. Now that she had the promise of food and a comfortable bed, not to mention a handsome companion, Hedra felt relaxed enough to be able to appreciate her strange new surroundings once again. And from time to time she was tempted to stop Vanora in her tracks in order to examine a particularly unusual flower or shrub.

Being a forest dweller and a natural-born lover of nature, Gideon was in no hurry to spur her on and instead delighted in watching the entrancing young woman take pleasure in the beauty of their surroundings. He couldn't rid his mind of the vision of her, as free and naked as a woodland sprite, giving herself to the sparkling torrent of the cascade. Unlike a woodland sprite though, this creature was a fully grown human and more arousing than any woman he had ever met before. Her body and her manner stimulated him beyond all reason and it was only his innate sense of timing that kept his emotions in check. She wasn't ready for him yet but later, after a plate of good rabbit stew and a goblet or two of negus, she would surely be as open to him as any village maiden.

During the ride Hedra eyed Gideon surreptitiously when she was certain he was otherwise distracted. Now that she had become used to his odd appearance she was very aware of the virility emanating from him and found his undeniably bestial aura incredibly attractive.

It was not a question of if they would enjoy each other's bodies but how soon. Half of her wanted to rip the clothes from her back, throw herself naked into the blanket of flora that covered the earth and beg him to take her there and then. But the other half was more circumspect. She supposed it was a legacy of her upbringing that she was prepared to wait for him to make the first move, although she was able to take comfort from the certainty that, when their time eventually came, he would not disappoint her.

Just at that moment a sideways glance from him disturbed her thoughts. 'You may be glad to know we are almost there,' he said with a smile.

Hedra nodded. 'I am – very.' She reached forward and stroked Vanora's mane. 'Nearly there, my beauty,' she whispered, 'we're nearly home.' Inexplicably, she felt a warm glow inside. Although she wasn't expecting a castle by any means, she couldn't help thinking of Gideon's habitat as home. It had a nice, natural ring to it.

The reality was far from a castle of course. In fact, the cottage built of rough-hewn logs was hardly more than a one-room hut. Primitive from the outside, inside it was warm and cosy, the large square room dominated by a huge canopied bed. Hedra found herself staring at the bed. It looked so inviting with its thick mattress filled with down and covered by a stout sheet of white dimity to match the curtains, and a warm layer of animal furs all stitched together to make one huge blanket.

Gideon didn't miss the way she stared at the bed. 'There will be plenty of time to make our pleasure after we've eaten,' he said.

Hedra whirled around to face him, her cheeks glowing a furious red. 'You forget yourself, sir. I have hardly slept in days; of course I find the sight of a comfortable bed enticing.'

At such a firm denial of her lustful thoughts, Gideon had to force himself to suppress the laughter that bubbled up within him. 'Oh, I see,' he said, 'in that case, please forgive me. It's just that here in Satyria we have no difficulty admitting to our desires – however lustful they may be.'

Opening her mouth to supply an instant retort, Hedra suddenly thought better of it. It was true, she did have lustful desires. She had heard tell that Satyria was thoroughly debauched but those tales came from a race of people who could hardly bear to touch their own bodies let alone anyone else's. Could it be that Satyria was merely free of guilt and inhibition? Might it offer her the freedom to explore the myriad cravings that she had been forced to keep in check?

'Yes,' Gideon said, surprising her and stopping her thoughts dead in their tracks.

'Yes, what?' she said, glancing at him with a quizzical expression.

He sighed and began to stir the pot of stew that hung from a pyramid of sticks over an open fire in the hearth. 'Yes, Satyria is everything you hope for.'

Hedra stared at him. 'How did you know what I was thinking?' she demanded.

He continued to stir the pot.

'I asked you how – ' Hedra repeated but he interrupted her.

'I read thoughts. It is a gift of my race, I assumed you knew.'

His disclosure shocked her. 'Of course I didn't know,' she said, her voice wavering in the midst of her confusion. 'How could I possibly know? By the mystics, I would not have allowed myself the luxury of unprotected thought if I had!'

Without waiting to hear his reply she rushed from the cottage and began to search frantically in the foliage surrounding the building, her fingers scrabbling amongst the tangle of stems and leaves. Finally she found what she was looking for, her eyes immediately picking out the distinctive blue-grey variegated colouring of a laissi plant that choked the trunk of a flowerless

55

shrub. Without hesitation she plucked a length of the thought-inhibiting vine and weaved it through her hair. Satisfied that she was properly protected, she went back into the cottage.

Gideon was still in the same place, stirring the stew, his broad back looking even more imposing in the confines of the tiny room. He glanced up as she walked across the room and sat in one of the straight-backed wooden chairs by the side of the cottage's only other significant piece of furniture, a small square table. 'What a damnable pity,' he said, rebuking her gently. 'You have spoilt my fun.'

Feeling a little more confident, Hedra smiled. 'Please forgive me, noble sir,' she said, aiming the words at him like poisonous darts, 'but I believe I am entitled to a modicum of privacy?'

Gideon looked far from put out by her sharp retort. 'I wish you would call me by my name,' he said lightly. '*Sir* is so formal.'

There was silence for a moment, then Hedra saw the folly in her behaviour and threw back her head and laughed. 'Very well, Gideon,' she said. 'I shall call you by your name and you will feed me before I expire from hunger.'

At her words he turned to looked at her, his eyes travelling over her body in blatant appraisal. 'I believe you have enough flesh on you to survive another star-twinkle or two,' he said, his tone of voice as warm as his scrutiny.

He was in no hurry to serve the stew and Hedra was forced to wait patiently until it was cooked to his satisfaction, her gaze travelling through the small oblong window by her chair. It had grown very dark outside the cottage, the forest no more than a grey army of sturdy trees whose massed ranks harboured a way of life that only came about during darkfall. From within the forest's dark interior she could hear the distinctive calls of wild birds and animals and for the first time she

56

thanked the generosity of the fate masters that she had been spared another night under the stars.

Inside the cottage it was a very different story. Gideon had gradually added more wood to the fire, stoking it up nicely so that its flames lit up the interior with a comforting rosy glow. And now the distinctive scent of black locust twigs mingled harmoniously with the enticing aroma of their supper.

Hedra's stomach growled suddenly and she made no attempt to hide it.

Gideon glanced around, smiled, then reached for two dishes fashioned from beaten silver into which he ladled generous helpings of the stew. 'It would be a very poor state of affairs if I kept you waiting any longer,' he said, setting down the dishes on the table and pulling up a chair to sit opposite her.

Grateful that she had food in front of her at last she bent her head forward and sniffed the rising steam.

'What is it?' she asked.

Gideon smiled and said, 'Just eat it and enjoy it.'

'I can't eat something if I don't know what it is,' she persisted but Gideon was implacable.

'Just do as I tell you and eat,' he said firmly.

Hedra stared at him for a moment and opened her mouth to argue but all of a sudden her stomach growled even more forcibly than before. With a shrug of her shoulders she decided to give in gracefully and dipped the roughly beaten metal spoon he had given her into the dark savoury mixture. Its texture was smooth and thick like molasses and when she put out the tip of her tongue and tasted it, she realised straightaway that the meat was rabbit.

'Why did you refuse to tell me if it is only rabbit?' she asked, perplexed.

Gideon regarded her thoughtfully over his bowl for a moment before replying. 'I considered it would be no bad thing if you started to learn a little obedience and perhaps a little trust.'

'I am a princess,' Hedra said hotly. 'I am the one who demands obedience.'

'Is that so?' Gideon said. He placed his spoon down on the table and leaned back in his chair.

His stare unnerved her and presently Hedra began to fidget. Despite her recent hunger she too put down her spoon. 'Do you not believe that I am a princess?' she demanded.

She noticed that, like the Satyrian earth, his eyes were ochre-coloured and now they glowed warmly as he spoke. 'Of course, why should I not believe you?' he said.

'Because you do not treat me with the respect I deserve.'

'Oh, but of course – the respect you deserve,' he said, his tone mocking. Reaching across the table he suddenly ran one large hand across her breasts. 'This is Satyria, here you must earn respect.'

Hedra was speechless. She gazed down at the hand which still rested upon her breasts over the thin fabric of her gown. His nails were thick, opalescent and once more she was reminded of his bestial nature. Suddenly she shivered and felt her belly gripped by longing. Raising her eyes tentatively to meet his she said, 'What would you have me do to earn your respect, Gideon?'

To her surprise he removed his hand. 'Do?' he said, a smile playing about his lips. 'All I expect you to do is to concede that here in Satyria you are like any other woman. That is to say, you are neither better nor worse than the finest lady or the lowliest village maid. Above all, what you must do is be true to your own desires. I have little time or inclination for elaborate games.'

Hedra was dumbfounded. No one had ever spoken to her that way before. Her first reaction was that he had insulted her beyond measure and she should have nothing more to do with him. Her second was to admit that she wanted him and the whole Satyrian way of life very badly indeed. As if to add credence to her thoughts she felt the telltale wetness gather on the brink of her sex and her body began to warm and expand in tune with her mental desire.

'I want you,' she said in a hoarse gasp. Reaching out with her hands she stroked them over the muscular ridges of his naked chest and stomach. 'I want all you have to offer.'

As she caressed him, Gideon allowed his eyelids to flutter to a close and he simply gave himself up to the pleasurable sensations that overtook his body.

Feeling emboldened by his response, she rose from her chair, moved around the small table to him and sank down to her knees in front of his tensely poised body. Her hands never left his torso and all the time she continued to stroke and caress him she heard a strange keening sound that, she was shocked to realise, was coming from between her own lips.

Never had she felt desire so strongly. It was as though her whole body had come alive for the very first time – an awakening. Her entire being felt like a single tightly compressed flower bud, that opened out, petal by petal, to reveal a warm, soft inner core and a naked longing of such intensity that she was certain it could never be assuaged.

Gideon sat perfectly still, allowing her to touch him yet making no move to reciprocate.

Hedra felt as though she was undergoing a trial of some kind, a test of her own erotic limits she supposed. Oh, how she loved the feel of him, the iron-hard musculature, the curves and valleys of his arms and torso. Shuffling closer to him on her knees, she pressed her body against his legs, luxuriating in the warmth that emanated from them and the way it permeated the layers of her robe and skin. She touched him more boldly now, running her fingertips over the ridges of his tautly muscled abdomen, moving upward to circle the dark brown areolae. Then his nipples. Ah! She nearly laughed aloud as they hardened so readily under her touch. His body's responses made her feel so skilful, encouraging her to be ever more inquisitive.

Now her fingers ventured to his throat, tracing the prominent tendons, the boldness of his throat-apple. As she reached and touched she could feel his knees pressing into her stomach and even under the covering of her robe her breasts seemed to hang in mid-air, so full-blown and heavy all of a sudden that she couldn't ignore them. Touch me, she willed him, as she had done to the Chivalrous Knight before, explore my body as I explore yours. With impish intent she plundered her hair and pulled out the length of vine. Then she willed him again.

All at once his hands were upon her, all over her. They cupped her breasts and squeezed them, the skilful thumbs easily working her nipples into such a state of excitement that they chafed against the delicate fabric of her robe. Then they roamed her shoulders and her back, down her arms and up again, moulding and squeezing the pliant flesh.

To Hedra, whose body had so long been denied the erotic caress of another, it was the purest, most unutterable bliss. Heedless of her own sense of shame, she arched her back and thrust her breasts deeper into his hands. Now it was she who was bestial, between her thighs her most intimate parts swelled and throbbed and issued forth an unending stream of moisture. She could feel her own arousal, indeed she could smell it as though it were the finest scented oil and her body had been doused in it.

Gideon buried his face into the soft cleft between the globes of creamy flesh that swelled above her bodice. He pressed his lips against her skin before opening them and licking her with long, smooth strokes. 'You taste so fine,' he growled into the depths of her body with a passion so fierce that she felt his words reverberate through her to the soles of her feet. 'I want to devour you. To taste and suckle every part of you until your flesh becomes too tender to bear my touch.'

Hedra groaned. His words inflamed her as much as his caresses. There was nothing she wouldn't do for him, nothing he couldn't do to her – nothing. She began to rip savagely at her clothes, the once-fine robe now only a hindrance, a barrier between her skin and his. 'Help me,' she said hoarsely as she tried to tear the front of her bodice.

Gently Gideon removed her hands and replaced them with his own. In one, great bear-like wrench he ripped the fabric asunder and allowed it to fall in tatters around her waist. Now her breasts were bared to his hungry gaze and thrust forward as she arched her back still more. His eyes devoured her, her nipples so proud and swollen, like huge raspberries, that he could not keep himself from tasting them. First one, then the other, licking and sucking at them – the fruit of her body ripe on his tongue.

Hedra moaned when she felt the first caress of fire-warmed air touch her naked skin, her cries of pleasure becoming louder and more frantic as she watched him feast his eyes upon her and then take her aching teats between his lips. Her nipples were as red and juicy as his tongue, flesh upon flesh, camouflaged by the rosy hue of desire. The sight inflamed her even more and she clutched wildly at his mane of hair, bringing him closer to her naked torso as she thrust herself wantonly against him.

His hair was surprisingly soft and silky and she wound her fingers into it like garlands of woodland flowers, all the time urging her body closer and closer to his. His tongue and lips were driving her mad with lust, working on her desperate flesh like a suckling animal, covering her breasts with wetness that dried instantly on contact with the air. And his tongue was so strong. It pushed at her breasts, forcing them upwards so that he could lick at the undersides.

Lower down, her pleasure parts were on fire, the throbbing flesh awash with her own juices. His hands gripped her shoulders now and she felt herself parting her legs and rubbing her lower body against his knee.

61

The agony was exquisite, a mounting pleasure that increased in intensity with each star-twinkle.

To her dismay he stopped lapping at her breasts. But then, in the next moment, he moved forward in his chair and sank to his knees in front of her, his mouth now moving to suck and lick her throat, the wet flesh moving along her collarbone, up behind her ears and around her hairline. One huge hand lifted her hair away from the back of her neck and she felt the soft caress of air and then his mouth and nose nuzzling her, his tongue sliding wetly over her skin, covering every inch.

She inclined her head to the side, offering him the long pale sweep of her neck. Her breasts chafed hungrily against his bare chest, which she could now feel was covered in a light down that was not visible to the naked eye. Sensation heaped upon sensation as his mouth and hands began to roam her body at will and she gasped a moment later as both his hands suddenly gripped her shoulders and pulled her tightly against him.

His very nearness invited her to stroke him with her breath and she allowed her eyelids to flutter closed as his lips pressed hers open and his thick, pink tongue snaked inside her mouth, tasting her from the inside. Lower down, she could feel the hard length of his excitement pressing into the softness of her belly and her own pleasure bud answer in return with a fierce pulsing. She felt lightheaded with excitement, her moisture flowing freely, readying her body for his pleasure gift.

As they continued to kiss he turned her around and gradually eased her down so that she lay on her back on a fur rug in front of the hearth. His hands pulled at the remainder of her robe, easing it over her hips, down her legs and away from her body. Now she lay naked before him, her only covering the soft glow of the fire and the shadow of his huge body as he hovered over her.

For a moment he did nothing more than look at her, his ochre-coloured eyes flicking backwards and forwards over her torso, scanning every inch. A slow smile started at his lips and spread across his face to reach his eyes.

'You are a beautiful woman, Hedra,' he said, speaking the words solemnly as if they were an indisputable truth.

She glowed warmer than the fire at his unexpected compliment and found her thighs parting as if of their own accord. 'Touch me, Gideon,' she said, urging him with her voice as well as her thoughts. She raised her hips a little from the fur rug. 'Touch me.'

Propping himself on one arm he kneeled between her legs, the outer flesh of his huge muscled thighs grazing the insides of her own legs as he stroked his free hand slowly across her breasts, down her stomach and over her belly, his fingertips lightly meshing with the soft violet fleece of her pubic hair. It looked and felt like the finest sugar strands and for a moment he delighted simply in stroking it, in running his broad fingers over her mound and lightly tickling the puffy lips beneath.

Hedra squirmed under his touch. It was so delicate, so refined that she felt she would scream aloud with her desire for him to display the rougher, bestial side to his nature that she felt certain existed. Beside her the fire crackled and cast out a comforting rosy glow, although the heat of it was not too hot upon her skin and it certainly could not match the cauldron of passion that churned within her.

Across the ceiling and around the walls she could see the shadows that the flickering flames created, like long tongues licking at the rough hewn wood, whilst beneath her she could feel the soft fur of the rug caressing her naked skin. It tickled her ankles and the backs of her knees and, further up, it tantalised the soft flesh on the inner parts of her legs. Her buttocks clenched and unclenched rhythmically, almost of their own accord and she arched her back, pressing her shoulders into the soft fur, offering herself up to him.

Gideon did not have to read her thoughts to know that she was ready for him. He could see her desperation and, when he finally allowed his hand to venture between her parted thighs, he could tell instantly that physically she was ready for him too. He knelt up, rearing over her like a great beast. The hand between her legs worked her swollen pleasure lips apart and he began to stroke the moist flesh between, his fingertips sliding over the hard nub of her pleasure bud before plunging into the wet opening below. With the other hand he unfastened his brief loincloth and threw it aside.

Hedra stared at him wide-eyed. She noticed immediately that he sported no underclothes and immediately his erect phallus sprang free, its huge dimensions entrancing the princess who had previously been used to nothing larger than her own Pleasure Stone. Despite her chaste upbringing a hiss of desire issued unbidden from her lips.

Without intending to do so, she found herself gazing at his groin as if in a trance. Despite her usual boldness she blushed as his phallus twitched slightly and seemed to grow bigger than ever under her gaze. All at once she didn't know what to do. With the few other men she had known she had been the one in a position of strength – princess of the land they visited. Now however, she was alone in a strange land, in a strange forest, with a huge creature who appeared at first glance to be barely more than a lowly animal. And yet, there was something about him that set him apart. Something almost refined, as though he was far descended down a lordly line.

Gideon leaned forward and pressed his lips once more against her mouth and he noticed how, straight-away, her lips opened and her eyes closed. She tasted sweet, like nectar cake, and he ground his lips down upon hers, his tongue plundering the inner depths of her mouth. His desire for her was now almost unbearable, like a pain. He felt as hard as steel, his erect phallus a burning rod that sought to plunge her very depths.

Unaware of the true extent of his hunger for her, Hedra simply revelled in the sensation of his naked body brushing her own. Reaching up to him she ran her palms over his shoulders and down the sides of his arms, delighting in their obvious strength and the hardness of the musculature beneath. She allowed her fingertips to linger on his forearms for a moment, tracing the outline of the muscle and sinew beneath the taut skin then, after a few moments, she ran her hands back up his arms and over his shoulders again.

This time her hands sought to stroke the long mane of hair that fell down the length of his back and delighted her immeasurably. As she did this he continued to explore her mouth with his and, after a few blissful star-twinkles had passed, she finally dared her hands to leave his hair and travel down his back to cup the mighty globes of his buttocks. They felt like iron beneath her delicate fingers and she trembled at the prospect of his powerful thrusts.

The whole of her body screamed out to him now. He hovered over her, one huge arm supporting his weight whilst his other hand roamed remorselessly between her legs and over her breasts, pinching and rolling the hard pink buds that crowned them until she began to moan and squirm with unrestrained delight.

'Please, Gideon,' she gasped urgently, 'let us make our pleasure! I need to feel you inside me.'

When he didn't respond to her demand immediately she reached down between their bodies, questing his solid phallus with her fingers, sliding them over the bulbous head on a slick coating of his own excitement juice and stroking them up and down the long, thick stem.

His body trembled in response to her touch, the juices within him bubbling with excitement. 'Witch woman,' he growled, his eyes burning with undisguised lust, 'priestess of pleasure!'

He took his hand away from her breast then took control of his own hardness and introduced the swollen tip to the edge of her hot, hungry sex. It started to yield to him immediately and yet he still wished to prolong each tormenting moment.

Hardly able to bear the suspense, the feel of him so close and yet so far, she spread her thighs wide in invitation and he thrust his lower body toward hers, entering her so powerfully that it took her breath away.

The way he filled her was magnificent. His phallus was so broad and long that she felt stretched to the widest extremes, yet she did not hesitate to buck her hips beneath him, to encourage stronger and faster movements. The rhythm of their clashing bodies pulled and tugged at the soft flesh around her pleasure bud and she felt herself rising to her zenith quickly, the heat overtaking her just a moment before the spasms of gratification began.

Hedra tossed her head from side to side and cried aloud, her eyes opening wide as he grasped her breasts and kneaded them in time with his thrusts. His pleasure-making was manic. It was bestial as she knew it would be – pure, unrestrained gratification. Feeling the heat build rapidly within her she screamed and attained her zenith a second time. Then he too cried out aloud – a long, drawn-out bellow of release that echoed around the walls of the small cottage and invited answering calls from the wild beasts of the forest.

He throbbed inside her for a long while until, gradually, his hardness diminished and their ragged breathing returned to normal.

Hedra smiled and stroked his long mane of hair before he rolled away from her and surprised her by picking her up in his strong arms and carrying her to the bed.

Laying down beside her he pulled her limp body back against him in a fiercely protective gesture and covered them both with the fur blanket. Nestled in the warmth of the animal skins they slept, smiling and replete, while the moons came up and sank down again to be replaced by the first golden sun of morning time.

When she awoke it was to discover him nuzzling between her legs. With a cry of pleasure, she spread her legs wider and ground her hips as his long, thick tongue snaked over the furrow between her thighs and entered the musky depths of her body. It was as though he wanted to discover her body all over again and when he finally entered her it was with as much passion as he had shown the night before. Hedra churned under his great bulk. His pleasure-making was exquisite, driving her to greater frenzies of delight as she greeted her climax.

Eventually, he rose from the bed and left her feeling sated and deliciously comfortable snuggled in the depths of the huge bed, her naked body wrapped in soft fur. He stretched his glorious body with obvious satisfaction and smiled down at her.

'By the mystics, you are a beautiful sight to behold, my princess,' he said.

'And you, my fine king of the beasts,' she replied, a dreamy smile playing about her lips and softening her gaze.

He left her with a kiss that he blew from his lips and allowed to hover in mid air between them. Her smile became broader at his action and she rolled on to her side to watch him as he moved about the room, clearing away their dishes from the night before and preparing a new day meal of fruit and bread. Then, when he placed it on the table, she rose reluctantly from the comfort of the bed and ate, her body naked, her mind at peace. At some point during the night she had allowed certain thoughts to take shape and now they had crystallised and set.

'Gideon,' she said, 'I have reached a decision about something.'

He raised his head to look at her, his warm eyes watchful, his mouth still chewing on a piece of nut-bread as he nodded to her to continue.

'I shall not be travelling on to Piosia,' she said. 'I did not want to go there in the first place and now I am certain.' She paused to assess his reaction but his expression was inscrutable. 'I intend to find a niche of my own here in Satyria, somewhere I can properly call home. But firstly I must write to my father. It is only right that I send him word of my intentions.'

'Do you think it is a wise plan?' Gideon asked her at long last. He reclined in his chair and studied her as she nodded her head enthusiastically.

'Oh, yes,' she said. 'Here in Satyria I can truly be myself.'

'Satyria is not like Piosia, or Parsimonia,' he pointed out needlessly. 'The . . . ah, way of life is very much different.'

Hedra smiled broadly, her hands moving to stroke her own breasts. She considered her nipples for a moment as they hardened into tight buds between her fingertips, then she raised her head to stare at him candidly. 'That is why I owe it to myself to stay,' she said. 'I cannot find the sort of happiness I seek in a land that does not permit the natural pleasures of the flesh.'

Gideon nodded. 'You are very welcome to stay here for as long as you wish,' he said, glancing around the small room. 'There is not too much space but I cannot say I find the idea of sharing my living quarters with you at all repulsive.'

'Particularly your bed,' Hedra added.

He laughed softly. 'Particularly my bed.'

She recognised the look in his eyes and a sudden flame leaped within her. Already his ways were becoming familiar to her and in moments he was on his feet, scooping her up in his arms as though she were nothing more than a featherweight, before dropping her unceremoniously on to the bed. It was time for the pleasure to start all over again.

# Chapter Five

$H$edra wrote to her father on a piece of coral-tree bark that looked just like a pale pink sheet of parchment.

'We shall have to journey to the village to find a harbinger to deliver it,' Gideon said, handing her a thick crystal cup of rose-hip tea.

Her fingers remained wrapped around the steaming bowl as she gazed up at him and asked, 'Is the village a good way hence?'

'No,' he replied, 'on horseback we should make it there and back during the period of the second sun.'

'I shall need something to wear,' she said, glancing down at her naked body, 'but the small amount of clothing that I brought is little more than a heap of tatters.'

Gideon picked up her bag and emptied its meagre contents on the table. He saw immediately that she was right in her assessment. Apart from her comb, mirror and hairbrush, the beetle-shaped bottle of scented oil and a few mother-of-pearl hair combs, the rest of her things were beyond use.

'I have my jewelled girdle. I could sell that to buy some new clothes,' she suggested.

'But you still need something to wear to the village in

the first place,' he said, almost at a loss to know what they should do.

For a few moments they both stared at the pile of clothes in silence, then Gideon found himself staring at the thin muslin curtains that were draped across the window in a single swathe. In an instant he was on his feet and releasing the curtains from the gold hooks that held them.

Hedra stared at him. 'What are you doing?' she said in amazement. 'Have you suddenly lost your senses?'

He turned to her and held the gossamer fabric in front of him. 'Your new gown, my princess,' he said with a smile.

She stared without comprehension at the length of muslin, then she realised his intention and rose to her feet so that he could wrap the material around her body. It circled her slim form a couple of times and once it had been fastened with a plaited girdle of golden fox hair it looked to all intents and purposes like a proper robe.

'It is perfect. Just fit for a princess,' she exclaimed delightedly, turning this way and that so that the delicate fabric billowed around her bare legs like a white cloud.

Gideon smiled, enjoying her pleasure and the sight of her draped in the fine muslin. If anything, the semi-transparent fabric merely served to highlight her sinuous form and the fact that she was naked underneath. But it was no matter, she was properly clothed and they would be in the village for hardly any time at all.

She followed him outside the cottage, paused to pick a fresh length of laissi vine to decorate her hair, just in case, and mounted Vanora. The unicorn had been peacefully eating her fill of delicious oat grass but now she whickered with joy at being able to serve her mistress.

Gideon mounted Rowan, who also grazed close by and, riding side by side, he and Hedra started to make their journey down the dusty road that led away from the forest in the direction of the nearest village.

Hedra found the scenery to be quite flat and boring for the first few miles but then it began to change hue and form. The ground became more undulating, with small hillocks covered by thickly growing blood-red grass, and they had to cross many small culverts which were constantly filled from tiny waterfalls that trickled down the hillsides like narrow ribbons of silver.

Presently the road widened and was bounded by lush meadows filled with a profusion of wild flowers which were punctuated every so often by rows of rough wooden huts that looked as though they had collapsed against each other like a fallen house of cards. Hedra shuddered at the prospect of living in one of those hovels. Indeed, she thought, the dilapidated buildings made Gideon's cottage look luxurious in comparison.

'We do not have much further to travel,' he said, mistaking her sombre expression for one of tiredness.

She leaned forward and patted Vanora's silky neck before turning her head to smile at him. 'I am glad, I feel quite excited at the thought of being surrounded by people once again.'

It was true. All of a sudden it occurred to her that she had spent too much time in solitude – or near solitude if she counted Gideon's quiet presence. She was not destined to live the life of a recluse, she realised. She needed the hustle and bustle of a busy castle around her and the gay revelling of a banquet or ball. If there was anything about her old life that she missed, apart from her father of course, it was the vibrant life and colour of the royal court that she had simply taken for granted before.

When they finally arrived at the village she found it was everything she had hoped for and more. Smiling, laughing people, hearty and ruddy of complexion, spilled from every open doorway. Children danced merrily around the brightly coloured maypole on the village green, chased each other down the main street

71

squealing loudly with delight, and played hoop and stick or ninepins. And the provision stores fairly groaned with good things: brightly coloured fruits and vegetables, fine fabrics, delicious sweetmeats and huge iced cakes. When her excited gaze alighted on these in particular, Hedra's mouth watered.

'I love cake,' she murmured to Gideon, her eyes glittering brightly in anticipation. 'May we buy some?'

'Of course, if my princess loves cakes, then cake she shall have,' he said indulgently. He had brought with him several brace of partridge and rabbit to sell and he dismounted and turned for the crooked doorway of the small butcher's shop. 'I shan't be but a moment,' he assured her.

As soon as he entered the shop Hedra also dismounted and tethered both Vanora and Rowan to a nearby hitching post before wandering along the main thoroughfare, hungrily taking in all the sights and smells of the bustling village. She was just watching the village cobbler working on a pair of tall black-leather riding boots and wondering to whom they belonged when a clattering of hooves and huge clouds of dust signalled the arrival of a horseman.

She glanced up and suddenly felt her stomach clench with trepidation. The rider had reined in his horse to a slow walk and now the huge ebony steed approached her, its velvety skin covered in a thin layer of white foam, its wide nostrils snorting out clouds of steamy breath. Instinctively, Hedra backed away.

'Stay there, young woman!' the rider commanded and she stopped immediately in her tracks, her heart beating wildly.

A moment later the horse drew alongside her and she was able to see that the dark-haired rider was a knight of some description but unlike the Chivalrous Knights he was clad entirely in black: from the thickly padded shoulders of his black leather jacket to the gleaming soles of his black leather boots.

He was obviously not intending to engage in combat,

she surmised, as he wore no armour of any kind, although from his waist hung a long white-gold scabbard, decorated with gemstones and filigree and from the top of the riding boot directly in front of her face projected the jewel-encrusted handle of a dagger.

The knight stared down at her. 'From whence do you hail, wench?' he said, his voice as dark and threatening as thunder.

Hedra swallowed deeply and forced herself to reply boldly, although her voice emerged as little more than a nervous squeak. 'Parsimonia,' she replied. 'I am Princess Hedra.'

He considered her in silence for a moment, as though weighing up the truth of her reply, then he said, 'What business have you in Satyria? It is not usually a place that Parsimonians care to visit.'

'I realise that, sir,' Hedra said politely, 'but my kingdom was threatened by the plague. I was on my way to find sanctuary in Piosia when my self and my band of Chivalrous Knights were waylaid by a scurrilous king. I managed to escape but became lost.'

The knight suppressed a smile. 'Scurrilous you say? No doubt it was King Randolph who attacked your knights.'

'I have no knowledge of his name,' Hedra said, 'but it was indeed King Randolph who taunted us with the plague. My father, King Hector, did everything in his power to encourage him to agree to a peaceful solution but alas to no avail.'

'That sounds like him, the rogue,' the knight asserted. He gazed down at her, taking in her beauty and her youthful innocence. 'As a Parsimonian, and a princess at that, no doubt you are an innocent?' he said.

She considered his assumption. Of course, she was far from an innocent. Her virginity had been lost to her for quite some time, yet for some reason she felt as though it would be in her best interests to simply agree. Raising her eyes to meet his she nodded silently.

The knight reached down to her, his hands huge as

73

they grasped her arms and pulled her off her feet, dragging her bodily over the saddle in front of him.

For a moment she was stunned, then she began to struggle and squirm upon the uncomfortable ridge of the saddle.

'Stop that at once!' the knight commanded and horrified her by delivering two stinging blows to her buttocks. 'I shall take you back to the castle,' he said firmly. 'You may as well join the vestal virgins and let Lord Gerard decide your fate.'

She felt her face glowing as warmly as her behind. How dare he show the temerity to smack her without her instructing him to do so first? It was beyond her comprehension that she should be treated in such an off-hand manner.

Squirming angrily under the palm that pressed down against the small of her back, she managed to turn her face to glare up at him. 'Unhand me, sir!' she demanded. 'Let me down at once!' In answer, the hand pressed even harder upon her back. 'How dare you, let me go!' she said and began to struggle and shout savagely, her eyes glittering with the force of her anger.

Again, two stinging slaps were delivered to her rear and the knight leaned right forward to whisper harshly in her ear, 'Be silent, girl, or I shall have you stripped and placed in the stocks for a public whipping,' he said. 'I'll wager your Royal Highness would not like to become a public spectacle? Think of the shame!'

To her horror, Hedra felt a sudden rush of moisture flow unbidden from her body. Her buttocks were still smarting but his words affected her more. The thought of being whipped naked and in public suddenly seemed to her the most terrifyingly delicious prospect. It was clear Satyria was indeed a barbaric land and one in which her royal lineage would not afford her many privileges.

'Very well, I shall go with you,' she said, 'but do not expect me to like it.'

Although she could not see the evidence for herself,

her reply amused the knight and a slow smile spread across his face. 'It is of no consequence to me whether you like it or not,' he replied, as solemnly as he could. 'It is what may please your Lord and Master Gerard that should matter to you from now on.'

With that the knight wheeled his horse around, dug his spurs into its glossy flanks and galloped out of the village – the swift hooves of his steed carrying them relentlessly towards the distant, shadowy form of the castle.

From inside the meat vendor's shop Gideon heard a kerfuffle taking place but thought nothing of it. The shop's hearty owner, with his bullish face and generous, muscular body that made him look like a prime head of cattle, glanced up from counting out a princely sum into Gideon's hand. His face broke into a broad smile.

'Lord Gerard will have a new maid to deflower come darkfall if I'm not mistaken,' he said with a knowing glint in his eye.

'What makes you say that?' Gideon asked. He wasn't really concentrating on anything other than the generous amount of money the vendor had offered him for his wares. It seemed that the locals had taken a particular liking to partridge and were prepared to pay well for the luxury. He continued to eye the golden coins in his palm until the noises that had occurred outside the shop began to take on real significance in his mind. He hastily recalled the sound of a horse's hooves clattering upon the cobbled stones, a stern voice and the higher pitched voice of a young woman. A young woman in a state of distress. Hedra!

To the amazement of the vendor, Gideon dropped his handful of coins on the broad wooden counter and ran from the shop. To his right he could see nothing. He looked up the road to his left. All he could see in that direction was a cloud of dust. And there was no sign of the princess.

'The young miss was taken, Sir,' the old boot mender

called out, disturbing Gideon's frantic thoughts. ''Twas a knight who came. The maid didn't have any say in the matter.'

Gideon slumped against the nearest wall. There was no point in going after them. The knight's steed would be swift and its hooves used to the rough terrain. They would be long gone by now. He thought for a moment, of how he should react to the situation. It was a shame to lose Hedra so soon after they had met. She had been warm and sensuous and fun to be with. But he knew deep down that she would not have stayed with him for too long. Her future was destined to include the finer things in life, things he could not give her. And, in all honesty, he did not fear too greatly for her safety either. She was strong of body and of will. He did not doubt for one moment that she was well equipped to take care of herself.

The thought made him smile, albeit a little wistfully, and he turned to go back into the shop. He would conclude his business and find a harbinger to deliver the princess's missive anyway. After all, who could tell? Perhaps one day, if the fate masters looked kindly enough upon him, he would meet up with Hedra again.

The road to the castle was long and steep, a meandering ribbon of barren wasteland covered with a thin layer of bright yellow dust and lined with unspeakable perils. For the most part Hedra remained in blissful ignorance of the shadowy dangers that lurked behind every tree and shrub, conscious only of the strong male body that held her fast and the unaccustomed movement of the great black beast beneath her.

They left the village far below them and the forest became only a distant vision – a ragged fringe of treetops that hung from the edge of the grassy gown that covered the rest of the undulating land. And ahead loomed the castle, a ghostly apparition perched like a vulture atop a craggy mountain and shrouded in blue-grey mist.

'Is that where we are headed?' Hedra called behind her unnecessarily. She already knew the answer but felt anxious to break the silence that had separated her from her captor since they left the village.

'It is, Princess, it is,' he said. Leaning forward he spoke into the back of her hair as it whipped around his face like a swirling cloud. Then suddenly he increased the pressure of his hand upon her back as his steed faltered slightly on some loose shale.

She couldn't help noticing how he enveloped the word 'princess' in a mocking tone, as though he did not quite believe the truth of her claim to royal birthright. It angered her and yet amused her. Let him treat her badly at his peril, she thought to herself with a wry, inner smile. The day could not be too far hence when he would come to her and beg her forgiveness for doubting the word of a ruler's progeny. She could wait.

All at once, her thoughts were disturbed by the sudden appearance of a small legion of Glarbs – thigh-high creatures of the outer limits whose elfin features were almost completely obscured by the large hoods of their roughly woven cloaks. Hedra knew they posed no real threat but the creatures' small bodies impeded their passage, several being trampled under the merciless hooves of the knight's horse. And their inane calls and piercing cries were irritating to the ear.

'Go away, you confounded wastrels!' Hedra raged at them, kicking out blindly at their scrawny bodies before turning her head to demand that the knight give her his sword. 'I'll smite the little wretches and slice them in two,' she declared with the bitter venom of one who means exactly what she says.

'Now is that any way for a princess to behave?' the knight said, his words deliberately mocking her once again. 'I avow, Lord Gerard will have sport with you.'

Hedra trembled at his words, although her anger was overlaid with a powerful sense of excitement. It seemed that the very threat of the infamous Lord Gerard sent her mind reeling and her lower body surging with the

77

heat of desire. 'If you will not slay them, I shall,' she retorted, referring to the squalling Glarbs who still plagued them. 'They are turning my veins into cauldrons of boiling claret and their noise pains my head unbearably.'

'I think the sweet princess exaggerates her claim,' the knight said. He mocked her a third time and on this occasion she lost her temper completely and turned swiftly to lash out at him. It was a rash move. With a cry of dismay she immediately slipped from the horse and fell headlong to the ground.

Straightaway the Glarbs surrounded her. Like a living blanket they covered her body, their ragged talons tearing at her hair, her skin and her makeshift robe.

With a bellow of rage designed to frighten the lowly creatures away, the knight leaped from his steed and began to lash out with his sword, slicing mercilessly at anything that stood between him and the princess who, far from laying meek and helpless as he expected, fought and screamed abuse at her attackers.

As the small creatures hesitated for a moment she rose from the midst of the violent horde, like a beautiful flame-bird rising from its ashes, and the knight recognised at once that his captive was not simply another village maid.

Realising their attack was useless, the thwarted Glarbs scattered and the knight mounted his horse once more and pulled Hedra up to join him. This time though he allowed her to sit upright in front of him, his left arm encircling her slender waist tightly, and for the rest of the journey he appeared to treat her with a new respect.

She noticed the change in his manner but said nothing. Nor did she employ a sarcastic tone of voice when she thanked him most kindly for his attempted rescue, however unnecessary his gallantry may have turned out to be.

* * *

78

By the time they arrived at the Satyrian castle evenfall was already well and truly upon them and the forbidding stone construction seemed to Hedra to be little more than a huge, dark shadow. Upon their approach the drawbridge was lowered with a great clanking and squealing of chains that badly needed oiling and the knight's horse galloped across at great speed, its hooves clattering on the rotting timbers. Immediately, the drawbridge drew up to a close behind them and she found herself trapped in the confines of the castle proper.

Turning her head this way and that she noticed straightaway that, from the perspective of the outer courtyard, the castle was not that different to her home in Parsimonia. Once they had entered the huge black-iron portal, however, it was a different story. Instead of being covered with rich, warming tapestries the grey stone walls were mostly left bare and the flagstones were similarly uncovered.

She realised the knight was deliberately avoiding the main halls and passageways as he led her through a maze of gloomy corridors, their misery only relieved by the occassional torch flickering upon the walls and a tarnished shield or wooden plaque positioned here and there.

The knight strode swiftly, the leather soles of his boots hardly making any sound on the flagstones and Hedra found herself almost running to keep up with him. Finally, he paused outside a huge pair of oak doors. Each one had a diamond-shaped hole cut into it at eye-level and now he peered into one of them and rapped sharply on the wooden door three times.

Hedra waited, one foot tapping impatiently. Her curiosity was aroused by her new surroundings and she longed to be able to see what he could see. She raised herself on tiptoe and tried to peer over his shoulder through the second diamond but he turned his head, his shoulder forcing her to move away. It was the first time she had really looked at him and now she saw,

with a tremor of lust, how purely handsome he was –
his skin smooth and swarthy, his features well shaped
and precisely placed upon the canvas of his face.

'I . . . ah, I just wanted to see in there,' she said, her
heart beating rapidly. 'Is that the vestal chamber?'

He nodded. 'It is indeed,' he said, 'and you shall see
in there soon enough. In fact, I wager that in a week or
two you will be heartily tired of your surroundings.'

Hedra's heart sank and she wondered at the hidden
meaning behind his words. Did he suspect that she was
not an innocent after all? However could she have given
him that impression?

Whatever it was he believed, he still continued to rap
his knuckles against the wood every star-twinkle or so.

Eventually she heard the sound of shuffling feet
behind the door and the soft *swish-swish* of the hem of a
long gown sweeping the bare stone floor. The sounds
came closer and closer then a moment later there was
the further sound of keys being jangled together, and
the distinctive rattle of one being placed in the keyhole
and turned. With a loud creak the door swung open
away from Hedra and the knight and he stepped
forward across the threshold and motioned to her to
follow him.

When the door closed behind them again, Hedra
noticed a tall woman, middle-aged but quite beautiful
still with long white hair gathered into topknots upon
her crown. Hedra smiled automatically but the woman
did not reciprocate. Instead she pushed past her and
the knight and began to lead the way down the
passageway.

To Hedra's mind the woman seemed to glide along.
She held her back perfectly straight and stiff, her head
erect upon a graceful swan-like neck. Her gown was of
a dark green silk, with long tight sleeves and worn
unfashionably full – over a heap of petticoats, Hedra
surmised. She wore no other items of clothing, no lace
kerchief or shawl and no girdle of any kind; nor did she
flaunt any jewellery or hair ornaments.

She stopped at the first doorway they came to and indicated with her hand that Hedra should enter, although the knight did not attempt to cross the threshold of the room but stood just outside the doorway and spoke briefly with the woman who nodded in response and occasionally said, 'Yes, I see,' and, 'Of course, that goes without saying.'

Eventually the knight stopped talking and it was obvious to Hedra, from his lip movements and the way he inclined his body, that he was bidding the woman goodbye. Just before he turned on his heel he glanced inside the room where Hedra stood, hands clasped meekly in front of her.

'You will be comfortable in the safekeeping of Mistress Quigley,' he said. It was not a question but a statement. Nevertheless Hedra nodded. 'Good,' he said, satisfied. 'We may or may not meet again, Princess.' Then he was gone.

Hedra stared after him, her eyes fixed on the empty place where he had once stood. All of a sudden she felt bereft and a long sigh broke from her lips.

The woman stepped into the room and closed the door carefully behind her. 'You are tired, Princess,' she said, then nodded as Hedra's eyes widened. 'Yes, Sir Drago has informed me of your origins. I have heard tell of you and I have no reason to doubt your claim.'

At the woman's words Hedra breathed another sigh but this time of relief. Perhaps this would mean that she could expect proper treatment, mayhap a few luxuries. However, her hopes were dashed in seconds when the woman spoke again.

'Remove your robe, girl, and stand upon the chair.'

Hedra glanced around. The room was completely empty except for a single wooden chair that stood in the centre. It was illuminated by a pool of light that fell from a trio of candles set in a simple iron chandelier. The ceiling ornament was nothing like the luxurious crystal and gold chandeliers that had graced the castle where she had been brought up and she shuddered at the idea of standing there naked and vulnerable in front of this sharp-eyed woman.

'What are you waiting for, girl!' Mistress Quigley said, her icy tone breaking through Hedra's reverie. 'I believe my command was simple enough to understand.'

Hedra turned her eyes to meet the cold, fish-eyed gaze. 'I understood you well enough, mistress,' she said as calmly as possible. 'However, I have no intention of complying.'

Mistress Quigley's glassy stare narrowed. 'You have no choice,' she said, 'unless you wish me to eject you from the castle. Or perhaps you would prefer to be left to the mercy of the Glarbs and hobgoblins, not to mention the many species of wild animals that roam hereabouts?' She gave a thin laugh and placed her hands upon her hips, her body assuming a victor's stance.

With a deep sigh, Hedra acknowledged defeat. She could tell this woman was implacable and she had no desire to leave the safe confines of the castle. 'Very well,' she murmured, and with trembling fingers began to loosen the fox-hair girdle. Within moments her robe had reverted to nothing more than a muslin curtain, the delicate fabric a white pool around her feet.

Mistress Quigley watched her disrobe and nodded with satisfaction at the sight of Hedra's nakedness. 'Now, on to the chair quickly, girl,' she said, clapping her palms together smartly and instantly reminding Hedra of the slaps the knight had delivered to her buttocks earlier that evening.

On shaking legs she walked across the room to the chair and climbed awkwardly, her movements designed to try and conceal her body from the woman's prying eyes. However, she knew she had lost the battle when the older woman crossed the room to stand directly in front of her and ordered Hedra to stand with her feet as far apart as the dimensions of the seat would allow.

Biting her bottom lip to try and quell the cry of shame

that threatened to burst from her lips, Hedra shuffled her feet apart, her hesitant movements displaying her unwillingness to comply. She stared at the ceiling, trying in vain to ignore the fact that she had never revealed her body to another woman before and that right at that very moment Mistress Quigley's eyes were scanning her with undisguised interest.

'You have a good shape,' the woman said at last. 'Firm and youthful, yet womanly as well. It is an enviable combination. I'll wager Lord Gerard would pick you out from the largest selection.'

'Selection?' Hedra asked faintly. She winced as the woman suddenly reached out and cupped her breasts, her sharp fingertips pinching the nipples until they stung with pain.

'Selection of virgins,' Mistress Quigley said, pinching her nipples even harder. 'Lord Gerard takes it upon himself to personally deflower all the vestal virgins. You could almost call it a favourite pastime of his.'

At the woman's words, Hedra felt her sex contract and moisten. Oh no, she thought, her cheeks suffusing with warmth, please do not let my body betray me now. She concentrated her mind on quelling her feelings but in the next instant Mistress Quigley released her nipples and bent forward to peer between her open legs. Two bony fingers probed there and Hedra felt the shaming rush of further moisture and a familiar pulsing sensation between her pleasure lips. Please do not let her decide to look at me there, she prayed silently to the fate masters, please do not allow her to discover the evidence of my desires.

'Open yourself to me, girl,' Mistress Quigley demanded but more softly this time. 'Spread your pleasure lips and let me see your secret treasure.'

Hedra's cheeks flamed with mortification now. She couldn't bring herself to comply, yet she knew she could not refuse.

'Do it, girl, show yourself to me,' the woman said,

her tone denying any further hesitation on Hedra's part.

Hesitantly, she reached down and touched herself, her fingertips delving into her soft fleece and stroking her outer pleasure lips. She parted them carefully and oh, so slowly, trying to prolong the final agonising moment when she would reveal the true extent of her shame to Mistress Quigley's keen eyes.

'Further, move them further apart,' the woman urged, her voice sounding slightly hoarse. 'Now keep your fingers out of the way. Let me see you properly.'

With her eyes tightly closed, Hedra held herself open to the woman's inspection. She could feel the odd warmth of a stranger's breath upon her innermost flesh and her mind and body cried out for Gideon. It had been different when he had looked at her and touched her there – very, very different. This was horrible, the worst possible exposure and yet still her body responded to the humiliation as though it was enjoyable. Her pleasure bud swelled larger and the moisture gathered within her and trickled down her inner thighs. Despite her agony she let out a soft moan and the woman glanced up at her.

'You feel the indignity of this and yet the pleasure too?' she said. 'That is good, very good.'

All at once she reached out and pressed her thumb hard against the swollen bud and Hedra felt an instant rush of heat and wave upon wave of overwhelming pleasure. Despite the degradation of her response she pressed herself against the woman's thumb and let out a series of tiny mewling sounds as her body spasmed again and again. Eventually, the heat subsided within her and she became aware of the woman's bony fingers probing inside her body.

'You have not the physical proof of your virginity,' she said at last, her fingers probing deeper just to make certain.

Hedra blushed harder. She hadn't thought the humiliation could get any worse but it seemed it could.

'I . . . er . . .' she began but Mistress Quigley interrupted her.

'If you are accustomed to riding a horse, it is quite understandable,' she said, her tone almost reassuring. To Hedra's relief she removed her fingers and straightened up once again. 'You may get down now.'

Nodding her thanks, Hedra climbed down from the chair. 'I have a unicorn, Vanora,' she said, suddenly remembering that she had been forced to leave her beautiful steed behind in the village. She hoped Gideon would take care of her.

Mistress Quigley nodded. 'It is of no consequence,' she said. 'There are always other forms of "proof" that you can use.' Now she had attracted Hedra's interest but she had no intention of expanding on the subject. Instead the older woman instructed Hedra to pick up her length of muslin and carry it with her. 'I shall give you a couple of new gowns,' she said. 'You shall not be needing that, although it was quite becoming.'

Hedra thought she almost detected the inkling of a smile but Mistress Quigley was already striding out of the door. Further down the corridor they stopped outside another room. This time it proved to be a sort of dormitory where six beds were positioned three abreast and end to end, with only a narrow space separating each one.

'You shall sleep here,' Mistress Quigley said, indicating the nearest bed, then she added, 'are you hungry?'

Hedra nodded. 'Very,' she said.

'Wait here, I shall send one of the other girls with a platter for you.' The woman pointed to a tall wooden cupboard that separated Hedra's bed from the next. 'You will find a nightgown in there and your new dresses. Please see to it that you change every day. Dirty gowns are collected by the laundrywoman while you are breakfasting, which is just after the rising of the first sun.' Suddenly she glanced out of the window where the darkfall had already blanketed the sky. 'I must leave now,' she said. 'The other girls will answer any questions you may have.'

As soon as Mistress Quigley had gone, Hedra opened the cupboard and took out the voluminous cotton nightgown. It was very plain, she noticed, decorated only around the neckline with a fragile yolk of creamy tatting. After she had pulled the nightgown over her head she sat on her bed and stroked the lace thoughtfully. It could be worse, she supposed: the vestal chamber was clean and warm and she had fresh clothing and a comfortable bed. And presumably the other girls would be friendly enough.

Nevertheless, she couldn't bear to think of staying there for too long. The prospect of becoming chaste again was not a beguiling one, nor was the idea of spending her days surrounded by the inane chatter of young girls. She much preferred the attentions and conversation of a man.

Naturally, her thoughts turned to the infamous Lord Gerard. Obviously his word was law here in Satyria and this made her wonder about the king – if one existed at all he must either be very old or weak to allow a lord to rule his land.

All her questions about Satyria were answered over the next few days. The girls with whom she shared her dormitory were only too willing to divulge information, their chatter sometimes driving her to distraction but nevertheless proving useful, even diverting at times.

She learned, to her disappointment, that Lord Gerard was currently away from the castle. Although she found she was right in her assumption about the incumbent king – he was both old and feeble-minded and as he had no other successor Gerard, the son of his much younger half-brother, was the effective ruler of Satyria. Furthermore, the castle was apparently populated by a variety of courtiers who were not lords and ladies in the traditional sense but instead were known as Watchers, Clansmen and Disrobers.

'I do not understand any of this,' Hedra said, shaking her head in bewilderment. 'This is not like any kingdom I have heard of before.'

At that the other girls had laughed. 'That is true enough,' one of them, a tiny red-haired girl called Serona said. 'Either you love the Satyrian way of life or hate it. It is brutal and licentious but exciting all at the same time. Or so my mother has told me,' she added hastily. 'Since the age of twelve I have not been outside the vestal chamber.'

Hedra stared at her wide-eyed. 'You have been here for six years?' she said, knowing the girl was eighteen. 'But how can you bear to wait so long to be chosen?'

The girl laughed. 'It is not so bad,' she assured her. 'I have always known that Lord Gerard would not choose a virgin younger than eighteen. I am sure my time is very close.'

'Have you seen Lord Gerard?' Hedra said, unable to resist asking her. 'Is he very handsome?'

To her surprise the girl trembled visibly and blushed. 'Oh, yes,' she said in a breathless voice, 'very handsome. And very forceful,' she added. 'My mother told me that he spanks his women daily . . .'

Again, at the very prospect of such treatment, Hedra felt her sex moistening. There must be something wrong with me, she thought. I should not be so excited at the prospect of chastisement. Yet she remembered the Chivalrous Knight who she herself had chastised and how aroused he had become by her harsh treatment of him. Suddenly, she realised that Serona had not finished speaking.

'. . . and he allows the Decadent Knights free and liberal use of the women in the royal court,' she said in conclusion.

'Decadent Knights?' Hedra asked.

Serona looked surprised. 'Yes, his knights,' she said, 'they are Decadent Knights. Did you not know?' She laughed and continued, 'I believe they are aptly named. Their tastes and sexual predilections are most debauched by all accounts. I really cannot wait to serve them.' She became dreamy, her eyes taking on a slight haze as Hedra stared at her in amazement.

If what the girl said was true, she would surely be stretched to the limits of her sexual endurance. Again Hedra shuddered and found herself glancing at the door. She could hardly bear to wait for Lord Gerard's return and hoped fervently that Mistress Quigley's estimation was correct and that he would indeed select her immediately in preference to all the other virgins in the vestal chamber.

# Chapter Six

*T*here was no possible way Hedra could have missed the exact moment of Lord Gerard's return to the castle. A cheer went up as he and his troop of knights on horseback appeared on the horizon and from that point on the castle and its grounds were buzzing with activity.

Within the normally sedate confines of the vestal chamber the excitement in the air was unmistakable and she could hardly hear herself think over the incessant chatter of the other girls. But what surprised her the most was the extent of the preparations in anticipation of Lord Gerard's visit to the chamber: armies of servants cleaned and scrubbed the whole place from top to bottom and the girls devoted themselves to bathing and beautifying. She watched agog as they shamelessly paraded about completely naked, massaged each other's bodies with aromatic oils and lotions and even combed each other's pubic fleece.

When Serona offered to rub blackberry oil into Hedra's fleece to soften it and bring out the violet colouring, the princess declined as gracefully as possible. 'No, really,' she said, 'I have bathed well enough. I would rather face Lord Gerard as nature intended.'

The other girl laughed at Hedra's reticence. 'Methinks

you will have to learn very quickly to be less ashamed of your body,' she said, carefully stroking a palmful of silknut oil across her own breasts as she spoke. 'There will be no room for modesty in Lord Gerard's chambers.'

Hedra found herself trembling inside at the girl's words. She hadn't ever thought of herself as being modest, quite the opposite. And yet she supposed that some vestige of Parsimonian law must have lodged itself in her mind. Perhaps she wasn't as bold as she assumed herself to be – at least, not by Satyrian standards.

It came as a surprise to everyone when Lord Gerard summoned the virgins to parade before him in his throne room. Hedra knew well enough by now, from information given to her by the other girls, that he usually visited the chamber to make his selection. Even the normally dour Mistress Quigley was all of a flutter at the new order.

Just as Hedra had finished dressing in a clean robe – a plain white satin shift – the older woman came to her and handed her a small bundle of bleached linen.

'What is it?' Hedra asked immediately, feeling that the contents of the bundle were soft and pliable.

'Do not squeeze it like that, girl,' Mistress Quigley warned her. 'Wrapped inside the linen is a chicken heart.'

'A chicken heart!' Hedra said. 'Whatever do I need a chicken heart for?'

'It is the "proof" of your virginity,' the older woman said mysteriously. 'You must conceal the bundle in your hair, like so.' Hedra's curly hair had been gathered up in loose twists and ringlets secured on top of her head with marcasite clips and combs and the woman tucked the bundle deep inside one of the twists. 'There now,' she said, leaning back a little to admire her handiwork. 'It cannot be seen and, unless you are very active, it is unlikely to be dislodged.'

'Well, what must I do with it?' Hedra said. She still really had no inkling of the woman's scheme.

'When Lord Gerard finally takes you,' Mistress Quigley began, her pinched white face suddenly looking uncommonly flushed, 'you must reach into your hair and extract the heart without him noticing, then hold it underneath you and crush it between your fingers. When he withdraws and you rise from his bed, you will leave your "proof" behind.'

Hedra stared at Mistress Quigley. For a moment she was speechless. It was an admirably devious plan and, like all the best schemes, oh, so simple.

There were fourteen virgins above the age of eighteen in the vestal chamber and, as they gathered in the small lobby, Hedra found herself eyeing each one as a potential competitor and viewing their individual merits. Some of them, she had no compunction in admitting, were just plain ugly – there was no point in trying to varnish the truth, whilst others were on the borders of being pretty but perhaps were a little on the plump side, or their faces were slightly too angular, their features too irregular for them ever to be considered beautiful.

There were amongst the group, however, a number, perhaps five or six, who were very attractive indeed, particularly one – a girl of nineteen like Hedra herself, whose straight corn-coloured hair was so long it almost reached the backs of her knees and whose pale green eyes twinkled and sparkled with all the devilment of one who is goblin-born.

'That is Bella,' Serona explained in a whisper, noticing the way her companion eyed the other girl with undisguised dislike. 'All the girls here believe she is the favourite to be chosen by Lord Gerard today.'

'Is that so?' Hedra said under her breath. 'Well, we shall see, shall we not? We shall see.' She would allow Bella to be selected over her dead body.

From somewhere deep within the bowels of the castle a gong sounded, agitating the waiting girls and spurring

Mistress Quigley into action. 'Quickly, girls, follow me in single file,' she said, pushing her way through the throng and unlocking the outer door.

To the melody of trailing hems and slippered feet whispering upon the bare flagstones, the virgins filed out of the vestal chamber and followed the older woman through a series of narrow passageways until they reached the main body of the castle. All at once it seemed there was far more space and light, and decorations appeared on the walls and thick rugs upon the floor.

As they neared the throne room they began to chatter excitedly amongst themselves, disguising their words behind slim white hands as they glanced over their shoulders to the ones behind.

Hedra remained silent. She couldn't deny the rabid fluttering of her heart, nor the fierce clenching and unclenching of her stomach. Her excitement was for many reasons, not least the actuality of being within vaguely familiar surroundings. It might not have been the Parsimonian royal court but it was still a royal court nevertheless.

She glanced around. Here in the hub of the castle it was still not as luxurious as the place of Hedra's dreams. But the tapestries that hung upon the walls were richly embroidered and bright and varied in hue and the carpet beneath her feet was thick and warm. Also this hall in particular was ornamented by proper chandeliers – huge crystal and gemstone confections holding a thousand tiny candles that transmitted their flickering light to the farthest corners of the vast stone room.

About twenty paces in front of them a pair of tall oak doors loomed. They were very narrow, their entire width no broader than the antlers of a stag, yet they were so high Hedra had to drop her head right back to make out the scalloped lintel.

Apart from Mistress Quigley and the virgins the court did not appear to contain any other living creature. Now, however, a figure appeared. Clad from head to foot in a long loose robe, the head entirely covered by a large hood, the figure moved silently to the double doors and opened them, gliding forwards across the threshold into the room beyond.

Mistress Quigley and the girls followed, all still walking in single file, their excited chatter hushed at the prospect of finally coming face to face with their eventual lord and master.

Having been lost in her own reverie, Hedra found herself last in line but she took the opportunity to properly take in her surroundings as she entered the throne room. Straightaway she realised nothing could have prepared her for the sight that met her eyes.

The throne room was a vault – a vast, round, stone-built chamber, the perimeter punctuated by grand archways and with a domed ceiling higher than any tree she had ever seen. At the top of each archway was a trio of further archways, the centre one slightly larger than its partners. These were windows through which precise rays of sunlight shone, each one meeting like thirty-six crossed swords at the very centre of the room.

Hedra had been staring around the summit of the room; now she followed a trail of light, lowering her eyes to meet the most terrifying vision. In the dead centre of the room, on a circular dais, was the most monstrous throne she had ever seen. Formed entirely from yellow and white gold, the throne was broad and deep, the arched back high. Intricate scroll-work decorated every surface and on the arms of the throne were cast two golden masks of beasts that she had never seen before. The sight of them made her shudder. The bestial faces had slanted, narrow eyes and long channelled noses that continued into fangs, which in turn went on without end, curving under the base of the throne.

And on the very top of the throne perched another carving, again of a creature Hedra had never seen before, of an evil bird-like face and tiny body from which three long bat-like wings protruded at either side. She shuddered once more but now she and the other girls were being ushered forward by the hooded figure, closer to the throne. As she drew nearer to the monstrosity, Hedra was able to make out the third astonishing sight – the man who sat upon the throne, waiting in silence for the innocents to approach him, Lord Gerard himself.

Hedra found herself staring and staring, she couldn't help it. Her eyes and mind had hardly been able to take in the dramatic scenery around her and now she was faced by a living being, a man whose very appearance took her breath away entirely and turned her whole body to liquid fire.

Her desire for him was instantaneous. Not just because of his looks – every bit as darkly handsome as the knight who had captured her in the village – or his dramatic garb: black leather from head to foot, relieved only by a breastplate, shoulder-pads and necklet of heavily engraved silver. But it was the aura that surrounded him which inflamed her passion, an aura that was powerful, majestic and breathtakingly sensual.

Hedra felt her mouth go dry and her sex spasm with desire. She could barely contain herself, every part of her screaming out for him. She wanted to run forward, to rip off her gown and throw herself naked at his feet. She wanted to feel those huge, leather gauntlet-clad hands roaming her desperate flesh, to experience those piercing sapphire-blue eyes burning into her with an intensity of interest that was for her alone. But most of all she wanted to hear him speak, to hear his dark, silken voice – as she knew it would be – tell her how much he wanted her, how much he desired her and how hard he intended to take her.

Without realising it a small gasp burst from her lips at the very thought and Lord Gerard glanced up. As though her prayers had been answered he turned his head to stare directly at her, his deep blue eyes glittering with something indefinable. Was it interest, was it lust? Hedra hoped desperately that it was both. He stared in silence for a moment, his expression hard and inscrutable, then he turned away.

'Let us proceed,' he commanded of no one in particular.

It seemed some of the girls already knew what was expected of them. But then Hedra realised that, of course, they would have been in this situation before, perhaps several times. She watched aghast as the girls at the front of the line moved forward one by one to walk backwards and forwards across Lord Gerard's line of vision, their bodies swaying as sensuously as possible. Then, at his unspoken command, each one stepped forward, gathered up the front of her dress and displayed her lower body to him – all the girls turning around to show him the curve of their buttocks when he indicated to them to do so.

Hedra was appalled by this. These girls were true innocents and yet they showed off their bodies without a hint of shame. She, on the other hand, had made her pleasure with several men and yet could not bear the thought of displaying herself so wantonly. Not to a complete stranger, who sat in silent judgement in the centre of this vast and inhospitable chamber.

One by one the girls continued to step forward and go through the same routine as the others. Occasionally, Lord Gerard would halt them for a moment and reach out to run an assessing hand over their fleece, or their buttocks; sometimes between their legs. And then he would nod, without passing comment, and bid them to continue.

Each time this happened Hedra felt her breath catch in her chest. Beneath the thin satin shift she felt her nipples harden into tight little knots, like cherry stones, and lower down her sex swelled and throbbed unmercifully, the juices flowing freely from her each time she became transfixed by the sight of black leather fingers probing innocent white flesh.

Slowly she inched forward. The time seemed to drag and yet flew quickly past. She measured the passing of time with each rise and fall of her chest, each shuffling step as she neared the throne.

Bella walked up to him now. Tall and proud she stood before him, her back arched slightly so that her breasts jutted forward through the thin satin covering of her robe. Hedra thought she detected the slightest flicker of interest cross Lord Gerard's face and she burned inwardly with desperation and hatred for the beautiful girl, the only one who now stood between her and their lord and master. If he chooses her, Hedra found herself thinking, if he chooses her, I shall . . . I shall . . .

'This girl is most interesting,' Lord Gerard said suddenly to Mistress Quigley, his words slicing through Hedra's train of thought.

No! Hedra screamed silently. No, not her!

Rational thought deserted her as, suddenly, she found herself running forward, her slippered feet slithering on the dusty flagstones. She didn't intend to harm Bella but somehow she managed it anyway. As she rushed up to the dais her feet slid from under her and she found herself clutching at air, then her fingers caught the ends of the girl's long hair and held on for dear life.

'Ow, ow, ow!' Bella started to yell in a most undignified way and, as Hedra fell headlong toward the floor, she noticed a look of disgust pass across Lord Gerard's face.

He waved the unfortunate Bella away and leaned forward to peer at Hedra's prostrate form. She lay across the dais in front of him, her robe rucked up around her thighs which were still outstretched from her ungainly fall.

Lord Gerard put out one booted foot and placed it solidly in the small of her back. 'Do not move,' he commanded, although Hedra fancied she could no more move from that undignified position than fly back to Parsimonia entirely unaided.

'I cannot move, my lord,' she mumbled angrily into

the flagstones, her words further muffled by a mouthful of her own hair.

'Good,' he said. With the toe of his other boot he poked at the hem of her robe, lifting it higher and higher until her thighs were completely exposed and then higher still until Hedra was able to feel a cold draught of air waft across her naked buttocks.

'Oh, oh!' she cried, the flush of mortification flooding her whole body.

He tapped the leather sole of his boot upon her buttocks and they quivered. He leaned further forward and watched as he tapped them a second time, only this time a little harder and they quivered all the more.

'Please,' Hedra said tearfully but still he kept tapping her with his boot and watching the answering ripples of her flesh with interest. Using his feet upon a maid was not something he had ever thought of doing before and now it entertained him immeasurably. And the girl herself? Well, she was interesting, he thought, with her violet hair and impulsive introduction.

He nudged the toe of his boot between her buttocks and the girl moaned. He found this interesting. Most of the innocents made no sound whatsoever but merely suffered his attentions in silence. It almost made him think that she felt humiliated by this ritual and yet the other girls, although technically virgins, had been raised to look upon their bodies as a source of enjoyment, not shame.

Questing his boot further, he slid it between her legs and found the crevice there to be very moist indeed. He pulled back his foot and glanced at the toe of his boot. It was covered with a distinct film of creamy white nectar, the juices of arousal. Again that was interesting, he thought. However much she may protest, it was clear that her body was enjoying the attention. He took his feet away and commanded her to stand.

Hedra rose awkwardly to her feet. She felt so disadvantaged, standing there before him and so dishevelled. And she felt blazingly angry with herself. How could

97

he possibly want her now, after the shameful display she had so far made of herself? Suddenly she realised he was speaking to her and she raised her eyes to find herself drowning in twin pools of sparkling blue, like the oceans she had only ever heard about from the mouths of explorers.

'Who are you, girl?' he said. 'From whence do you hail?'

She had difficulty in harnessing her breath and in finding enough wetness in her throat to aid her vocal cords, yet somehow she squeaked out a reply.

'Ah, Parsimonia,' he said sagely, 'that might explain it.'

'Explain what, my lord?' she said, looking every bit as confused as she felt.

He shook his head impatiently. 'It is of no consequence,' he said. All at once he rose to his feet, his imposing stature overshadowing her.

In his dark presence Hedra felt small and almost helpless. It was not a state of mind to which she was accustomed and in the next moment he proved his physical strength by picking her up as if she were no heavier than a flutter moth, and throwing her over his broad shoulder.

'I choose this one,' he said, glancing first at Mistress Quigley, who nodded, and then at the other virgins gathered before him, their expressions crestfallen.

Hedra found herself smiling, her lips pressed against black leather, her stomach contracting from the chill of the protective plate of silver upon his shoulder. She could feel his arm gripping her tightly around the backs of her knees and his other hand resting protectively upon her buttocks. The heat from his gloved palm seared through the thin covering of her dress and into her skin and without thinking she squeezed the twin globes of flesh together. For that she received an answering pat from his hand that sent fresh tremors of anticipation running through her.

98

At least she had managed to entice him. Now she would have to learn how to manage him.

If he could have read her thoughts it would have amused him to learn that Hedra had, in those early stages, not yet learned that he was not a man to be managed, or controlled. As he strode from the throne room and along the wide passageway leading to his personal chambers, several hooded figures scurried and darted about, like eager rodents, anxious to do his bidding. Finally, although Hedra couldn't see it, they came to a huge wooden doorway which the hooded figures held open so that Lord Gerard and his female burden could enter. Still carrying Hedra on his shoulder, he strode through a couple of outer rooms until he reached the sanctuary of his bedchamber.

As he walked, Hedra tried to raise her head and look around but her hair was coming loose from its pins and combs and falling across her face in thick tendrils. Realising that her head movements were only making matters worse, she kept as still as possible and prayed that her hairstyle would stay in place long enough to keep the existence of the hidden chicken heart a secret.

When they reached his bedchamber, Lord Gerard threw her down upon the high bed – a majestic confection, ornately carved from solid oak and draped in rich tapestries and velvets the colour of emeralds and rubies. He stared down at her as he removed his sword, still sheathed within its scabbard, and casually threw it into a corner of the room before disposing of his armour plating in a similar fashion.

'Remove your robe, please,' he said, as he walked across the room to a small sideboard upon which stood a number of silver goblets and a flagon of wine. He poured the wine into two goblets and turned around. Despite his request, Hedra had not moved an inch and now he stared coldly at her. A shadow passed across the stained glass window, blotting out the sun for a moment. 'I said remove your robe.'

Hedra quaked under his piercing stare. 'I . . . I . . .' she started to say but he raised his hand.

'No matter,' he said. 'I understand that you could be feeling a little nervous.'

Her lips had just begun to curve into a smile at his thoughtfulness when he lunged forward suddenly, grasped the neckline of her dress and ripped the garment clean away from her. Immediately she felt her body contract into itself. Using her hands she tried to shield her nakedness from his sight but his attitude was uncompromising. The phantom of lust descended over him.

'Move you hands,' he commanded, his eyes growing-dark. 'Lay back and spread your legs. I want to be able to see my new prize properly.'

Hedra began to shake her head slowly from side to side. 'I cannot,' she whispered, but yet again he displayed that he had no time for modesty.

Leaning over her he pushed her roughly backwards, pulling her arms apart as he did so to expose her naked breasts, then lowering his hands to drag her legs wide apart – so wide that Hedra winced as her muscles began to burn. Gazing down at her, he nodded with satisfaction.

'Now why could you not have done that yourself?' he said to her, his tone mocking.

Hedra was in no mood for derision yet she was unable to retaliate. She felt overcome by the most powerful feeling of shame. It burned in her cheeks and suffused her breasts and throat with a rosy glow. Tears smarted in her eyes and she could hardly bring herself to look at him, or to look down at herself, to see what he could see.

'I have a powerful need for release,' he began to confess, climbing onto the bed to kneel between her parted legs. 'I have been on a crusade for some weeks and unfortunately did not come across that many wenches upon my travels.' All the time he spoke, he tugged and fiddled with the laces at the front of his leather breeches. 'But now I have you,' he continued, 'I can take my satisfaction and relieve you of your burden at the same time.'

'My burden?' Hedra said in a low murmur, her eyes transfixed by the working of his fingers.

'Your virginity, my lovely Hedra,' he said, laughing and remembering her name. 'After the terrible deed is done I shall enjoy playing with your body and giving you your due punishment, but for now . . .'

Hedra stared wide eyed as his phallus suddenly sprang free from the opening at the front of his breeches. The shaft was long and broad, topped by a helmet of livid purple. Before she could speak or utter a protest of any kind he lunged forward and sank himself inside her to the hilt.

All at once she gasped; her body was wet enough and ready to welcome him, yet the intrusion was so sudden that it took her breath away. Moments later, she found herself raising her hips to meet his thrusts and he groaned with undisguised pleasure at the naturalness of her response. It was almost too late when she remembered the chicken heart but, at the last moment, Lord Gerard closed his eyes and she quickly pulled the bundle from her hair, unwrapped the heart with fumbling fingers, and crushed it beneath her. In the same instant, he reached his zenith and she moaned loudly in return and quickly threw the small scrap of linen under the bed.

She was glad she had not forgotten about the chicken heart because he seemed intent on seeing the result of his action, her 'proof'. Withdrawing from her, he rolled her away from the spot where she had been lying to observe the sticky spot of blood for himself. Then he told her to get up and stripped the soiled coverlet from the bed.

'I shall have the seamstress cut out this patch and sew it to all the others,' he declared proudly. 'I'll wager my favourite wall hanging will encircle the entire circumference of the Great Hall before the year is out.'

Hedra stared at him, aghast. 'You cannot mean it,' she said. 'That is the vilest thing I have ever heard.'

His response was to laugh, an infectious rumble that even made her smile despite her horror. 'If that is the vilest thing you have ever heard,' he said, pushing her back onto the bed, 'then you have not been in Satyria long enough.'

Before she could answer, he sat down on the bed and pulled her until she was laying face down across his thighs.

'What are you doing now?' she asked, her pleasure parts beginning to throb anew at the sensation of warm leather beneath her nakedness.

'You really are an innocent, aren't you?' he said, clapping his leather-covered palms together before smoothing them over the taut mounds of her buttocks. 'Naturally I am going to punish you now.'

'But what for? I haven't done anything wrong!' Hedra exclaimed.

She started to struggle, twisting her upper body so that she could treat him to a vicious glare – one of her specialities – but he merely laughed again and pressed one hand against the back of her neck so that she was forced to hang her head down, the ends of her violet hair trailing over the dark green rug beneath his feet.

When the first slap came and the second she tried to jerk upwards and when he delivered the third and fourth slaps she began to squirm from side to side, trying to avoid his huge leather-gloved hands as they stung her tender flesh and set it aglow. Ten smacks he delivered to each buttock before he stopped and began to smooth his hands over her flesh, testing it, soothing it. By the seventh or eighth slap, Hedra couldn't remember which, she noticed how pleasant the warmth in her rear had become, how much she began to welcome it. And, when he started to smack her again, she found herself raising her bottom to meet his hand.

All the time he slapped her she felt her pleasure parts swelling and growing thick with arousal – even during

102

the first period when she didn't enjoy the chastisement he dished out so readily. And she felt sticky with her own nectar and the remainder of his fluid. Carefully, she eased her thighs apart a little, telling herself that it might alleviate the discomfort somewhat.

The second bout of smacking stopped and she felt Lord Gerard's surveying hands upon her again, stroking her burning flesh tenderly, gently easing her buttocks apart and stroking a finger down the cleft in between. His finger dipped lower, circling the outer edge of her sex, the black leather skimming over the slick moisture that had gathered there.

Hedra moaned, she couldn't help herself. Her sex was on fire, desperate to feel him inside again and her clitoris throbbed unmercifully. She felt more of his fingers upon her lovelips, spreading her open wider and wider. Cold air joined his fingers to touch her there, drying the moisture on contact. But no sooner did it dry that her desperate body made more, filling her up with creamy nectar that ran from her opening and coated the puffy outer lips, somehow working its way into the crevice of her split-peach pleasure parts. The touching and the caress of air and the efficient workings of her own body almost drove her mad until, at last, Lord Gerard pushed her gently from his lap so that she fell in a limp heap onto the rug. 'On your hands and knees,' he commanded her but more gently now. 'Legs apart.'

Silently she obeyed him. Her whole body trembled, her legs and stomach weak and quivering, and her arms almost too limp to support her body.

He knelt down beside her and began to stroke a hand down the long sweep of her back, over and over again, along her spine and over the curve of her flaming buttocks.

She flinched when he touched her there but in the next instant she moaned as he pressed his fingers into her hot sex and slid his other hand beneath her body to caress the heavy weights of her breasts, holding and

103

kneading first one then the other until she thought her desperate nipples would burst. Still tormenting her breasts with one hand, he began to stroke her outer sex, smoothing the creamy juices over the puffy flesh, his fingertips gradually spreading her pleasure lips wider and wider apart until the found the hard nub of her pleasure bud.

At once she spasmed as she reached her climax, the intensity of it surprising her almost as much as the immediacy of her response. Forcing down her sense of shame she pressed her sex hard upon his fingers and rocked backwards and forwards against his palm until the waves of delight began to subside.

As she began to spasm, he released her breasts and reached out to cup her chin, turning her face around and leaning forward so that he could press his lips against hers and taste her gasps of pleasure.

'You have a lot to learn, my dear Hedra,' he said, easing himself into a sitting position and pulling her limp body against his, her face turned up to gaze at him, 'but be certain of this, every day I am here you shall receive my caresses and every day your punishment.'

Hedra opened her mouth to speak but he silenced her. 'I am not finished; you may not speak,' he said a little more firmly than before. 'It is fitting that you should learn your place from the earliest moment.' He gazed down at her, his face suddenly softening into a smile. 'I am pleased with you,' he said. 'You have conducted yourself well and already proved to me that you are not simply another vestal virgin, or a simple Satyrian maid. You are a princess, that much is obvious, by your bearing and your beauty. But,' he narrowed his eyes a little, 'despite your royal parentage I am your lord and master now. You are answerable to me and only to me, is that understood?'

Hardly able to take in his words, Hedra nodded dumbly.

'Very well,' he continued. 'I intend to make you my

lady. I cannot treat you as one of the others and, indeed, I believe you have the ability to conduct yourself well in such a position of authority. I shall explain everything to you in due course but be certain of this, you will obey me in everything. If I tell you to bare your body to me you shall, if I tell you to pleasure me you shall, and if I tell you to give your body to another, you shall. Is that understood?'

This time she managed to gasp out a reply. 'Yes, but – '

'There is no but, Hedra,' he said, interrupting her. 'In the last instance I refer particularly to my Decadent Knights. They may have leave to enjoy your body – you will not refuse them. By the same token,' he added, 'no one else in the royal court is permitted to refuse you. Male or female, you are entitled to use the courtiers' bodies as you wish.'

'Really?' Hedra exclaimed. 'Any of them?'

Lord Gerard nodded. 'You may beat them, manacle them, or have them spreadeagled naked in the courtyard if that is your amusement for the day,' he said, 'and, of course, you may order them to pleasure you in any way you desire.'

Excitement surged through her at Lord Gerard's revelation. It overlaid her misgivings about putting herself at the disposal of the Decadent Knights. Fancy that, a whole castle full of people to have fun with and exactly how she wished!

# Chapter Seven

*T*heir pleasure-making continued throughout the silent, mysterious hours of darkfall, each of them delighting in the other's body and sharing in the discovery of new pleasures. Finally, at the rising of the first sun, Lord Gerard left her to sleep for a few hours while he attended to matters of court.

'I shall select a personal attendant for you and send her along to prepare you for your formal introduction to the rest of the court,' he said as he clothed himself in a fresh costume.

From the enveloping warmth of his bed Hedra watched him, her mind and body suffused with a sleepy haze of contentment. Despite the number of exquisite zeniths she had attained and the times he had taken her – sometimes tenderly, sometimes forcefully – she couldn't help feeling new stirrings of arousal. As he walked about the room she could see the tight muscles of his thighs and buttocks working beneath the supple leather and the interesting bulge at the front of his breeches that did not call for the adornment of a codpiece.

'Come back to me, my lord,' she pleaded, reaching out a hand to him, 'my body still burns for you.'

At her words, he turned and smiled, his blue eyes

glittering with barely assuaged desire for the wanton young woman who graced his bed so divinely. Her plea tempted him but nevertheless he shook his head. 'Alas, I cannot, my lady Hedra,' he said. 'Matters of the kingdom have to take precedence on occasion and you need to rest and recoup your energies for this evenfall.'

Giving in gracefully, she stared after him as he left the bedchamber, although her eyes still lingered on the heavy oak door long after it had closed behind him, resting there until the moment when they began to droop with tiredness and she gave in willingly to her body's demands for sleep.

The second sun was already high in the sky, its rays casting a jewelled brightness through the stained-glass window of the bedchamber, when Hedra was roused from her slumber by the gentle tap-tap of a hand upon her bare shoulder. Turning over sleepily, she struggled to open her eyes and found herself gazing up into the slanted yellow eyes of an elfin girl.

Struggling to clear her mind and vision, Hedra sat up and saw that the girl was of no more than fourteen or fifteen. Her slight form was clad from head to foot in a loose black satin robe and her hair was as dark and glossy as a raven's wing, the short hairs feathering gracefully around her gamine face and the nape of her long, slim neck.

Just as Hedra opened her mouth to enquire who she was and the purpose for her visit, the girl stepped back from the bed and waved her hand in silent indication that Hedra should rise and follow her.

Although a little embarrassed by her nakedness, Hedra slipped from the high bed and followed the young girl through a second doorway in the bedchamber that she hadn't noticed before. To her amazement it led into a bathing room of astounding luxury.

For a moment she forgot herself and simply gazed around the circular room with undisguised awe. Her wide eyes skimmed the walls and ceiling which were draped entirely in black silk, the sumptuous fabric pleated and gathered into generous swags that fell to the pure crystal floor and gathered there in dark, bottomless pools. The ceiling was domed, its spherical centre multicoloured crystal that cast a rainbow of natural light over the room's focal point, a sunken bath carved from ebony marble.

Stepping forward hesitantly, Hedra noticed that the bath was already filled with bubbling rose-coloured water and she closed her eyes to block out her other senses, allowing herself to just wallow in the fragrant steam so redolent of a flower-filled woodland glade.

'I hope it is to your liking, my lady?' the young girl said, her tone anxious. 'It is the special minerals that make it bubble so and emit the fine scent.'

Hedra opened her eyes reluctantly and reassured her. 'Oh yes,' she said, 'it looks wonderful and smells so enticing I shall be there in an instant. But first tell me, who are you – are you my attendant?'

'That is so, mistress . . . er?' the girl replied, faltering for a moment.

Hedra murmured her name and tested the water temperature with the toes of one elegantly arched foot.

'Mistress Hedra,' the girl said softly, trying out the name upon her lips before adding, 'I am Jade. Lord Gerard has indeed chosen me to be your personal attendant. I hope I do not displease you. It is a great honour to be chosen.'

Hedra turned her head. 'You please me very well so far,' she said.

Jade's anxious expression softened with relief and she extended a tiny hand to her waiting mistress. 'You must be fatigued, allow me to bathe you.'

She guided Hedra into the water and made sure that she was comfortably immersed before disrobing herself – stepping out of narrow pointed slippers and shrugging away the voluminous black silk robe that had been secured with a wide belt of stiffened black velvet.

As she floated weightlessly in the mineral-enriched

water Hedra watched the young girl, although she tried to disguise her interest in the emerging body. The waif-like form was tiny but still nicely rounded, the breasts high and firm, like two halves of grapefruit, with nipples so dark they blended into the surrounding aureola. And the waist was tiny, the stomach flat. For a moment Hedra felt slightly envious of her attendant's shape but in the next instant reassured herself by glancing down at her own body through the mists of the steamy water.

At that moment, Jade turned around completely to face her and started to walk towards the bath.

And it was then that Hedra noticed the girl's most unusual physical trait – the oddly denuded appearance of her intimate parts where she bore not even the slightest trace of a fleece. She found herself staring quite openly at the little fleshy purse as Jade came closer and eventually managed to ask, 'How old are you?'

The young girl raised her thin, arched eyebrows in surprise as she lowered herself into the opposite end of the sunken bath. 'Surely you know I am a Kelf?' she said. 'I have been alive from the very beginning of time.'

Hedra was intrigued beyond measure by the reply. She had never come across a Kelf before although she had heard tales of them. Original keepers of the Fantastic Lands, of which Satyria and Parsimonia were only two, the Kelf race had gradually receded into the wilder lands at the outer limits. Nevertheless, some clans still lingered in the new kingdoms and she had been intrigued by the Kelf legends which were coloured by the magical abilities of the race and the Kelf's natural inclination towards artfulness. At once, she realised Jade could prove to be a very useful ally in the future.

Gradually her thoughts of Kelfs diminished and she simply wallowed blissfully in the enveloping water. After a while she stretched out her legs and rotated her ankles in mindless contemplation until, to her surprise, Jade reached out, clasped the feet close to her chest and

109

began to massage them, her thumbs moving over the softened skin in tiny circles. Sighing with contentment, Hedra watched as her attendant added a little azure-coloured oil to the palm of her hand from one of a dozen delicately carved crystal flagons that were grouped at the side of the bath and resumed the massage. She seemed to be thinking as her delicate fingers expertly worked the muscles and sinews and hundreds of tiny bones and Hedra immediately wondered at the thoughts of one who lived as an immortal being.

Eventually Jade relinquished Hedra's feet, her task completed, but when she noticed her mistress's slight frown of disappointment she asked, 'Are you not happy with my work, mistress?'

'Of course,' Hedra said, quick to reassure the anxious girl. 'Would you mind attending to my hands in the same fashion?' She raised one arm from the water and spread her legs so that the Kelf could move closer and sit between them.

Jade immediately did as her mistress bade her, massaging each hand with equal dexterity. And when the hand massage was finally completed, she picked up a large natural sponge and added a few drops of the blue oil to its surface before deftly sliding the sponge along the length of Hedra's arms, taking it from shoulder to fingertip in smooth, continuous strokes before attending to the rest of her body in the same fashion.

Jade's ministrations were so relaxing Hedra found herself drifting back into the grip of slumber and she had to force her eyes from closing. She couldn't help but sigh with pleasure as the young girl attended to her body. With drooping eyelids she allowed her mind to drift, her floating body weaving slightly in the heavy water, responding to a silent melody of desire that built gradually as the anticipated moment of Lord Gerard's return drew ever closer. With difficulty, she raised her hand to signify that she had received enough treatment and slowly she rose to her feet, her silken body graceful

110

as it emerged from the water and hesitated for a moment with all the heart-stopping splendour of a living statue.

Glancing around, she stepped regally away from the sunken bathtub, pausing only to allow the young girl to cloak her with soft fabrics. On Jade's instructions she moved, gliding like an ice dancer across the crystal floor towards a low bed set upon a raised dais and draped in blood-red satin. Dropping the fabrics carelessly she lay down flat upon her back.

As soon as she was comfortable Jade approached, her damp body now wrapped in a short red silken robe. Taking great care she eased her mistress's thighs apart and to Hedra's embarrassment, peered closely between them. Immediately, the Kelf's expression showed concern. 'Oh, mistress,' she murmured softly, 'your secret parts look so sore.'

She placed her fingertips delicately on the soft flesh and palpated it slightly, her lips pursed with concentration.

Recoiling for an instant from Jade's touch, Hedra nodded dumbly. All her mind seemed able to concentrate on was the fact that it was the girl who felt between her legs and not Lord Gerard or indeed another male. She felt her stomach tighten as the tiny fingers gently parted her outer lips and touched the sensitive tissue that had just been exposed. Her sex moistened of its own accord. Jade's fingertips brushed her pleasure bud and, although the touch was only light, it was enough to arouse her.

'I'll attend to that properly for you, mistress,' Jade said. 'Please grant me leave to fetch some soothing puffmint balm.'

To Hedra's surprise, her most secret flesh felt suddenly bereft without the girl's touch and she felt tempted to put her own hand there instead. But before the thought had time to crystallise Jade returned bearing a small, emerald-green glass vial which was covered with an intricate filigree of silver. The vial also bore a

111

tiny silver stopper secured by a thin chain, which Jade now removed. Holding the vial aloft she allowed a stream of pale green lotion to trickle onto her mistress's pleasure parts. Then she replaced the stopper carefully and set the vial upright on the end of the bed, her manner almost reverent.

Hedra recoiled as the ice-cold lotion hit her flesh. The liquid sizzled and tingled as it anointed her most sensitive places, emitting a keen minty aroma and inciting a chain reaction of sensation that coursed throughout her whole body. Twisting and turning upon the satin-covered bed, her body in the grip of pleasure, she cried out shamelessly.

The Kelf caressed and calmed her, all the time whispering in a strange tongue that Hedra did not recognise. It was pure bliss to feel the deft fingertips upon her once again, working their magic as they smoothed the puffmint balm into every tiny portion of her quivering flesh. Relaxing into pleasurable abandon she spread her legs wider, anxious to aid the girl in her duties.

'There, is that not a sorcerer's potion, mistress?' Jade said with a smile as she allowed her fingers to slide slowly and rhythmically, taking their time to blend the lotion into that most tortured part of her mistress's body.

Hedra could only whimper in reply. She felt as though she could die from the intensity of such pleasure. The satin upon the bed felt cool and luxurious beneath the perfumed satin of her skin and somewhere in the distance she could hear a hypnotic humming sound. Muted, though clearly existent, it seemed as if perhaps twenty or thirty voices intoned a single incantation that helped to lull her into a blissful trance.

'Those are the Disrobers,' Jade said, anticipating her mistress's question. 'Their chant predicts the return of the Master.'

At the Kelf's words, Hedra felt her stomach tighten even further and her sex began to throb anxiously with barely controlled desire. She desperately wanted to touch herself but her attendant's hands still occupied that part of her body, arousing her, yet in such a way that did not provide the hope of imminent relief. With a huge sigh she arched her back and opened her thighs still further.

As if it were a cue, the young girl spread Hedra's outer lips with the finger of one hand and eased back the hood of skin that shielded her clitoris. Using the soft pad of a single fingertip, she began to delicately pat the tiny nub of flesh.

A deep groan of desire tore from Hedra's lips. She could hardly bear the torment of the girl's touch, yet neither could she bear to lose it. In response, her legs stiffened and her pelvis rose slightly from the table.

As her mistress moved, Jade made a slight clicking sound with her tongue against the back of her teeth and drew back the skin surrounding the delicate bud even further. Bending her head in concentration she continued her rhythm – she loved her work but sometimes found it difficult to deal with the impatience of a master or mistress.

All that Hedra could think of right at that moment was the sudden rush of heat which grew and grew and threatened to overtake her body completely. Desperately she tried not to concentrate on the tiny portion of flesh that trembled under the young girl's practised ministrations; it would be too shaming to reach her zenith in such a way.

Suddenly, loud footsteps sounded outside the doorway, the unexpected noise dissipating the haze of sensation that surrounded her. She turned her head and in the next mometn the imposing figure of Lord Gerard filled the doorway. Their eyes clashed.

'Master!' She and Jade exclaimed in unison but with a different inflection. Jade was surprised and a little fearful, whilst Hedra felt suffused with desire and relief at the sight of him.

Lord Gerard crossed the room in a few strides, a long leather cape billowing out behind him. His boots made little sound on the crystal floor. Standing at the side of the bed, his feet placed firmly apart and his gloved fists upon his hips, he nodded to the young Kelf who quickly withdrew into the background. Then he turned and looked down at Hedra, his eyes sweeping her naked body as though reminding himself of her particular charms.

'You are feeling well rested, my lady?' he said, dropping down beside her. He knelt on the floor with one knee and rested an arm on the opposite thigh before reaching out with the other hand to cup Hedra's chin and tilt her face upwards to receive his kiss.

Hedra had felt her breath catch at the sight of him and now she almost swooned as he touched her. It was almost as though she had forgotten the power of his presence in those brief hours they had been apart. Yet at that moment, as he bestowed a searching kiss upon her lips, she wanted desperately to feel his arms about her and to experience the sensation of his naked flesh pressed against her own.

'I am indeed rested, my lord,' she replied, when at last he allowed her to regain her breath, 'and I find myself strongly desirous of you.'

'Indeed?' he said and allowed himself a smile that travelled to the corners of his eyes. 'Then I am honour bound to put my lady out of her misery.' With that, he rose and swept her up into his arms, carrying her once more to his bedchamber.

Hedra lay in his arms, her body limp with desire, but to her surprise he didn't take her straightaway to the bed but set her down upon a low footstool which was covered in a rich red and gold brocade and placed her on her knees.

The footstool was quite close to the hearth where a recently lit fire was still flickering into life, its tiny flames only just growing stronger and more potent. As Lord Gerard turned this way and that, positioning Hedra so that her palms were placed flat on the floor, her knees spaced wide apart and the rounded swell of her buttocks jutting into the air, the draught caused by his cape fanned the flames still further.

'Master?' she said, her one-word query made in a tone that displayed all the trepidation and excitement that flickered inside her like the dragon's breath that stroked the walls of the hearth.

'One thing you need to learn is patience, Hedra,' he said as he ran a firm hand along the length of her spine. 'Patience and obedience are the two things that will keep you in my good graces.'

Although she could not see him, she sensed him walk around her, studying her. There was no possibility of shielding any part of herself from him like that; it was the most shaming of positions and the blood rushed to her cheeks with an immediacy that had nothing to do with her head being lower than her heart. Despite her humiliation she thrilled to the thought of the dark expression on his face and between her legs she began to swell and tingle as she imagined the way he must be looking at her.

Walking around in front of her he squatted down, cupped her chin to tilt her head up and pulled aside the curtain of violet tresses that covered her face.

Straightaway she noticed that in his other hand he held a broad leather belt which he held up for her inspection then stroked across the tips of her dangling breasts.

'No, you cannot – ' she began, realising his intention, but he silenced her.

'Not every punishment will be the same,' he said. 'Today I will grant you only three strokes but I think that will suffice to accustom your recently awakened flesh to the kiss of my belt.

'No, please, master, I beg you,' she cried, finding herself trembling at the very prospect.

He kissed her gently on the mouth and released her chin before rising to his feet and walking around her.

'Be quiet, Hedra,' he said, stroking his hand over the

115

smooth mounds of her buttocks. 'I promise you will enjoy it.'

Hedra felt her body melt under his touch but before she had the chance to utter another syllable, he brought the belt down upon her naked flesh. Although she was aware that it sounded worse than it felt, the stroke of his belt made her scream out. And each time it left a fiery trail across her tender flesh that quickly turned into an answering echo of pleasure that rippled throughout her entire body. The stinging in her buttocks transmitted itself to a heavy, lustful ache in her breasts and her sex began to swell with desperation, oozing with the proof of her arousal.

'Please, my lord,' she said breathlessly after he had delivered the three promised strokes, 'I cannot bear to stay like this. I am desperate for your touch.'

He did not allow her to move but the answering caress of his fingers questing between the outer lips of her pleasure parts drove her to the brink of madness. A dark wave of lust engulfed her and she thrust her nether regions towards him. She paid no heed to the wantonness of her actions; she wanted him to touch her – all of her.

'You conduct yourself well, Hedra,' he said. 'I believe you rightly deserve to reach your climax.'

To her delight she felt his fingers slide between her legs and open her pleasure lips wider and wider and, in the next instant, she nearly swooned as the glorious caress of his tongue swept over her tortured flesh, snaking around her clitoris until she began to groan aloud with unrestrained desire. As wave after wave of sensation engulfed her she bucked and ground her hips until the pleasure peaked and she fell headlong onto the carpet, her mouth opened wide in a hoarse scream.

And while she still lay panting breathlessly upon the green velvet, he covered her with his fully clothed body and took her without mercy, driving his hardness into her as she wound her legs about his waist and urged her body up to meet his.

She felt as though she could never get enough of him, that her body would never be satisfied. In the short time that she had known her lord and master he had awakened desperate, primeval urges within her that had been denied for such a long time. Now she felt truly alive and, as if a veil of deceit had been lifted from her eyes, she was able to properly regard her own body and the bodies of others as instruments of pleasure.

She and Lord Gerard lay together for a while afterwards, their faces bathed in the glow from the fire as they spoke words of adoration and desire to each other and he told her a little bit about his early life and his position as virtual ruler of Satyria.

'It was not a place to which I was born and raised,' he said, stroking her naked body almost absently as he spoke. 'I started life much the same way as any other young cove, although I was born into the court and of a noble bloodline.'

'And what of the king?' Hedra asked.

Lord Gerard smiled and shook his head. 'He is old,' he said bluntly, 'and feeble. Everyone knows it and even he himself acknowledges that his authority is no more than that of a titular head. I make all the decisions. It is my word upon which the Clan folk of Satyria are bound to act.'

'I have heard tell of the Clansmen,' Hedra said, remembering the awed tales of visiting travellers to her father's castle. 'But who are they, what is their purpose?'

'Aside from the Kelfs, the Clansmen and their women-folk – the Watchers – are the true subjects of Satyria,' he replied. 'All others here are immigrants from other lands, or inter-breeds, hybrids of two other races.'

'Then who are the disrobers?' Hedra asked. 'What is their station?'

'The disrobers are not a race,' Lord Gerard explained. 'They are usually Clansmen or Watchers whose appointed task it is to serve the Decadent Knights, to assist them to remove their armour after battle, that sort of thing.'

'Ah,' she murmured with a smile, 'it is all becoming clear to me now.'

To her surprise Lord Gerard pushed himself up and rose to his feet, extending a hand to help her do the same. 'Speaking of the royal court, it is time we prepared ourselves to greet them,' he said. 'They are most anxious to meet their new lady.'

He picked up a tiny crystal bell from the lintel over the hearth. Inside the clear dome it had no clacker, yet when he shook the instrument from side to side, Jade appeared instantly in the doorway to the bathing room.

'Yes, Master?' she said, as Hedra examined the silent bell in wonder.

'Your mistress is ready to be prepared for presentation at court,' he instructed. Then he turned to Hedra and added, 'Go with Jade but do not tarry; our pleasure-making has cost us dearly in time.'

Despite her new-found confidence in matters of the flesh, Hedra still blushed at his words but when she glanced up she saw that his expression was relaxed and his deep blue eyes crinkled with suppressed laughter. Instead of returning his smile, she deliberately simpered coquettishly and replied, 'Perhaps, sir, I should find myself a partner who is quicker to arouse and does not demand such complete and utter satisfaction?'

At that he lunged forward to slap her naked behind which quivered tantalisingly just below the wispy ends of her violet hair but she darted away from him into the sanctuary of the bathing room, her tinkling laughter echoing around the crystal dome like icicles touched by the breeze.

Despite her teasing she was mindful of his words and bathed herself in a matter of star-twinkles. The second sun had begun its descent and now the centre of the room was cloaked in a pale orange light, the perimeter falling into shadow.

Just as Hedra finished drying herself, at her own insistence, Jade brought forth her outfit for the evening. Unlike her previous dress it was not a robe of some kind but a costume fashioned from pure-white parmerian hog-hide, brushed and treated to be soft and velvety to the touch.

Jade held it against the front of her mistress's body and cinched it tightly around her waist and ribcage, pulling her sinuous figure into an even more defined sand-vial shape.

Hedra glanced down. The tightness of the garment had forced her full breasts into generously swelling mounds that Jade now draped with a finely worked fichu of golden chainmail. And, working deftly to secure the costume with tiny horseshoe clips of gold, the young girl used another length of chainmail to veil Hedra's fleece, taking it between her legs to cover her buttocks.

'There,' she said at last, standing back to admire her handiwork, 'you look superb if I may say so, mistress.'

Pausing only to slip her feet into a pair of boots worked in supple golden leather and which reached her thighs and sported high, pointed heels of pure gold, Hedra walked back into the bed-chamber and viewed herself before a full-length looking-glass. To her surprise and pleasure she felt a whistle of breath behind her, followed by the familiar sensation of Lord Gerard's hands gripping her waist tightly, his fingertips touching as they encompassed her tiny waist.

'Do I please you, master?' she asked, as she treated his reflection to a foxy smile.

'Please me?' he growled darkly in her ear. 'The sight of you makes me want to throw you to the floor and ravish you all over again.'

He slipped one hand between her legs and Hedra felt the tormenting pleasure of the fine gold chain being rubbed against her most tender flesh. And she groaned aloud at the piquant pain as it pinched and nipped the delicate folds, Lord Gerard's fingers rolling it over her

119

pleasure bud until her greedy body spasmed against him.

'Take care, my lady,' he murmured softly, 'this costume cannot disguise your desires.' He pinched her hardened nipples through the chain mail and brought the fingers of his other hand to her lips for her to taste the creamy proof of her arousal.

Hedra lapped hungrily at the musky nectar and took his fingers deep inside her mouth, sucking hard upon them. Reaching behind her she rubbed the leather-covered bulge that nudged between her buttocks.

With a sigh of regret he removed her hand. 'Alas, we are already late,' he said, gazing longingly at their reflections, 'but I shall enjoy looking at you. In that costume you are covered and yet supremely exposed. The torment of delay will only serve to heighten our enjoyment later.'

Hedra nodded. 'I believe you, master,' she said, 'but know you well during the long hours to come how much I desire you.'

At that moment they were disturbed by a knock on the door to the bedchamber and at Lord Gerard's instruction a young, sandy-haired page stuck his head through the doorway and announced that the royal court was all assembled.

'Tell them my lady and I shall be there in all haste,' Lord Gerard instructed the page. Turning Hedra around, he offered her the crook of his arm. 'Come, my darling,' he said softly, 'your subjects await you.'

Hedra felt a sudden rush of excitement at his words. Although she was a princess by birth and had been revered by the Parsimonian courtiers, as such she had never really enjoyed a position of true power. Now she sensed that her time was at last upon her.

'Lead the way, my lord,' she said, taking his arm and straightening her body to assume an even prouder stance, 'and let my reign begin.'

* * *

They walked together through the wide passageways and great chambers of the castle, Hedra's golden heels clicking loudly on the bare flagstones, until they reached the vaulted splendour of the throne room. Upon the centre dais, beside the monstrous throne where Lord Gerard was accustomed to sitting, was a second throne, slightly smaller but every bit as magical as the first.

Hedra stepped up to the throne and ran an assessing hand along one of the arms, the warm yellow gold fashioned in the image of a bat, its pointed face forming the very front of the arm and its folded wings the remainder. Its opposite number was to the same design and the narrow back of the throne rose up to a sharp point around which a golden cobra curled sinuously, its hooded head a diadem – the throne's crowning glory.

'It is wonderful, my lord!' she breathed, her face glowing with pleasure. 'May I have your leave to be seated?'

'Of course,' he replied and took her hand to guide her up to the throne, whereupon she sat down gracefully and he took his rightful place beside her.

They made an imposing couple and as he instructed the waiting pages to bid the courtiers to enter, each person paused in the grand doorway and gasped aloud in awe.

Hedra soon became accustomed to being an object of wonder and of reverence and was happy to nod and smile and bid welcome to her subjects. She noticed how quickly the vast chamber filled with bodies robed and gowned in the finest silks, satins and velvets and bedecked in a fine array of gold and gemstones. The courtiers swirled about the room in glittering, shimmering waves, their chatter muted yet animated and she couldn't help overhearing their spoken astonishment at her beauty. On hearing this she smiled; it pleased her greatly to know that they regarded her thus.

She watched as Lord Gerard spoke with a few of them, his handsome face occasionally breaking into a smile that raised his desirability still further in her eyes. Beneath the scant leather and chainmail of her costume, her body still burned for him and she was aware how her breasts and most secret parts still recalled the sensation of his touch. As Lord and Lady their obligation was to deal with court affairs, as mortal beings and as lovers their allegiance was to the pursuit of pleasure.

As soon as there came a lull, Hedra leaned sideways and whispered to Lord Gerard, 'May we eat soon, my lord?' I have not consumed a single morsel since I left the vestal chamber.'

A shadow of surprise passed across his face. 'Please forgive me,' he murmured in reply, 'I had not realised.' He glanced up and added, 'See the arrival of the Decadent Knights. I have invited two of them to dine with us.'

She nodded. 'That is good,' she said, her lips forming a wicked smile, 'otherwise I might have found myself too overcome by lust to bother with food after all.'

He laughed then – a loud rumble that echoed around the lofty vault and made everyone stop what they were doing and glance up in surprise, their own faces breaking into smiles. It wasn't often that the courtiers heard the fearsome Lord Gerard give way to laughter.

A moment later two Decadent Knights approached. One of them Hedra recognised immediately as Sir Drago, the knight who had captured her in the village. The other was a most fearsome sight and straightaway she found herself forgetting the lesson of her good breeding and recoiling in horror.

'Be not afraid, my lady,' the knight said at once, stepping forward and bending to one knee in front of her. 'My serpentine appearance is merely the result of a spell cast by a spiteful enchantress from another land. I am indeed a mortal beneath this terrible façade and I am assured by Zendik the sorcerer that my state is only temporary.'

The fact that he spoke as a mortal convinced her and yet she gazed at him openly, trying to reconcile his words with his appearance. There was no denying his looks were awesome: hairless skin formed from yellowed scales like that of a snake, lidless eyes flat and beady, while the rest of his features – his nose and ears – were so reduced in size and flat to his smooth, elongated skull that they almost appeared non-existent. Yet for all that he displayed a certain beauty, an inner strength that overshadowed his outward appearance and attracted her to him far more than handsome looks ever could.

'I apologise, sir,' she said when she had recovered her composure. 'I was indeed startled for a moment but I do not find you repulsive.'

The knight laughed in reply and she noticed a thin forked tongue flicker around the dark inner cavern of his mouth. The sight of it made her shudder with awful excitement and for an instant she found herself imagining how that tongue would feel were it ever to seek out her hungry flesh.

# Chapter Eight

$T$he rising of the silver crescent moon signalled the
end of their presentation to the royal court and Lord
Gerard rose to his feet, motioning to Hedra to do the
same. Without further ado the stately couple bade
farewell to the gathered throng, stepped down from the
throne dais and made their way to his private chambers.
This time they were accompanied by Sir Drago and the
serpent-knight who introduced himself as Sir Jagared.

On discovering that Lord Gerard's private apartment
was actually quite extensive and included a small ban-
queting-room, various sitting- and writing-rooms and a
bedchamber for her own personal use, Hedra realised
how little she had actually seen of the castle and
resolved to explore properly the following day. But first,
she thought with an inner frisson of excitement, there
was still the long period of darkfall to come.

The banqueting room was dominated by a round oak
table that rested upon a single plump pedestal and
would easily seat eight. Around it were gathered a
number of stately oak chairs, with high narrow backs
and diamond-shaped seats upholstered with red velvet.
And on this occasion the dining table had been laid
with fine linen and a sumptuous array of gold and
crystal. Almost the whole of the wall to the right-hand

side as they entered was taken up by a stone hearth in which a welcoming fire had been lit, whilst dozens of tiny gold and white candles flickered from a central crystal chandelier and torches burned brightly on all four walls. The whole ensemble was one of comfort and luxury and, at the invitation of a servant boy, Hedra found herself sinking into a deeply padded chair with a sense of anticipation.

The knights and Lord Gerard took their places around her, Sir Drago taking the seat to her right and Sir Jagared to her left, with Lord Gerard next to him. And when they were all seated comfortably a half-dozen servants entered bearing golden platters heaped high with food.

Her mouth watered at the sight of them and the smells that issued forth and she greedily accepted a portion of everything that was presented to her: succulent slices of grouse and partridge, venison and wild boar; crisply roasted root vegetables and crunchy green leaves, as well as a golden, jewel-studded goblet filled to the brim with a rich, ruby-red wine.

'To your health!' Lord Gerard said as soon as they were all served, raising his goblet into the air and in the next instant drinking deeply.

'This is an excellent wine, my lord,' Lord Drago said, nodding approvingly after he had tasted his wine and swilled it around his mouth. 'If I am not mistaken it is from the Koolabrak caverns.'

'Correct, my friend,' pronounced Lord Gerard with a smile. 'The Koolabraks treat their wine better than their women – and it shows.'

The three men laughed and Hedra glanced from one to the other with amusement. To her the wine tasted no better and no worse than any other she had ever imbibed; each sip coursed down her throat and into her stomach like molten lava and touched her famished brain with goblins' fingers. Consequently, after half a goblet or so she felt decidedly warm and took to laughing prettily at every comment directed at her.

As she concentrated on her food the men discussed a variety of matters all connected with the running of Satyria and she took little notice. However, when the conversation began to hum with familiar notes she paused in her chewing every now and then to listen properly to what was being said.

'He has no right to threaten us so,' Lord Gerard was saying. 'We have nothing special here in Satyria. Nothing that he could possibly want.'

'Oh, well,' said Sir Drago, 'you know King Randolph, he is a barbarian after all – what difference does it make to him?'

'And he is determined to become the ultimate ruler, do not forget that,' Sir Jagared added, his beady eyes apparently blank as he slewed his head from side to side to pay proper attention to his fellow knights.

'Did you say King Randolph?' interrupted Hedra, suddenly realising what, or rather who, they were talking about.

The three knights paused in their conversation and stared at her.

'We did,' replied Lord Gerard at last. 'Why, does his name mean something to you?'

'Indeed it does,' she said, dropping her fork with a clatter and raising her voice slightly. 'He is the scoundrel who theatened my kingdom and scattered its subjects to the four corners of the Fantastic Lands. Indeed, it is the result of his infamy that I came to be here in the first place.'

Lord Gerard looked thoughtful. 'I had not realised,' he said. 'To be truthful, we have not really talked about your origins, have we, Hedra?'

'To be truthful, we have hardly spoken at all,' she replied with a careless wave of the hand which held her wine goblet and almost spilling some in the process. 'We have been far too occupied with other things to bother with conversation.'

Her laughter carried around the room and she found herself shifting uncomfortably on her chair, parting her

126

legs slightly as she remembered every moment of time she had spent with her lord and master so far. All of a sudden she felt hot and her costume seemed unusually restrictive. Also it seemed, she had suddenly become the object of everyone's attention.

'As you already know, I am Princess Hedra of Parsimonia,' she stated, when no one else chose to break the oppressive silence. 'I fled my kingdom when King Randolph threatened us with the Monomanian plague. Then my small band was raided on the way to Piosia and I managed to escape. I found myself across the border in Satyria and for several days lived in the forest until a kindly woodsman named Gideon took me in and the following day took me to the village where Sir Drago here captured me and brought me to the castle. The rest you know,' she added, glancing wickedly at Sir Gerard.

To her surprise, he did not grant her an answering smile. 'You say a woodsman took you in?' he said, leaning forward on his elbows, his dark eyebrows knitted in contemplation.

'That is so,' Hedra replied. 'What of it? It was very kind of him.'

'It certainly was,' he agreed, 'but simple woodsmen are not renowned for their kindness, nor for their chivalry.' He paused for a moment before adding, 'You came to this castle as an innocent and passed your time in the vestal chamber?'

'Yes,' she replied hesitantly. 'Thanks to you it was short-lived, but what of it?' It was disconcerting to find that her light-hearted remarks were not having the desired effect. He still seemed withdrawn and disturbingly serious-minded. 'What of it, my lord?' she persisted with a harder edge to her voice.

'Nothing,' he said, resuming his meal, 'it is nothing. Now, please, everyone, enjoy your supper before it becomes cold.'

It was as though the very air around them breathed a sigh of relief and they all took up their knives and forks once again. There were a great many courses to get through and Hedra found herself drinking more and more wine with each one. Thankfully, she noticed, Lord Gerard's mood seemed to have lightened once more and the four of them exchanged frivolous banter across the dining table. To her further amusement, she noticed how Lord Drago appeared very taken with one of the serving girls – a pretty-faced maid of generous proportions whose chestnut hair was woven into a single thick braid and whose grape-green eyes sparkled above rosy-apple cheeks.

She is as luscious as a basket of fruit, Hedra thought to herself, with a pang of desire that shocked her and she couldn't help feeling slightly envious when Sir Drago showed no compunction about touching the girl at every available opportunity. As she reached across him to refill his goblet, he reached out and cupped her generous breasts and when she bent over the table he ran his hands over her behind, smoothing her long linen skirt over the sumptuous mounds beneath.

'What is your name, girl?' he asked her at one point as she served him a dish of sliced forest fruits.

'Lindy,' she replied with a giggle. He was touching her quite openly now, running a hand up the inside of her dress, caressing her from ankle to thigh.

'Lindy,' the knight repeated, 'Lindy, you are beyond doubt a comely wench. Come and sit here, tarry with me for a while and let me taste that luscious mouth.'

The girl did as she was commanded and sat upon his lap, arranging her skirts modestly about her.

Hedra glanced sideways to look at her. As the knight said, she was indeed comely. Her dress was the same as all the other female servants wore, a long full style made of plain cream linen and puffed up with many layers of petticoats underneath. Around her waist she wore a tight cummerbund of stiff black velvet, similar to the one Jade had worn but much plainer, without the addition of jewels. Laced at the back, it cinched her waist in tightly and pushed her full breasts upwards and together so that they spilled forward, her modesty only just protected by a carefully arranged muslin shawl that draped around her shoulders and tucked into the top of the cummerbund. The garb was simple yet enticing, enhancing her natural curves.

Sir Drago wasted no time in kissing the girl, pressing his cruel mouth against her soft, berry-red lips and forcing her to yield to him. She arched her back in reply, offering his open eyes the creamy swell of her breasts and the deep valley between. With a soft groan he cupped the breasts and ground them beneath his hand, his fingers seeking out the nipples which hardened visibly beneath the thin muslin.

Hedra felt an answering tug of arousal deep inside her and she glanced hopefully in Lord Gerard's direction. Both he and Sir Jagared were watching their companion but as Hedra moistened her lips provocatively Lord Gerard's expression darkened and he ordered her to go to him.

'Come here, Hedra,' he repeated as she rose to her feet, 'stand in front of me.' He pushed his chair away from the table a little as she approached and for a few moments contented himself with looking at her, his eyes feasting upon the sight of her semi-revealed body in its unusual outfit. The high boots made her much taller and now the veiled portion of her fleece was almost level with his eyes. Deftly he unhooked the tiny horseshoe clips, turning her around and around until her lower body was completely bared. 'Remove the rest of it,' he ordered, nodding at the chainmail that cloaked her breasts and shoulders, 'let us all see those fine breasts.'

With trembling fingers, she uncovered herself as he commanded and stood before him, shivering slightly on her high golden heels, only too aware that his stern countenance was afforded a good view of her fleece at the front, whilst Sir Jagared had the equally close-up perspective of her naked buttocks.

As if upon an unspoken command, the two knights

129

began to simultaneously explore the enticing cleft in front of them. Lord Gerard parted Hedra's pleasure lips and ran a moistened finger along the inner folds of her sex, stroking and stroking the silken petals until her mouth became slack and issued a shameless groan that made him smile darkly. At the same time, Sir Jagared had parted her buttocks and ran his snake-like tongue up and down the deep groove, flicking the forked end around the tiny puckered opening until she cried out once again.

She breathed heavily, parting her legs further and further to receive as much of their attention as she could. It was delicious torture, feeling two sets of hands and then two mouths upon her at the same time. Like men who had not eaten for a week, they feasted greedily, covering her most sensitive parts with their wet sucking mouths, diving their tongues inside her until she thought she would go mad with ecstasy.

It was a common misconception to think that a serpent's touch would be cold and clammy, yet she still felt a frisson of surprise the first time Sir Jagared's hands came in contact with her naked flesh. His touch was cool certainly but not repulsive by any means. And it was only when she actually caught sight of his yellow-scaly fingers moulding themselves around her body that she remembered his strange appearance with a slight jolt of apprehension.

I cannot believe this is happening to me, she thought from time to time. And if the sharpness of her perception had not been softened slightly around the edges by the effects of the wine, then she might have behaved with a little less abandon. Yet, as it was, the heady sensation of two pairs of hands separating and probing her body was exquisite and she simply opened herself wider and wider to their touch.

The dreamlike quality of the long blissful moments continued, drawing silken veils over the hidden realms of her own private pleasure. And while all this was taking place she watched through heavy-lidded eyes as

Sir Drago ordered the table to be cleared quickly and then pushed the serving wench face down upon it and raised her skirts to expose the quivering mounds of her naked buttocks. The light from the candelabra flickered warmly across her rosy flesh, touching it with tiny incandescent fingers that seemed to make her moan and squirm with increasing fervour.

Hedra watched the girl and the knight with hazy interest, noticing with continuous tremors of excitement how his fingers spread the creamy flesh of her thighs open wide to reveal a juicy red sex and fold upon fold of darker pink. The princess found herself transfixed as the fingers of one of his hands became lost in the plump fruit of the girl's pleasure parts, two of them disappearing inside her up to the knuckle. And, using his free hand, he fumbled with the lacing at the front of his leather breeches and practically tore the material apart in his effort to release the throbbing hardness confined within. Suddenly his phallus sprang free like a fearsome, angry beast and Hedra felt herself spasm at the sight, a powerful orgasm overtaking her as every one of her senses was satisfied to the extreme.

Sir Gerard and Sir Jagared left her to rest for a moment, to lean weakly against the table and watch as they disrobed completely. The black panther and the serpent, she thought to herself, eyeing their separate forms. Both were magnificent, hard and muscular, their buttocks tight, their stomachs flat, and both eyed her as their prey. Nectar dripped from her waiting sex, which throbbed and hummed a sensuous madrigal of desire. She leaned back against the table and spread her milky thighs wide.

'Come forward, my fine knights,' she offered huskily, 'come forth and take your pleasure.'

Sir Drago glanced at her as she spoke, she noticed. Although his phallus was now sunk deeply into the serving wench he seemed for a moment to waver, as though her offer was more tempting than the banquet he was already enjoying.

'Be not disquieted, sir,' Hedra whispered to him, her posture as she reclined across the table as wanton and inviting as her smile. 'We have all night and my body is barely awakened.'

Little did he know it but she wanted him with a potency that was akin to physical pain. She had desired him ever since he had captured her in the village and thrown her across his horse – ever since he had smacked her on the behind for resisting him. A fierce surge of heat flooded through her and to her relief at that moment Lord Gerard advanced and entered her waiting body with a powerful thrust.

'You are truly beautiful, my lady,' he murmured urgently into her ear as he took her hard. 'Eternity would not be time enough for me to assuage my desire for you.'

His body pounded against hers, sending fiery darts of ecstasy throughout every portion of her eager body and she peaked at his words, her whole being glowing with passion, her sex on fire as it enfolded him and milked him of his pleasure gift. With one sharp-nailed hand she raked his shoulders and with the other she reached out blindly to grip Sir Drago's arm, his muscles spasming underneath her palm as she contracted around her own lover.

Eventually Lord Gerard withdrew from her and a moment later Lindy screamed out her own release beside them. After this they all paused to recoup their senses and drink some more wine until Sir Jagared reached for Hedra and took her. This time she could not hide her senses from his true appearance. His beady eyes roamed her body as she writhed under him, her legs hooked around his waist so that she could pull him deeper and deeper inside her. His large, scaly hands gripped and kneaded her screaming breasts, his forked tongue snaking and flickering around her swollen nipples until she felt they would explode.

She felt his pleasure mounting, his movements becoming more frantic, his sharp teeth nipping at her desperately engorged flesh. In a final surge of lust she arched her back and to her it seemed the ultimate pleasure that Lord Gerard should choose that moment to claim her mouth with his own.

It was some time later that she lay upon the table top, at last feeling blissfully sated and sublimely happy as Lord Gerard stroked her hair and murmured words of adoration. Beside her she was aware of the presence of the servant girl and eventually, with a feeling of great languor, she turned her head.

The girl was fully naked now, her ripe body a soft invitation of sensual delights. Lord Gerard had taken her but Hedra had not minded; she had enjoyed hearing the girl's cries and moans of pleasure, knowing all the while how she felt, how wonderful it was to have such a man pay attention to the body. He was knowledgeable and skilful in bringing a woman pleasure and all Hedra could think was that she was the luckiest woman alive.

Sir Drago had, at long last, served her own body very nicely, his pleasure-making every bit as exciting and fulfilling as she had anticipated but neither he nor Sir Jagared could compare with her lord and master.

'Are you all right?' she whispered to the girl.

The two knights could be heard somewhere in the room, talking once more about King Randolph and his heinous threats to their land, but at that moment Hedra could not give a care about the infamous king. Lord Gerard kissed her neck and murmured in her ear that he was going to get some more wine to which she turned her head and smiled dreamily at him before turning back to look at the girl again.

'Oh, yes, mistress,' Lindy breathed in reply to her question. 'They are truly fine knights, are they not?'

Hedra smiled more broadly and found her eyes transfixed by the sight of the girl's lips moving as they spoke the words, a twin succulence of ruby wetness. She licked her own lips and edged closer to the body beside her. With sudden abandon she rolled over and pressed her mouth against the girl's. To her delight the girl responded, returning her kiss with fervour and pressing her naked body against Hedra's own.

It felt odd, Hedra thought, to feel another's breasts caressing her breasts, the hard pink tips jousting with each other as lower down their pleasure parts clashed, the soft fleecy curls meshing and tangling together as their limbs tangled in natural response. And yet she forced her body harder against the girl's, anxious to feel enveloped by her soft, creamy flesh. Her hands moved freely over the girl's naked body, roaming over her smooth shoulders and down the length of her spine to cup the fleshy globes of her buttocks.

Lindy's knee moved between her legs, her thigh rubbing against the soreness of her well-loved flesh, her sex still hot and sticky from the pleasure gifts bestowed upon her by the three knights.

'Hedra!'

She heard her name but she chose to ignore it, her fingers had just discovered the girl's pleasure bud and she didn't want to be disturbed.

'Hedra, come, we must go now.' It was Lord Gerard who murmured directly into her ear and she turned her head. In truth she felt slightly delirious – delirious from the wine and the pleasure-making and now the wonder of this new discovery. 'Hedra, we must sleep, I have a lot to accomplish on the morrow.'

'Oh!' she pouted, rolling away from the girl and allowing herself to be swept up in his arms. 'I was enjoying myself, my lord.'

'I know,' he said gently and with a smile. 'But you can enjoy yourself again tomorrow and the day after and the day after that, if you so wish. But now we must retire. I want you once more to myself before we give way to slumber.'

'It is an enticing prospect,' she murmured sleepily, nestling against his hard body as he carried her from the room, 'and one I do not believe I could possibly resist.'

* * *

Lord Gerard's pleasure-making was every bit as wonderful as she hoped and he left her early the next morning with a fierce kiss that bruised her lips.

'I do not expect to return before darkfall,' he said, his fingers closing around her waist as he pulled her torso up to meet his sinful mouth, his eyes drinking in the sight of her nakedness as though he had never seen it before. 'Believe me when I say I hate to leave you alone in this bed. I would rather spend the coming hours with you.'

Hedra arched her back further and encouraged him to slide his questing tongue lower and lower over her belly until it reached the anxious zone of her womanhood, the small nub of flesh eager to receive a new day's gratification. 'Then do not go, my lord,' she pleaded, 'tarry in this warm nest awhile.'

'Do you mean this nest, or this?' he asked wickedly, firstly glancing at the bed they occupied and then cupping her pleasure parts in one hand, his fingers gently plucking at her fleece.

'Both,' she murmured, 'either. All I know is I want you always and for ever.'

'You shall have me later,' he said and dropped her eager body back onto the bed. In the next instant he rolled over and smacked her naked buttocks playfully until she cried out in protest.

'That is not fair, my lord,' she said with laughter in her voice though her eyes gleamed wildly with arousal, 'you must not tease me so. You know how fiery that makes me feel.'

'Then perhaps I should pick you up and dunk you in a cold bath,' he said, motioning to scoop her up in his arms, at which she kicked her legs and squealed aloud.

'No, sir, dare you not!'

'Then I shall, just to tease you all the more.'

Without further ado he gathered her up and carried her across the bedchamber and into the bathing-room to a chorus of her excited screams and pleas for mercy. But once there she noticed, with an inner sigh of relief, that the deep tub was filled with warm, fragrant water as it had the day before and that Jade was standing meekly in attendance. For a fleeting instant, Hedra wondered if the girl had been standing there in such a pose all night and the next moment dismissed the very notion as ridiculous.

'Bathe, dress, eat, explore, do what pleases you the most,' he said. 'Remember, the castle belongs to you now, you may do whatever you wish.' He paused and set her carefully on her feet before adding, and with a smile that melted her, 'Just be sure that you do not tire yourself too much, you will need plenty of energy to keep pace with me this darkfall.'

He watched her slide sensuously into the bath and left her with a final kiss upon her shoulder moments before it disappeared beneath the steamy water. When he had finally gone it was as though someone had blown out all the torches on the walls and Hedra felt his absence almost as keenly as his presence. With a small sigh she turned to Jade who smiled back sympathetically.

'No matter, my lady,' she said, trying to console her mistress, 'there is much you need to do today.'

'Oh, really, such as?' Hedra asked. She couldn't think of a single thing that she could consider pressing, or even pertinent that didn't involve her lord and master.

'There is the matter of your wardrobe for one,' Jade said, kneeling by the side of the bath to wash Hedra's hair in a matter-of-fact manner. 'I have taken the liberty of arranging for the seamstress to pay you a visit before the advent of the second sun and you may also wish to pay some heed to the decoration of your own bedchamber.'

'Oh, yes,' Hedra said, laughing suddenly as she remembered the existence of the apartment's other rooms and that one in particular, 'although I cannot picture myself ever making use of it.'

She was surprised when Jade shook her head sagely. 'You may not think so at the moment, mistress,' she said, 'but you should pay more attention to your own needs. It would not do to be seen as the master's lap-dog. If you will excuse the expression?' she added quickly.

'Of course,' Hedra said straightaway. 'I know that you mean well and have my best interests at heart. There is nothing wrong with a woman maintaining a little mystery, is there not, especially where a man is concerned?'

'Precisely, mistress,' Jade replied, rinsing the violet locks with warm, clear water.

Bearing in mind that the seamstress was expected to make a visit, Hedra completed her *toilette* with the minimum of fuss and allowed Jade to dress her hair while she broke the fast of darkfall with a mixture of nuts and segments of succulent xiben fruit.

'I miss cake, Jade,' Hedra said, glancing ruefully at her plate. 'Ever since I arrived at the castle I have eaten very little and what I have ingested has been far too good for me. I crave something wicked that is not attached to a man.'

She laughed aloud at her own little joke and was gratified that her attendant understood immediately and laughed along with her. Jade's laughter was most pleasing, she decided, light and refreshing like rainfall upon dry leaves.

'Then order it, mistress,' the girl said as though it was the most obvious thing in the world. 'You heard what the master said. You are Lady Hedra of Satyria, you may have whatever you desire.'

'Mmm,' Hedra murmured thoughtfully as she ate the last piece of fruit and began to lick her fingers, 'I shall do just that and I shall ask for some sweetmeats and I shall send someone to the forest to look for my unicorn, Vanora, and bring her here and – ' Her list of desires was interrupted by a sharp rap on the door to Lord Gerard's bedchamber.

'That will be the seamstress no doubt,' Jade said. Leaving her mistress's side she walked across the room to open the door.

137

Hedra glanced up just as an old woman entered. She was dressed from neck to ankle in a serviceable dress of plain black cotton. Over one arm she carried a basket and in her other hand she held a length of measuring tape. Behind her followed a young man clad in typical male servant's clothing of rough brown woollen breeches, white cotton shirt and a tabard of red and white stripes with the Satyrian ram's-horn motif embroidered in the centre.

At that point Hedra was still wrapped in a large cream-coloured towel; however, on the old woman's instructions she dropped it to the floor and stood with her arms and legs spread wide in order to be measured. To her surprise it was not the woman who measured her but the page who stepped forward and with trembling hands encircled her naked breasts with the narrow tape. As his fingertips brushed her nipples they immediately awakened from their slumber and Hedra had to force herself not to sigh aloud. Instead she stood patiently as he continued to wrap the tape around her and call out the relevant measurements to the seamstress, who noted them down on a scrap of parchment with a stick of charcoal.

The page took a great many measurements, moving lower and lower down Hedra's body until he was forced to sink to one knee in front of her. His face was level with her fleece and she had to clamp her mouth tightly closed as his fingertips reached into the valley at the top of her inner thigh to hold the tape there while he measured the inside of her leg. His warm breath stroked her and she shuddered with a new desire.

To the seamstress's annoyance the point on her stick of charcoal broke at that moment and she frowned at the offending item in her hand. 'Please accept my apologies, my lady,' she said in a voice that was almost as gnarled as her fingers, 'I shall have to fetch a fresh piece before we can continue.'

Hedra inclined her head. 'Do as you must but please make haste, I do not have all day,' she said imperiously, as though she had a hundred important appointments to get through before her master's return.

On a whim, she instructed Jade to arrange for a fire to be lit in her own bedchamber and as soon as she was satisfied that she and the page were quite alone, she smiled down at him, her expression benign yet uncompromising. 'Do not move,' she ordered.

'Mistress?' the young man murmured in surprise as she gripped his wrist and moved her feet a little wider apart.

'I want you to pleasure me with your mouth,' she instructed him huskily. 'Do not take all day about it, we have little time and I crave the touch of your soft lips upon mine.' If the boy had been in any doubts as to her meaning, she lowered her hands and began to stroke her pleasure parts softly, parting them so that he could see the hard nub of flesh nestling within the pinky folds. 'Lick me,' she said.

The caress of the lad's tongue was wonderful, she thought; so soft, so hesitant and yet so effective. In no time she felt the heat begin to gather within her and countless dark fantasies jostled in her mind.

'Oh, yes,' she moaned, 'oh yes, you wicked, wicked boy!'

Her hands clutched his hair and she urged her body against his soft, wet mouth. Her zenith was just a fragment of time away and she arched her back and forced her trembling legs to hold her upright as the familiar waves of pleasure coursed through her body. Eventually, the waves ebbed and she started to compose herself, pushing the page's head away from her and stroking her hands tenderly over his thick dark hair, smoothing back from his furrowed brow.

'Mistress, I . . .' be began, his face a picture of confusion and wonder.

'Hush,' she murmured, affording him a smile. 'What is important is that you served me well. Now tell me your name.'

139

'Peregrine, my lady,' he replied, rising awkwardly to his feet.

Hedra noticed with a smile how he hurriedly arranged the front of his breeches as he stood upright, pulling at them as if they had suddenly become too constrictive. It was too bad, she thought, Jade and the old seamstress would return at any moment; he would just have to think of more mundane things until he was able to find relief at some other quarter.

'Well, Peregrine,' she said, 'I shall not forget you and perhaps you will have reason to visit my bedchamber on some future occasion?'

'I hope so, mistress,' he muttered fervently, 'indeed, I truly hope so.'

At that moment their conversation was interrupted by the appearance of Jade, who informed Hedra that a fire was warming her bedchamber even as they spoke, and then the seamstress returned armed with at least a dozen sticks of charcoal in a long wooden box.

'I am so humbly sorry, my lady,' she croaked. 'I hope the delay has not fatigued you. I promise it will not happen again.' Displaying several broken and blackened teeth, she gave what Hedra supposed was a smile and rattled the box of charcoal as proof of her claim.

Obviously I look a little more flustered than I realised, Hedra thought to herself with amusement as she readied herself for the page to start measuring her again.

'Please do not berate yourself, old woman,' she said, aware that her pleasure bud automatically started to pulse as soon as the young man's fingers moved anywhere near the tops of her thighs, 'I had other matters to attend to in your absence.'

When the measuring was finally completed, Hedra admitted that she had no real idea of the sort of clothes she would be needing.

'Oh, that is of no consequence,' the seamstress assured her, 'I already have the master's instructions for your wardrobe.'

'Indeed?' said Hedra, raising an eyebrow. 'That is very kind of him but what can a man possibly know about a woman's clothing?'

'Did you not like the costume I made for you to wear last darkfall?' the old woman asked with a note of obvious surprise in her voice. 'The master assured me that the style would suit you admirably.'

Hedra had to concede that the costume had been a fine one and that she had felt extremely comfortable in it.

'Lord Gerard said that you are a powerful woman,' the seamstress added. 'He did not consider fragile robes to be your ideal garb.'

'The master knows me better than I know myself,' Hedra said thoughtfully, the words spoken almost to herself. 'I had not realised. I should beware of his knowledge.'

She smiled at the old woman and bade her good day and to the page she also bestowed a smile but one that was a good deal more knowing and more intimate. As soon as the two of them had left she turned to Jade who stood, as meekly and as patiently as ever, her hands clasped loosely in front of her.

Today the girl was wearing a long straight gown of red silk, the simple garment decorated around the waist and hips by a plaited belt of flat gold chain.

'You look nice, Jade,' Hedra said. 'Now what did the master leave for me to wear today?'

She hadn't noticed the package wrapped in oatmeal-coloured sacking that lay upon the bed. But now Jade picked it up and opened it. Inside lay a robe fashioned entirely from squares of white leather held together at the four corners by loops of gold. Hedra stepped into the robe and when she pulled it up her body she found it was very short and barely skimmed the underswell of her buttocks. 'Another modest little piece,' she said with a laugh in her voice that set the robe trembling. 'I do not think I am in any doubt about the way the master perceives me.'

141

All at once she imagined Lord Gerard's expression when he saw her and felt a dart of naked lust streak through her at the thought. Staring out of the window for a moment at the bright light of the second sun, just risen in the sky, she ruminated on how tedious a time she had to wait until darkfall. How can I bear to wait for him? she thought. How can I bear to be removed from him at all? And from that moment she decided that, whenever it was possible to do so, she would accompany Lord Gerard when he left the castle. Better to face danger together, she reasoned with conviction, than endure the torture of being apart.

# Chapter Nine

$A$fter a brief visit to her own bedchamber where she met with a trio of servants and gave them instructions as to how she wanted the room redecorated, Hedra decided to explore the rest of the castle.

It was fortunate that Jade had advised her to wear flat slippers because the grey stone edifice was indeed vast, much larger than the castle in Parsimonia, and proved to be a very frustrating place – as much a tribute to man's folly as to his imagination, for it had no rhyme or reason about it at all.

After much walking she soon found that the maze of corridors tended to lead back into themselves and return the explorer to the place he or she had started from; or that the many flights of stairs did not actually lead anywhere except a sheer drop, or indeed down again a few paces from the place they had begun to ascend. Corridors led to dead ends or blocked doorways and windows invariably looked out onto stone walls or the solid trunk of a tree.

With the exception of the central area where the great hall, the banqueting room and the throne room were situated – and, of course, the courtiers' private apartments – most of the castle was unfurnished and undecorated. Bare stone walls and dusty flagstones were the order of the day and with hardly a torch or candle set into a wall-sconce to light the gloomy way.

By the time the second sun had begun to drop from its apex Hedra was starting to feel decidedly tired and dirty, and sadly not in the way she enjoyed the most. Rounding yet another cold grey-stone corner she was relieved to see Jade, her tiny Kelf form appearing even more dwarfed by the shadowy vault that surrounded her.

Her face lit up when she saw her mistress. 'Oh, I am so pleased to find you here, my lady,' she said, her musical voice a chorus that seemed to echo endlessly around their heads. 'I did not anticipate you would be gone for so long.'

'No, nor I,' Hedra admitted, using the back of her hand to push a stray lock of hair away from her eyes. She glanced around. 'This place is incredible,' she added, putting real inflection into her voice so that Jade could not mistake the true meaning of her words.

The Kelf laughed, a sound which again echoed around them again and again. 'Let me show you the way back to your apartment,' she offered, turning on her heel. 'I have received word that a banquet is planned for this evenfall. It is to be a rather lavish affair by all accounts.

'I wonder that Lord Gerard did not mention it to me,' Hedra said, following in the girl's light footsteps. 'It was very remiss of him and I shall scold him for it when he returns.'

Jade glanced over her shoulder, an impish glint dancing in her eyes. 'I fancy if anyone is to scold or chastise it will be the master,' she said.

Hedra nodded, although her attendant did not see it. 'You are right, of course, my dear little Kelf,' she said, 'and I thank the fate masters that he conducts himself that way. It is a great relief to me to have met someone who is, at the very least, my equal.'

She understated the situation of course but it would not do to admit to a servant that she took great pleasure

144

in being subjugated. Some things were best kept private between a mistress and her master.

If Jade could have read her mistress's thoughts she would have laughed aloud. Chastisement and domination were not secret aspects of the Satyrian way of life, they were vital components – spectacles and pleasures to be brought out of the dungeons and bedchambers and exhibited to all. But Hedra was yet a stranger to the kingdom and could be forgiven for her naïvety.

The seamstress had proved herself a quick worker despite her frailty, Hedra found, as she eyed the half-dozen costumes arranged upon Sir Gerard's bed. Fashioned purely from animal skins and precious metals the garments were brief and outlandishly erotic.

'If you will permit me, mistress,' Jade said, 'I would like to suggest this outfit for the banquet.'

'Are you sure?' Hedra asked, eyeing the tight black-leather corset with a doubtful expression. She stroked the supple hide, her fingertips encircling the ruby studs in the centre of each pointed breast cup – a lewd indication of the fleshy nipples concealed beneath. 'I thought a gown of some kind,' she added, her voice trailing off as Jade shook her head decisively.

'Trust me, mistress,' she said, 'this will be perfect.'

Time seems to be moving at great speed, Hedra found herself thinking as she watched the great trio of moons rise high in the black velvet firmament and hover above the glass dome. The whole process of bathing and oiling and pampering seemed to be taking an age. And although she relished Jade's skilful attentions she could hardly bear each tormenting moment, knowing that Lord Gerard's return was imminent.

At last she heard him return to the castle: the clatter of horses' hooves on the drawbridge and in the court-yard outside, his heavy boots ringing on the flagstones, the metallic clash of armour and, finally, the tell-tale creak of the door to the bedchamber. Her heart raced and her stomach knotted.

'Quickly, quickly, Jade,' she urged, wanting only to be free of the girl and ready to fall into his arms.

He bested her, sweeping into the bathing chamber, his leather cloak billowing around him, while she still lay upon the satin-covered bed, her naked body only half oiled and perfumed.

She looked up as he stood over her, gauntlet-clad fists on hips, his muscular legs planted firmly astride, and she felt herself melt under his piercing sapphire gaze.

'Well, well,' he joked, 'what have we here – a comely maid laid out for me like a sacrifice upon a red silken altar?'

As he spoke she felt her body flame to the same colour as the sheet beneath her and a rush of fluid ran from her anxious sex.

His keen eyes missed nothing. 'My, what a shameful little wench you are,' he continued in the same light-hearted tone. 'I have no choice but to punish you most severely for your indiscretion.'

'Oh, master, please,' she breathed.

It wasn't apparent whether she intended to say please no, or please yes, but it mattered not one jot to Sir Gerard. He would chastise her anyway and they would both enjoy it. Like a large, leathery bat he swooped down upon her and gathered her limp body into his arms, carrying her away into his lair.

Hedra almost swooned as he touched her. The sensation of warm leather against her skin was an undiminishing pleasure. And the knowledge that his body lay beneath the erotic garb was almost too much for her to bear.

He spread her across the bed, face-down and spread-eagled, his dextrous fingers securing her wrists and ankles with thin silken cords the colour of pure gold. 'Try to move and you will only hurt yourself,' he warned as she squirmed upon the rich brocade coverlet.

Tugging at the bindings to her wrists she felt a chafing heat bite into her. 'Master,' she cried, 'it pains me!'

146

'Did I not just tell you it would?' he said, unfastening a clip at his throat to loosen his cloak. He dropped it carelessly onto a chair and disposed of his scabbard, boots and jerkin in the same offhand fashion.

Hedra turned her face to look at him. Every time she saw him she found herself transported on a wave of desire and this was no exception it seemed. His broad muscular torso gleamed in the candlelight and his large, clever hands now clapped together. They were still gloved, she noticed with a further surge of desire, and she knew only too well what they intended to do next.

She felt the mattress give slightly as he knelt beside her on the bed and, when she felt the first touch of a leather finger upon the base of her spine, her sex contracted sharply and began to throb with a fierce desire. Pressing her face into the coverlet she moaned. His fingers were tracing her spine and the cleft between her quivering buttocks, up and down, up and down, creating a relentless, fiery trail that transfixed her whole mind.

Her body was but one line. A narrow, white-hot spear of lust. She moaned again but louder, so that there was no mistaking her desire. Her whole body screamed 'touch me!' yet she would not give him the satisfaction of putting voice to the words.

'Your body flames, does it not?' he asked, in a silky smooth tone that drove into her with the lustful intent of a phallus. 'You want my fingers to seek you here and here.'

She felt him delve inside her, sinking into the melting wetness between her legs. Thrashing her head from side to side in silent ecstacy she refused to answer him.

'How sweet that you should try to resist me, my love,' he murmured, completely unperturbed. His warm breath surprised her as he pressed his rough cheek against hers, his lips brushing her ear, 'But you know already that I have you where I want you,' he continued, 'and I can *have* you whenever I want you – or not at all, the choice is entirely mine.'

147

He laughed wickedly and rose to his feet, moving to the cupboard the top of which bore a silver tray of goblets and a crystal flagon of wine.

'Make me suffer at your peril, wicked rogue,' she cried, finding her voice at long last.

'Oh, ho!' He turned around and laughed at her, throwing back his head to drain a goblet of wine in one fell swoop. 'And what should I fear of you, my lady, a thrashing perhaps – or a withholding of your body? I think not in either case.'

The wicked roar of his laughter reverberated around the room and Hedra knew she was beaten. It was not a cruel laugh though, there was a loving note there, an undertone of oneness and Hedra felt herself warming to him more.

'I want you, my lord,' she said huskily. 'All jesting aside, I want you.'

He moved back to kneel beside her upon the bed but this time his large, gloved hands covered her buttocks, the fingers widespread, kneading the firm flesh beneath.

'Are you ready to receive your punishment, my lady?' he murmured.

She replied at once, 'Is that what you desire?'

'It is.'

She nodded. 'So be it, my body is ready.'

Her buttocks thrust into the air slightly as he smacked her, her back arching in time with her moans. Fiery stings were left upon her delicate flesh and still she urged him to spank her more soundly.

'I deserve it, my lord,' she assured him between gasps of pleasure, 'I have been a very, very bad girl.'

'Have you indeed?' he said, smoothing the burning globes beneath his hands before resuming the chastisement. 'And pray tell me, how so?'

Hedra hesitated, her bravery deserting her for a moment. She didn't want to displease him and yet she sensed her news would only serve to enhance the moment. 'I ordered a servant to pleasure me,' she said.

'It was the seamstress's boy. I made him pleasure me with his mouth.'

'Indeed?' His eyes gleamed as he stared down at her, the cheeks on her face displaying shame, now flaming as brightly as those of her bottom, and yet her wet sex told a different story. 'And did you enjoy it? Did he serve his mistress well?'

'Oh, yes, my lord,' she said, gasping as his fingers grasped her buttocks and spread them wide, 'I reached my zenith easily.'

'Then what must I do?' he asked, pressing a finger against the tight opening, watching with interest as the muscles gave reluctantly beneath the pressure. 'Beat the young knave, or beat you?'

'Oh, me, beat me!' she cried, arching her back as his fingers went inside her, 'Please, master, smack my licentious body until it burns.'

Lord Gerard smiled. 'Your innocence was soon forgotten, was it not, my lady?'

'My what?' she exclaimed, momentarily forgetting the story she had perpetuated.

'Your innocence, Hedra, your innocence,' he said.

His finger turned and probed inside her, inducing cries of shameful pleasure to issue from her lips.

'It is all thanks due to you that my innocence has deserted me, master,' she managed to gasp. 'Now I simply crave your debauched attentions.'

His thrust his phallus inside her, taking her by surprise. His chest pressed against her back as he plunged and withdrew in the musky wetness beneath. 'You fancy you know the meaning of debauchery,' he hissed beside her ear, 'but mark my words, by this end of darkfall you will wonder at your own folly.'

His laughter radiated outward from their tangled bodies, harmonised with her screams of ecstacy and was carried away from the dark, craggy castle on the shriek of a carrion crow.

\* \* \*

149

The lavish array of the banquet surprised her into uncharacteristic silence. As she crossed the threshold of the wide doorway, her hand resting on Lord Gerard's arm, she found herself entranced by the sight that met her eyes.

Totally transformed, the gloomy banqueting hall was now suffused with light, the dancing flames of thousands of tiny candles casting their brilliance into every nook and cranny. Along the centre of the room was arranged a long, wide table bounded by serried ranks of high-backed chairs. Smothered by a thick tablecloth of blood-red velvet it groaned with the weight of its burden: platters of food, flagons of wine and negus and place settings for at least a hundred.

Hedra gazed at the opulence around her and whispered to Lord Gerard that she felt underdressed for the proposed occasion.

Reassured by Jade and then a nod of approval from her lord and master, she had donned the leather outfit, breathing in sharply as her attendant tightened it about her, pulling in her waist until her hips swelled either side like fleshy panniers. Although her breasts were partially concealed beneath the bodice, the two rubies perfectly positioned, she had no covering for her lower body – nothing at all to shield her fleece and buttocks. And on her feet and legs she wore the longest, tightest boots of matching leather, the heels as high and pointed as twin daggers.

'Be not disquieted, my lady,' he said in a low voice meant only for her. 'You have no reason to doubt your attire, I assure you.'

He led her to twin chairs at the head of the table – carved of oak like modest thrones, their seats thickly cushioned in a blue velvet of the same hue as Lord Gerard's eyes. She sat and he sat beside her, both their bodies held erect in a naturally regal posture. They stared silently at the open doorway and a moment later a carillon of bells and a blare of trumpets summoned the guests – other courtiers, Watchers and Clansmen, who were dressed in a wide array of costumes. Some were clothed quite modestly, in long robes of velvet or silk, and others in much scantier garb of leather and other fabric.

'I take your meaning now, my lord,' Hedra murmured as a woman entered and took a seat near to them. Her tall thin body was clad only in a series of narrow bands of leather, held together at the sides by circles of gold.

More leather-bound Watchers took up their places and another, much younger girl entered shortly afterwards, attracting Hedra's immediate attention. She wore hardly anything at all save a tight cummerbund of diamond-studded black velvet, and black opals that hung like a sweep's teardrops from her nipples and earlobes. Hedra glanced down, her shocked gaze taking in the further piercing and decoration of the girl's lovelips. She looks familiar, Hedra found herself thinking, surprised that she should presume to recognise anyone at all when she had hardly moved outside Lord Gerard's apartment.

Suddenly she realised with a sickening jolt that the girl was Bella, the innocent whom she had managed to defeat in the battle for Lord Gerard's attentions. There was no mistaking her now, the pertly pretty countenance, the long pale blond hair.

'Who is that girl?' Hedra whispered to Lord Gerard.

'Who, what girl?'

He glanced sideways, startled from an idle daydream that involved himself and a whole crowd of desperate, pleasure-starved young women.

'That girl.'

Hedra all but stood up and pointed at Bella and he glanced in her direction instantly. Bella had the grace to blush, Hedra noticed, but he, of course, did not.

'I believe she is called Beauty or Bella or some such pretty name,' he said, his tone displaying a disinterest that he genuinely felt.

He remembered her now of course; the deflowering

had taken place only that morning, in the brief interlude between the sun-up meal and his departure from the castle while his horse was being saddled. It had been very enjoyable but nothing special and nor was the girl.

Hedra glared venomously down the length of the table. 'Did you say I could do as I wished with the courtiers?' she asked.

Lord Gerard inclined his head. 'Indeed I did.'

'Then I wish her to be humiliated,' Hedra stated. 'I want her chained and manacled here before me and I want a whip!'

He looked startled, as well he might. He knew his Lady Hedra was not a delicate, wilting flower and yet she had surprised him once by her admission about the young page and now her behaviour surprised him again. In all truth, he had expected some legions of time to pass before she became fully immersed in the Satyrian way of life. Most did and they were not even Parsimonians by birth.

'Very well,' he said and crooked his finger to summon a disrober. 'Bring that girl forth,' he ordered, pointing at the unfortunate Bella, and bring my lady a restraining frame and horsewhip.'

The cloaked man nodded and set about his task, delegating with efficiency as the girl was lifted from her seat by two other disrobers and marched to the head of the table to stand unwillingly by the side of Hedra's chair. The disrobers held Bella fast, gripping her at the shoulders and elbows while they waited for the equipment to be brought.

Hedra turned in her chair and stared at the girl, her expression as regal and disdainful as she could manage. Inside she felt a burning anger but she dare not let it show. What folly it would be to disgrace herself at her first proper royal engagement and how stupid to let her lord and master know of her jealousy. Better he thinks me calm and worldly, she thought, watching with interest as a high wooden frame was carried into the room.

The disrobers brought the frame up to the head of the table and set it beside her, angling it so that it was in her direct line of vision were she just to turn her head slightly. Bella's slippered feet slithered on the flagstones as they positioned her against the frame.

'Front or back, my lady?' one of the disrobers asked.

'I beg your pardon?' she said.

Lord Gerard leaned across to whisper in her ear, 'He wants to know if you wish the front of the girl to be presented to you, or the back – do you care to whip her breasts or her buttocks?' he said.

'Oh,' Hedra gasped. She hadn't considered the possibility of a choice. 'Back, I think,' she said, turning to the cloaked man. She didn't want to have to look at Bella's face throughout the entire banquet, she reasoned, and buttocks were much more interesting to chastise.

She almost laughed to herself at that moment. It was as though she were used to delivering a whipping and yet she had only ever punished the Chivalrous Knight before and he hardly counted – she hadn't enjoyed the experience nearly as much as she intended to enjoy this.

In amused silence she watched the girl sob and squirm as the disrobers spreadeagled her and manacled her wrists and ankles to the wooden contraption, a flat frame made up of several intersecting bars of simple, forest wood supported by joists on the reverse. It held her upright and completely helpless, spread apart and available to Hedra's every whim.

As this was taking place the seats around the table continued to fill up with people, all of them murmuring in low voices and glancing first at the stately image of their new Lady and then at the unfortunate tableau represented by Bella.

One of the Clansmen near the head of the table called out to Lord Gerard, 'I see you have already selected our entertainment, my lord!'

'Not I,' Lord Gerard replied, with a slightly bemused

shake of his head. 'It seems our Lady Hedra wishes to enjoy a little sport.'

'My, my,' a Watcher interjected, 'we should all laud you, my lady. It has not been like this for many a long season, not since the old queen was upon the throne and in her prime.'

Hedra smiled and nodded, taking the praise as her due. 'I hope there will be many changes to the good around here,' she said, her glance taking in all the courtiers seated at the table and those still clustered in little groups beyond. 'Be certain of this, I like to work hard at my civil duties, and play even harder still.'

The air was thick with laughter and mutters of approval. Lord Gerard leaned across to Hedra and kissed her full on the lips in front of the gathered throng. 'Now you see why I selected her,' he announced to all, his face bearing a broad, prideful smile. 'She is magnificent, is she not?' He rose to his feet suddenly and raised his goblet in the manner of a toast. 'I give you Lady Hedra,' he announced, 'most desirable and fearsome woman in all Satyria!'

'Lady Hedra, Lady Hedra!'

The crowd rose to its feet and drank to her health and to her success as Lady of their kingdom and eventually the food was brought in on great, golden platters – whole roasted wild boar and venison amongst them – and everyone fell silent for a while, eating and drinking and generally taking their relaxation.

As he ate, Lord Gerard began a conversation with the courtiers nearest the head of the table and strove to include Hedra. However, her mind was on other things. Primarily she thought of the unfortunate Bella who had to suffer the further indignity of being fed by a servant, a cheeky young cove who wasted no opporunity to touch the girl upon the breasts or between her out-stretched legs whenever he thought no one was look-ing. He did not realise that Hedra observed his movements from the corner of her eye and gradually

154

she surprised herself by feeling sorry for Bella rather than angry with her.

It was too bad that, as she had been told, Gerard had taken her so soon after their first coupling but then she supposed it was inevitable; he had been about to choose Bella after all. And, of course, it was still his duty to deflower the vestal virgins. The act did not mean that he loved and lusted after her any the less; she realised that now and felt a little foolish.

When she mentioned to Lord Gerard that she had eaten her fill he called a disrober to step forth. In the man's outstretched hands there lay a whip, long and menacingly dark, with a single leather thong knotted at the end. Hedra stared at it wide-eyed and almost in a trance found herself reaching out to take it, her fingers curled around the woven leather grip. She glanced up at her master.

'I feel I have misjudged the girl,' she murmured, her stomach fluttering with trepidation. 'Perhaps I should show leniency this time.'

To her surprise and consternation, Lord Gerard threw back his head and laughed loudly. 'Do you not think that is a little cruel?' he said.

'Cruel?' she asked, her surprise evident. 'I thought I had just proposed a kindness.'

Lord Gerard laughed again but this time more softly. He took Hedra's free hand and urged her to rise from her seat. 'Come with me,' he said softly and led her over to the wooden frame. Gathering a handful of Bella's blond locks he pulled her head back a little. 'Look at her,' he ordered gently.

Hedra glanced unwillingly at the girl's tear-stained face. Even now fresh droplets bubbled in her eyes and trickled from the corners. She glanced back at the impassive face of her master. 'I see a girl who is much troubled,' Hedra said. 'I no longer wish to be the cause of her misery.'

'Then you shall not let her go,' he said, stroking a

finger down Bella's smooth white throat. 'She would not thank you for it.'

'Master, you are perplexing me,' Hedra said. 'I do not understand the logic of your claim.'

'See the wetness upon her face?' he said, releasing Bella a moment later.

Hedra nodded. 'Indeed I do, my lord, that is why – '

He interrupted her by placing a finger against her lips and she felt the fingers of his other hand curl around her wrist.

'Now compare it with the wetness here,' he murmured and to Hedra's shocked amazement he thrust her hand between Bella's legs and worked it back and forth along the slippery folds of her sex. Hedra gasped. The girl was indeed very moist and she could feel the puffiness of her pleasure lips and the heat emanating from them. 'She is aroused,' he added needlessly. 'Most Satyrians derive great pleasure from this treatment.'

With slight reluctance she allowed him to pull back her hand and watched in fascination as he brought her fingers to his lips, took them into his mouth and, his eyes holding hers, he sucked deeply. Deep inside her she felt an answering tug of desire and a rush of her own wetness. Her pleasure bud throbbed as his tongue wrapped itself around her fingers and sucked them deeper still, his eyes speaking volumes. She imagined him treating her most intimate parts in the same manner and knew he could read her thoughts.

He released her fingers, folding them within his own to just hold them for a moment. From far within her body she felt her heart beating hard and fast and heard the answering beat in her ears. His eyes burned her, as did his touch. And for a long moment she felt the two of them were transfixed in time and wished the banquet and its guests could fade away to nothing so that she and her beloved lord and master could be alone.

'Later, Hedra,' he murmured softly, reading her thoughts once again. 'My passion for you cannot be dimmed by time.'

She smiled lovingly at him but in the next instant their blissful interlude was suddenly interrupted by raucous yells coming from somewhere else in the vast chamber and they turned their heads simultaneously.

Further down the table, almost near the other end, a Watcher had been stripped completely and was now being mounted by a fearsome-looking Clansman, his torso broad and his face half-concealed by a bushy red beard. Far from being afraid of him, the woman was laughing and crying out her encouragement as he thrust into her and a group of other courtiers had gathered around to cheer the copulating couple onward towards their mutual orgasm.

'I fear I still have a lot to learn, my lord,' Hedra murmured. To which Lord Gerard nodded.

'Satyria is a unique place,' he assured her, as if she had not already realised it. 'There are very few kingdoms who place as much import on debauchery and pleasurable living as this.' He gripped her waist with one hand and raised the hand aloft that held the whip. 'Start the punishment now, my lady,' he urged, 'before our little friend becomes too anxious.'

Hedra glanced at Bella. Her body did indeed strain, she noticed, the twin moons of her buttocks almost pleading to be chastised. 'Very well,' she said with a smile and strode purposefully to stand at the side of the girl. Without further ado she raised her whip hand and brought the lash down with a whistle, striping the buttocks cleanly.

At that moment a great clamour sounded outside the banqueting hall and although Hedra did not pause in giving Bella her punishment, she glanced up as the double doors were suddenly flung wide open and a crowd of people surged into the chamber.

'What is going on here?' Lord Gerard cried. 'Who dares to interrupt our revelling?'

Bella let out a loud moan at that moment and Hedra glanced at her before sweeping her eyes to the new assembly. To her horror and surprise from the midst of

157

the gathered throng stepped a familiar and formidable figure – a tall broad-shouldered man dressed in sueded skins of brown and golden chainmail, his white hair and beard a sharp contrast to his dark, leathery face.

Her sex contracted sharply at the sight and in the next instant Lord Gerard took a vast step forward, his manner threatening. 'King Randolph!' he bellowed. 'What business have you here, vile scoundrel?'

The king threw back his head and laughed, a deep rumbling that shook the goblets upon the banqueting table and set the chandeliers a tremble. 'Vile scoundrel!' he cried, laughing all the more, 'I'll wager I have been called worse than that in my time. Why, 'tis almost a compliment you pay me, sir.'

Suddenly it seemed as though the air around the gathering darkened and became foul. The interloper looked around the chamber and caught Hedra's eye. A flicker of recognition crossed both their faces simultaneously and he strode forward, coming nearer and nearer to her while all she could do was stand transfixed in a pose that held her whip-hand aloft and her black leather-clad legs apart, her breasts heaving as though straining to escape the tight confines of the corset.

'Continue,' he commanded, coming to a halt only a few paces from her.

Hedra stared at him, her eyes wide, her lips devoid of words.

He repeated his command and added the words that galvanised her, 'What ails you whore? Are you afraid?'

'You pig!' she screamed and brought the whip down hard across Bella's buttocks. 'You filthy-mouthed gutter rat!' Heedless of the girl's moans and cries Hedra continued to beat her until she suddenly realised the folly King Randolph had goaded her into and she turned her attention upon him. 'Rotting piece of laver meat!' she raged – settling on what she believed to be the worst possible insult – and whirled around suddenly to bring the leather thong down hard across his chest.

He stepped back, surprised by the sting of the unexpected blow, then reached out and caught her wrist before she was able to stripe him a second time.

Hedra wasted no time in kicking out with the sharply pointed toes of her boots but he sidestepped her, his movements agile for a man of his size. And he further aggravated her by laughing all the while as she became more angry and more heated.

All this time Lord Gerard had been stunned into inaction. Looking on in amazement he had watched the scene unfolding between his beloved Hedra and the most debased man in all the Fantastic Lands. He had seen the spirit within her, of course, and learned that her lovely, womanly body concealed a feisty nature and a will of steel, yet he had never witnessed her giving such spectacular vent to her emotions.

'That will do, Hedra,' he said, coming to his senses, and raised his hand to restrain hers as the king had done. It surprised him that he should find himself in the position of defending the man and against his Lady of all people. 'What business have you here?' he added, turning to glare at King Randolph, who looked uncharacteristically relieved by the interruption to Hedra's performance.

The king glanced scathingly at the Satyrian Lord. 'Your time is up, Gerard,' he said, being deliberately rude. 'Prepare to be overthrown.'

Hedra glanced fearfully at Lord Gerard, who glared at the man in front of them. 'I do not think this is the place to hold such a discussion,' he said, so calmly that she longed to cry out her admiration for him. 'Let us repair to the antechamber.' He and the king moved away from the table in the direction of a side door and she automatically made to follow them. 'No, Hedra, wait here or go to my apartment and wait,' Lord Gerard murmured, glancing at her over his shoulder. 'This is a man's business.'

'You jest I hope, my lord?' she responded instantly.

159

'A man's business indeed.' She stressed the words in a derisory manner.

Realising she would not be dissuaded, he sighed. 'Very well, you may accompany us,' he said and added in an undertone, 'but I beg you to behave yourself, no talk of gutter rats or laver meat, or I shall have you ejected from the room, is that clear?' Despite himself he could not disguise a smile.

Hedra's lips curved in reply and her eyes danced impishly. 'As if I would, my lord,' she said in a low murmur and accepting his proffered arm, 'as if I would.'

# Chapter Ten

*T*hey were joined in the antechamber by a trio of
Decadent Knights, one of them Sir Drago, two of
the king's own knights and also a pair of strange-
looking women whom King Randolph introduced as his
'Bisextrix'.

'They keep me entertained,' he said by way of explanation, 'and warm during the long, cold nights while I
am on my travels.'

As the men took their seats around the sturdy oak
table and began to talk in low voices, Hedra found
herself intrigued enough to keep glancing surreptitiously at the two women who stood, like bodyguards,
just a few paces behind the king's chair. They were
indeed an incredible sight. Tall and lean of limb and
torso they were clad in very little: a few leather thongs
that wound carelessly about their arms, waists and
thighs and a cummerbund of brown leather, studded
around the upper and lower edges and redecorated by
a small golden replica of the king's coat of arms. On
their wrists they wore bracelets of beaten gold, etched
with scrolling, and a shield of similarly decorated gold
hung from a thong to disguise their fleeces. Their legs
too were clad in brown distressed hide in the form of
knee-high boots that laced up the back.

161

But it was the sight of their faces, or rather their heads, that amazed the princess and held her in awe of them. For almost the whole of their scalps were shaved except the very centre from which a long, thick hank of hair was gathered into a high tail and allowed to fall in strong ripples to the upper swell of their buttocks.

The Bisextrix noticed Hedra looking at them and turned around in unison to mock her with their eyes. 'A pretty piece of meat,' one of them muttered to the other and Hedra burned with indignation.

She longed to speak out but dared not. It was no longer a simple matter of avoiding Lord Gerard's disapproval. The situation was a tricky one, she realised instantly and, remembering the recent discussion between Lord Gerard, Sir Drago and Sir Jagared, recognised that they were on the brink of war.

Moving to a side table she picked up a flagon of sloe wine and carried it to the table where she filled a number of goblets with the fiery liquid. Most of the people present murmured their thanks but the Bisextrix merely leered nastily at her as they accepted the wine she offered and King Randolph held her eyes with a rock-hard stare, his irises glinting in the candlelight like chips of black marble.

He pointed to the empty seat next to him. 'Sit,' he ordered.

Hesitating for just a moment, she poured herself a goblet of wine and carried it to the place beside him. As she lowered herself upon the seat he reached out one rough, calloused hand and stroked it down the length of her thigh.

'We have encountered one another once before, have we not?' he said, although his expression did not alter as she nodded her agreement.

Gerard glanced in their direction, throwing her a look of surprise but Hedra kept the sight of him in the corner of her eye and continued to hold King Randolph's stare.

'I understand you are the rogue who threatened my land so convincingly that all but my father fled,' she said, her voice low and controlled despite the fierce anger that burned within her.

'That is true,' he said, 'but I was not referring to that incident.'

Hedra raged inside at his casual reference to the destruction of her kingdom as an 'incident' but still maintained her calm. 'Then you must mean the time you raided my band of knights?' she said. 'How unfortunate for you, yet fortunate for me, that I managed to escape your loathsome clutches.' She felt her self-control slip a little and reproached herself for it.

The king, however, appeared not to care. Insults did not bother him one jot. If anything, he found such retaliation amusing. 'But you have not escaped, have you, my dear little princess?' he said, the straight line of his lips now curving into a cruel smile. 'You are here now in my clutches.'

Clenching her hands into angry fists under the cover of the table top, she forced herself to speak in a level tone. 'You are here at our invitation, my liege,' she said. 'I would hardly call that having me in your clutches.'

'Then what would you call this?' the king replied, laughing. All at once he rose to his feet and, pulling a stunned Hedra with him, his great bear-like arms went around her and held her tightly against his body while his mouth pressed down on hers.

She struggled against him, hardly able to breath. Like that of his knights, his costume was one of leather and chainmail but his jerkin was studded with sharp chips of diamonds, rubies and other precious gemstones and now they dug cruelly into her flesh as he continued to hold her tightly.

Lord Gerard was on his feet in an instant. 'My liege, I must protest!' he cried but, as King Randolph released Hedra's mouth in order to reply, she shook her head vehemently and assured her lord and master that she was unharmed and was well able to look after herself. Pursing his lips, he sat down reluctantly and King Randolph looked into Hedra's face.

He noticed how brilliantly her eyes glittered and her cheeks flushed. And, against his chest, he could feel the fullness of her breasts and the way they heaved. All at once he found himself wishing his breeches were not so robust, otherwise he could have felt the softness of her fleece as well. One arm still gripped her around the waist but now he moved his other hand lower to grasp her buttocks. She squirmed a little but otherwise did not protest.

'If we had more time at our disposal I would not hesitate to take you, Princess,' he said, his voice a low growl as he spoke directly into her ear.

Hedra stared levelly at him. 'I would not allow it, my liege.'

'You would not have a say in the matter.'

'I have something to say about every matter.'

He paused and pondered what to offer next in this bout of verbal jousting. 'You are something of a virago, are you not?'

'If you say so, my liege,' she replied, laughing lightly. 'I prefer to think of myself as assertive.'

'Then could you rise to meet a challenge?'

'I have no doubt about it.'

'Then it shall be left to you to save Satyria.'

The cut and thrust of their debate wavered as Hedra suddenly felt lost for a reply.

'How so, my liege?' she asked finally but in a much subdued tone.

He released her abruptly and bade her to resume her seat beside him. Leaning one elbow upon the table top, he placed a thoughtful hand over his mouth and considered his answer carefully. 'On the morrow I shall place into your keeping three of my knights,' he said, 'fine and stalwart men who have served me well for many a legion.' He paused and glanced at her, accepting her nod to continue. 'Your challenge shall be to seduce all three,' he said and laughed aloud as Hedra's face took on a look that derided the challenge as being too simple to overcome. 'I do not just refer to their

164

physical seduction, my lady. You must seduce them into renouncing their loyalty to me and joining the ranks of your own Decadent Knights.'

Inside Hedra quaked at his words, although she kept her face impassive; just the faintest smile of confidence playing about her lips and eyes. 'And what may I expect in return?' she said finally. 'What inducement do you have to make me take up your challenge?'

'Complete freedom,' he replied candidly and added, 'I may be a harsh man but let no one deny that I am fair. If you succeed in this task I shall not threaten Satyria again – not as long as I live.'

'That is indeed a tempting offer, my liege,' she said, recognising that she had no real choice, 'but I fear I may require a little more inspiration than that. It is a difficult challenge and although I now bear allegiance to Satyria I am still concerned about the kingdom of my birth, Parsimonia.'

He looked thoughtful once again and took a deep swallow of his wine. Hedra grimaced on his behalf, knowing how much it burned the throat and yet he seemed not to notice and drank the fiery liquid as if it were the purest spring water.

'If you succeed and, know you now I doubt that you will, otherwise I would not strike such a bargain,' he said, 'I will grant unconditional safety to all Parsimonians. I am only interested in the gemstones contained within your kingdom's rocks; the people are of no interest to me. If you are successful I shall mine the land and allow your father to rule his people as he did before.'

This additional concession tempted Hedra a great deal and she wasted no time in accepting his challenge. 'Deliver your men straight to the castle dungeons,' she ordered imperiously, 'I shall deal with them from there.'

The gathering broke up a short while later. King Randolph bade his goodbyes to all Satyrians present and added to Lord Gerard that he envied him, that Hedra was a fine woman to have as his Lady.

'I know that,' he said, stepping forward to Hedra's side and putting a protective arm about her waist, 'but make no mistake that she is mine, and shall remain that way for ever.'

Hedra swallowed deeply. As much as she loved her lord and master she still regarded herself as independent of anyone and ached to remind him of this but she held her tongue and the moment passed.

As soon as they were alone Lord Gerard pulled her into his arms and kissed her fiercely, his large hands stroking her hair, her back, her buttocks. 'I feared for you for a moment,' he admitted, gazing into her eyes with the white hot heat of passion. 'Nay, I feared for all of us. You realise you have offered yourself as a sacrifice?'

Smiling warmly, although a lump constricted her throat, she said, 'All is not lost, my lord, and I hope you believe me when I say that I did what I thought best.'

'This is not easy for me to say, my darling,' he began, cupping her chin and tipping it upward so that the invisible aura of their lips touched, 'but I truly believe that I love you, although I had never before thought myself capable of such an emotion.'

'And I love you, my lord,' she said, and allowed the warm salty tears to flow at long last as he commanded her mouth with his own and cradled her in his arms for a long, long time.

Outside the room, in the main banqueting hall, the courtiers were well and truly lost in their revelling. Hedra and Lord Gerard peeped through the doorway and saw the tangled, writhing bodies – men pleasuring women, women pleasuring men, and men and women pleasuring others of their own gender.

'Do you wish to join them?' he asked.

She shook her head. 'I might have wished it before but now I would prefer something a little more intimate.'

He smiled his understanding and took her hand. 'Then let us take the back staircase,' he said. 'It leads directly to my apartment.'

The staircase was dark and narrow but Lord Gerard felt his way upwards, leading Hedra by the hand and as soon as they reached his bedchamber he pulled her into his arms once again for another searching kiss.

She gave her lips to him eagerly, helping him as much as she could as he unlaced her corset and then disrobed himself without releasing her. When they were both completely naked, their bodies glowing pinkly in the firelight, she sank to her knees in front of him, the fleshy tips of her breasts hardening as they brushed the length of his body. Gazing at the magnificence of his phallus she put out her tongue and tasted it, probing the little opening at the very top where a large salty droplet emerged.

A hiss of pleasure escaped his lips but she still kept her mouth upon him, licking and sucking and tasting all the time as he groaned deeply and clutched at her hair, his large, strong hands gathering it into handfuls before releasing it and gathering it again, each time a little more passionately than before.

She could feel his juices rising, surging just beneath the fragile covering of skin just as the blood flowed quickly through her veins, urged on by the rapid pulsing of her heart.

'Hedra, stop,' he commanded her but for once she ignored him, keeping up the remorseless caress despite his cries of pleasurable agony, taking her tongue around and around the swollen tip of him before sucking deeply and rhythmically.

She knew he would soon reach his crisis and yet cared not. She had never yet experienced the receiving of a man's pleasure gift in her mouth but now she welcomed it and urged it on, her body stiffening in anticipation just a star-twinkle before he groaned loudly and the hot, salty fluid drowned the inside of her mouth.

167

'You are a little witch,' he murmured softly a moment later, pulling her to her feet so that her naked body pressed full length against his, 'a beautiful, clever, little enchantress.' He punctuated the words with kisses pressed against her throat.

To her delight he was still hard and his strong phallus pressed insistently into the soft flesh of her belly and, as she arched her back further and offered herself to his soft lips, she prayed his desire for her would always be this enduring. They had barely set out on the course of their lives together and yet she already feared a parting, as though her inner eye could see something the conscious part of her could not. Make pleasure today for tomorrow we may breathe our last, she thought, although not with any sadness but more a *frisson* of urgency. Living for the moment was all that mattered to her now. She had seen how fragile a safe, secure existence could be; how easily it could be shattered upon the dreadful whim of one person.

Her thoughts drifted naturally to King Randolph as Lord Gerard continued to kiss her neck and shoulders and caress her quivering buttocks. The infamous king was indeed a scoundrel and a rogue. And yet . . . To the surprise of her lord and master, she shook her head vigorously. There should not be an 'and yet', in her thoughts, any desirous inclinations toward him were truly a scandal and should not be entertained under any circumstances.

'Love me, master,' she said urgently, anxious to dispel all thoughts of King Randolph. 'Take me to our bed and love me.'

He did not hesitate in acquiescing to her demand. Turning her and walking her backward just a few paces, he put his hands around her waist and lifted her slightly pressing her back upon the coverlet and raising her legs so that they linked around his neck. Her soft wetness was open to him, pouting with desire as always. He felt her with his fingers, hot and puffy and wanting. And then, in a moment, he was inside her, buried to the hilt, his hardness sinking with delight into the wet, pulpy tunnel of her sex – loving the way her body automatically gripped him and increased the flow of creamy nectar around him.

She had bewitched him, about that there was no doubt. Her body was delightful yet her mind and spirit entranced him more. Even if an evil enchantress gave her the appearance of a goblin he would love her none the less. He glanced down at her, at the way her grey eyes glittered like steel under the flickering light of the chandelier that hung over the bed, the light diffused through the red velvet canopy to cover her face and torso with a rosy glow. And her breasts heaved in such a beguiling way, the twin globes thrusting upward with each forward motion of his body as though coming to greet him.

'You are truly beautiful, Hedra,' he said with a slight gasp. Gripping her hips, he endeavoured to thrust deeper and deeper inside her, as though he longed for her to eat him alive. 'I can't help loving you.'

A smile flickered across her face as he said the words but she did not really acknowledge them as she might have done under other circumstances. Her climax was so close that it was the rhythmic thrusting of his body that mattered to her the most, not his thoughts, however wonderful or poetic. Later she would savour them. Hold them close to her like a bunch of the most exotic flowers. But at that moment, as her body strained to take more of him, it was sensation, not sentiment, that drove her to the peak of gratification.

They reached their zenith together and she released her grip on him and lowered her legs as he fell upon her, his lips pressing into the valley of her throat which was covered with a thin film of salty droplets.

He tasted her idly, his tongue venturing from between slack lips as he waited for his breathing to slow and the pace of his heartbeat to follow suit. Further down his body an ebbing pulse told him that a period of rest was the most sensible option to follow. Recover-

169

ing a little strength, he withdrew from her with some reluctance and crawled upon the bed, dragging her body to meet his under the warmth of the coverlet. With great tenderness he covered them both and held her tightly, his lips pressed against her hair as languor tugged at their eyelids and sleep claimed them until the rising of the first sun.

After bathing and eating, Hedra's main task of the day was to go down to the dungeon to see what King Randolph had left her and she found her guests locked in separate tiny chambers: three men, each handsome in his own way, and chained at the ankles to the bare stone wall.

The first rose to his feet as she crossed the threshold. She had to stoop to avoid hitting her head on the low lintel and when she straightened up she realised that his gaze had been transfixed by the sight of her breasts, swelling generously from the zig-zag neckline of a brown suede jerkin. Based on a man's garment, she wore the brief covering with her own inimitable style and without the addition of any underclothing. Consequently, her movements offered any voyeur tantalising glimpses of the dusky triangle at the tops of her thighs and the enticing curves of her lower buttocks. As she straightened up she noticed, with an inner satisfaction, how his gaze faltered before flicking down the length of her body right to the toes of her high brown boots.

'I am Lady Hedra,' she said without any preamble, striding forward boldly with her hand outstretched, 'and who might you be, sir?'

'I *am* Sir Jarl,' he replied in a slightly ironic tone, 'there is no *might* about it.'

Hedra fumed at his rudeness but said nothing. After all, he was one of King Randolph's men and therefore bad manners were no doubt to be expected.

'Very well, I am pleased to meet you, Sir Jarl. I hope we will soon be friends.' She forced herself to smile at him and to her relief he smiled back.

170

The look transformed him, softening his hard, craggy features and lending a sparkle to his deep brown eyes. He is quite passable a specimen, she found herself thinking, eyeing him carefully. At first she had not thought too much of him but now she saw his his slight, gaunt figure actually became him; the angles of his bone structure lent him a kind of grace that was almost feminine. And his hair, which at first sight she had considered nondescript, she now realised was quite a thick mane; deep brown and silky like the coat of a thoroughbred.

'Have you quite finished, my lady?' the knight said, interrupting her thoughts.

She looked at him askance and then allowed her face to soften back into a smile. 'I am so sorry, I was merely entranced by your appearance for a moment,' she said, stepping forward to stroke his hair lightly. 'You really are quite a handsome fellow, you know?'

Sir Jarl pursed his lips, amused by the young woman who stood so close to him and treated him like a prime head of livestock. He had no inkling of his purpose for being there, or how he was expected to behave. King Randolph had delivered himself and two other knights to the Satyrian castle with the simple instruction to follow their own instincts, whatever that meant. And since he arrived his treatment had been a series of contradictions. Firstly, being thrown into a cell. Then being brought an excellent meal upon a golden platter and with a whole flagon of rich, heady wine. This morning he had eaten equally well before being forced to suffer the indignity of being manacled and now . . . now he was suffering the appraisal and caresses of a beautiful young woman, so scantily clad he might reach out at any moment and touch her intimately.

'And you, my lady, are truly beautiful,' he murmured. He decided to do as his king had instructed him. Besides, for the time being it made for an interesting diversion; he had little else to do that day it seemed.

Hedra nodded, accepting his compliment as her due

171

– a response that amused him greatly. 'Do you know why you are here, sir?'

He shook his head. 'Indeed I do not,' he said. Glancing down at his manacled ankles and pursing his lips ruefully he added, 'And I know not what I have done to merit such treatment.'

Hedra smiled and dropped to her haunches, her fingers immediately reaching to stroke the reddened skin where it had chafed against the unforgiving iron. 'My deepest apologies, sir,' she said, rising to her feet once again. 'I shall arrange for you to be freed at once. In fact – ' she broke off as a thought began to formulate in her mind ' – I believe it would be far more commodious for us to continue our business in my own apartment.' She strode to the door, which the gaoler had locked behind her as soon as she entered the cell, and opened a small, arched flap just level with her face.

As soon as she called out, the gaoler arrived and, on Hedra's instruction, released Sir Jarl.

She turned to the knight who had sat down once again on a small wooden stool and was rubbing his sore ankles. 'I shall be but a moment,' she said. 'I just want to check on the others.'

Walking along the gloomy passageway behind the squat, bald figure of the gaoler, she mused how interesting it might be to spend some time in the dungeons with Lord Gerard. Purely in the interest of fun, of course. She had spotted some quite interesting items of equipment in some of the empty cells and made a mental note to suggest it to her lord and master.

The gaoler stopped abruptly in front of a low, oak door, just like all the others and, opening the flap cautiously, Hedra peered inside the gloomy little room. She felt her breath catch instantly. Seated upon a plain hard-backed chair, chewing thoughtfully on what was obviously the remainder of his sun-up meal, was the most handsome fair-haired knight she had ever seen. His appearance suddenly made her feel homesick for her native kingdom, for like the Chivalrous Knights of

Parsimonia his appearance was one of golden innocence; a beauty that was far too fair to belong to a man
and yet he had no female affectations.

His build was broad and muscular, his whole
demeanour stalwart and the aura that surrounded him
was very, very male. It was so strong she could almost
smell it and then she came to realise that perhaps this
masculine aura, coupled with feminine beauty, was a
characteristic of all King Randolph's knights. It seemed
more than coincidental that of the two men she had so
far seen, both were similarly endowed. And now she
came to recall, the two knights who had been present
in the antechamber the previous darkfall had also had
comparable attributes, although she had been too pre-
occupied to really pay any attention.

She moved swiftly on to the cell which housed the
third knight, who immediately confirmed her theory.
He too was quite fair-haired, although not golden like
the previous knight and he bore the same characteristics
of beauty overlaid with masculinity. Shivering slightly
with anticipation, she realised that perhaps her quest
would not be so onerous as she first thought.

Sir Jarl leapt to his feet once again as she returned but
this time she beckoned to him to join her. He left the
confines of the cell, avoiding the gaoler as best he could,
as though he suspected them both of trickery and
wondered if the round little man with the huge bunch
of keys would actually try to do him some harm. Hedra
laughed.

'Have no fear, sir,' she said. 'All you have to concern
yourself with from now on is pleasure. Make no
mistake.'

'You will understand trust does not come easily to a
knight in a foreign kingdom,' he said, still eyeing the
gaoler warily as he and Hedra walked side by side
down the long passageway to the main hall, 'especially
when he has been forced to spend the long hours of
darkfall in a cell.'

'Have you been mistreated?' she asked with a suspicious flick of her eyes in the direction of the gaoler, who waddled along in front of them, but the knight was quick to reassure her.

'Oh, no, my lady. It is merely the indignity I have had to endure, that is all.'

She smiled, satisfied, and at that moment they reached the vast cavern of the main hall. Taking him by the hand, she led him up the great sweeping stairway, its newels formed of great winged beasts, the body similar to that of a dragon but with the head of a ram.

'The ram is the symbol of Satyria,' she said conversationally when she caught him looking at the carvings. 'It is most apt.' Her lips curved into a smile and lights began to dance in her eyes as she remembered Lord Gerard's love-making, the desperate way he had taken her only that sun-up, before he left the castle. 'I'll keep you too weary to deflower virgins,' she had joked, enfolding him tightly with her whole body. 'Before long you will have to delegate the task to someone else.'

When she spoke the words he had merely smiled enigmatically and kissed her in reply but she still hugged the possibility close to her, with all the anticipation of a much longed-for gift.

Sir Jarl proved to be an adequate lover, responding with gratifying alacrity to her none-too-subtle overtures. Inside the safe haven of her own bedchamber, now decorated almost identically to the one she had in Parsimonia, she had poured him a goblet of wine and then proceeded to seduce him – sitting very close to him, touching him with increasing regularity and intimacy, leaning forward to kiss him lightly when he made a joke, making certain her breasts rubbed against his arm and chest as she did so.

Of course, he missed nothing. In fact she needn't have gone to such an effort. If she had simply lain on the bed and opened her legs he would have obliged. But it seemed she liked to play games and he was only

174

too delighted to go along with them; provided the outcome was the same, what did it matter?

It was therefore to her great disappointment that he refused her offer to join the Decadent Knights with almost as much speed as he had taken her body.

'But why not, sir?' she protested when he refused her a third time. 'They are a fine band of men and you will want for nothing.'

'I am already with a fine band of men and want for nothing. Why should I change allegiance?' he pointed out with a calm reason that made Hedra thump her fist against the bedpost in anger.

'Ow!' She rubbed her hand ruefully, glaring at him as he laughed aloud and reached for her a second time.

'Allow me to kiss you better, my lady,' he offered, moving down her body with skilful lips until he reach the musky-scented purse of flesh between her thighs.

'It was my hand that suffered the injury, sir,' she cried, squirming under him as his tongue probed her relentlessly, dragging her rapidly into the dark abyss of gratification until her protests died on her lips to be replaced by groans of encouragement.

She took him inside her body a second time, this time sitting astride him and riding him harder than if she were upon a horse and had a pack of slavering wild beasts on her heels. Yet still he would not relent and pledge allegiance to the Decadent Knights.

'Exciting though you are, my lady, and no doubt there are others who would keep me similarly diverted,' he said, 'I have ample women-flesh waiting for me in King Randolph's court.'

A short while later she took her leave of him. 'Why not take advantage of this soft bed and get some rest?' she urged him. 'I need to bathe and dress before Lord Gerard returns.'

He nodded quite happily at her suggestion and, she suspected, had fallen asleep before the door had even closed behind her.

Wondering if she had ever felt more relieved to see

Jade than she did at that moment, Hedra found herself sinking gratefully into the steaming bath tub and pouring out her heart to the sympathetic Kelf.

'It sounds to me as though you need something beyond the physical, if I may say so, mistress,' Jade said, kneeling by the side of the bath to soap her arms and shoulders. 'A foray into the realm of enchantment may not go amiss.'

Hedra exhaled slowly, spreading out her arms and arching her back so that Jade could slick the soapy sponge across her breasts. 'I truly think you may have the solution but I know of no enchantress, nor sorcerer and therefore have nowhere to turn.'

'Zendik,' the Kelf said abruptly, patting her mistress's shoulder to indicate that the top half of her body had been soaped.

Hedra rose to her feet, sudsy trails weaving quickly down her torso as she did so, leaving her magnificent body clean and glistening. 'I take it he is a magician of some kind?' she said, 'although I have not heard the name. Does he reside far from here?'

To her surprise Jade began to laugh softly. 'He lives within the shadow of the castle, mistress,' she said and added, 'Zendik is the king's own sorcerer. No one knows how old he is but there are those who say he is immortal and has been here since the beginning of time.'

'Is he a Kelf?' Hedra asked, but Jade shook her head.

'No, but he claims to have the secret to immortality and a great deal besides.' She paused to wrap Hedra in a bathing robe and led her to the silken bed. 'I could show you where he lives. On the morrow we could ride out together. He is not an easy man to deal with and mistrusts strangers. You may find it useful if I am there.'

'Stranger indeed,' Hedra said derisively. She moved her limbs obligingly as Jade went about her business, oiling and perfuming her entire body.

'You have been here only a short time,' Jade pointed

out. 'Therefore to a man who is as old as time itself you would seem to be a stranger.'

Hedra nodded. It was frustrating to have to wait before the matter could be resolved and even then, there were no guarantees that Zendik would have the answer she sought. 'Very well,' she said, turning her head to throw a smile at Jade, 'you and I shall ride to meet this Zendik as soon as the first sun has risen. I cannot afford delay in this matter. I still have two more of King Randolph's knights to deal with and there is so much at stake.'

# Chapter Eleven

*L*ord Gerard was surprised when Hedra rose early and told him that she had business with Zendik. 'I thought you would have seduced that knight easily. Do not tell me you have lost your touch?' he said, raising an enquiring eyebrow.

She laughed at his words, her full breasts heaving under the unfamiliar constraint of a bodice, for she had decided to wear conventional clothing for her journey outside the castle. Perhaps, she reasoned, as this Zendik was an old character, his heart would possibly be unable to cope with the sight of her dressed in her usual outrageous garb.

'Of course I seduced him easily, my lord,' she stated, with an airy toss of her head that made him smile inwardly, 'but I could not entice him that vital step further into becoming a Decadent Knight.'

'Then what do you plan to do?'

'Find out his weakness and act upon it.'

'How do you know he has a weakness?'

Hedra drifted across the room, her long amethyst skirts brushing the deep green carpet. Leaning across him as he still lay in the high canopied bed, she pressed her lips to his ear. 'Everyone has a weakness, my lord,' she whispered darkly. 'Even you.'

'Oh, yes?' he said, laughing and gripping her delicate face between his hands so that the tips of their noses met. 'And what is my weakness, pray?'

'Me,' she said simply.

A discreet knock at the door to the bedchamber interrupted them and, dropping a light kiss upon her lord and master's lips, she skipped away from him and went to answer it. It was Jade, fully dressed, for once, in breeches and a jerkin of moss-green sueded leather. In her hand she held a long silver dagger and as soon as Hedra saw it she exclaimed loudly, 'We are going to ask the old man for his help, Jade, not threaten him with his life!'

The Kelf laughed her tinkling laugh. 'This is not for Zendik, mistress,' she said. 'This is in case we are attacked along the way. I suggest you arm yourself with something similar.'

Hedra went back into the bedchamber. 'Jade thinks I should take a weapon of some kind,' she said to Lord Gerard.

He threw back the coverlet and swung his legs around until his feet touched the floor. 'She is right to suggest it,' he said, trying hard to ignore Hedra's interested gaze as it swept blatantly over his naked body. Striding over to a low, ornately carved oak chest, he lifted the lid and withdrew a thin, white-leather scabbard from which protruded a golden hilt.

'This weapon should suit you, my lady,' he said, fastening the scabbard around her slender waist, his hands deliberately lingering. It is longer than a dagger, yet shorter and lighter than a full-sized sword.'

As he stepped back, Hedra withdrew the instrument swiftly, slicing the blade back and forth through the air between them until she was satisfied that she had the feel of it.

'Thank you, my lord,' she said with a broad smile, 'this should serve me admirably.'

All at once, Lord Gerard became unusually sombre. Stepping forward he held the delicate hand that still

179

clutched the hilt of the sword and wrapped his other arm tightly about her waist. 'I pray you shall not need to use it,' he whispered urgently and, kissing her hard upon the lips, he moved his mouth to murmur into her hair. 'Take all good care, Hedra. It is the first time you have left the castle and I urge you not to do anything rash.'

She was touched by his concern but determined not to give away her feelings. Instead she replied lightly, 'I do declare, my lord, you treat me as though I were as fragile as a flutter moth. Surely you know me better than that by now?' With a second but much lighter kiss, she danced away from him and spoke briefly with Jade before turning back to gaze at him with a look that spoke volumes. 'Do not despair about anything, my lord,' she promised. 'By the time we meet again next evenfall your band of Decadent Knights shall have a new recruit.'

The ride from the castle compound and beyond was quickly dispensed with. Without threat from wild animal, or wicked foe, Hedra and Jade reached the ancient bell tower that Zendik had chosen as his quarters. Nestling in the green velvet of a woodland glade, the old structure was higher than a fir tree and built of crumbling white stone. At the very top, Hedra could just make out the bell itself, an instrument of blackened iron that swayed aimlessly in the grip of the strong breeze as though a pair of arms pulled continuously upon the frayed rope that hung from it.

'I declare, this is a desolate place,' Hedra said, glancing warily around. Although the glade itself seemed bright and friendly, all around them the tangled undergrowth seemed to harbour a life of its own; a thousand slanted yellow eyes that watched their every move.

Jade started to walk around the base of the tower, leading her horse. She and Hedra had each borrowed a steed from the castle stables, a chestnut for her and a dappled grey for her mistress. Now they tethered the horses to a low branch and left them a few handfuls of oat grass as the ground around them offered little to graze upon, only a few sparse tufts.

Hedra caught up with Jade and waited as the young girl raised the heavy black iron doorknocker, cast in the image of a sleeping dragon, and let it fall. Three times she repeated the action and presently they heard the sound of shuffling feet and a harsh, rasping cough. A moment later the door swung back to reveal the figure of an old man dressed from shoulder to ankle in a velvet robe of blue. His hair was white and straggly with a beard to match and for a brief instant Hedra was reminded of her father. The pang of recognition burned in her chest as she adjusted her senses to take in the fact that the person before her displayed none of her father's handsomeness, nor his nobility. In fact, she realised, he seemed quite dusty and unkempt, as though he had needed to brush a curtain of cobwebs from him before he rose to answer their knock at the door.

There was no time for sentiment, nor the tedious ritual of pleasantries and she set straightaway about introducing herself and Jade, although the sorcerer laughed and said he knew already who they were – he was, after all, a sorcerer, he said, laughing gruffly. The laugh turned into another series of wracking coughs and, waving his hand apologetically, he turned to lead them into the main vestibule and then up a narrow, creaking flight of stairs to a more comfortable room.

As they were in a tower, of course all the rooms were round and this one contained furniture that echoed the theme of curvature: a round wooden table, big enough to seat twelve, wooden chairs of all sizes but all with curved backs. And, taking pride of place, a sofa that meandered back and forth sinuously, one red velvet seat this side, one on the other, and so forth. There were four seats in all and Hedra thought it quite the most interesting piece of furniture she had ever seen. She moved across the room to it and sat down on the second seat facing into the centre of the room, Jade sat behind her and to the left side, facing a small flickering fire, and the sorcerer sat beside her.

'State your business, my lady,' he said, coming straight to the point. 'I have not time to delay on idle chit-chat.'

For a moment, she felt affronted by his rudeness and somewhat bewildered. It seemed incongruous to her that a man who claimed to be as old as time should be concerned with brevity. Using as few words as possible, she described her predicament and, when she finished, the old man nodded.

'I wonder at a man who does not find your willing body enough of an incentive,' he said, his wrinkled apple cheeks becoming redder as he looked at her.

She gazed back at him, sensing the subtle change in the atmosphere between them. For a moment he had ceased to be a magical being and had reverted to responding simply as a man.

'What would you do if you were in my shoes, Zendik?' she asked softly, reaching out her fingertips to toy with the straggly ends of his beard.

The old man cleared his throat a couple of times before jumping hastily to his feet. Crossing the room swiftly, he approached an object that stood in the corner shrouded by sacking. With a flick of the wrist he pulled away the covering to reveal the most beautiful full-length looking-glass that Hedra had ever seen.

She gasped aloud, her eyes roaming the ornate silver frame depicting fairies and elves in bold relief, their tiny, sinuous bodies engaged in all manner of lewd activities. Just the sight of them made her sex tingle and she had to fight hard to resist the urge to squirm upon the red velvet seat.

'It is fabulous,' she breathed, leaning right forward to see it more clearly, only too aware that by doing so her breasts were forced to swell more obviously above the straight neckline of her bodice.

Old and wily Zendik missed nothing. He recognised her appreciation of the looking-glass, even though she did not yet know its true purpose, and he realised that she was unconsciously making a bargain with him. It was not a transaction that he was about to refuse. It had been many a decade since he had enjoyed the charms of a young woman and to have one as lovely as the Lady Hedra beholden to him was too good an opportunity to let slip through his creaking fingers.

All of a sudden Jade turned in her seat and spoke out. 'I know you of old, Zendik. Surely that is not just any looking-glass. What is its special purpose?'

The old man turned his head in her direction. 'You Kelfs are an inquisitive lot,' he said, but his tone bore no accusation. 'There is truth in what you say. The looking-glass does have one peculiar attribute.' He paused for effect and waited until both young women urged him to continue. 'This particular little beauty is like a fresh-water pool,' he said. Holding out his hand to Hedra, he bade her to rise and step up to the looking-glass. 'You see yourself, do you not, my lady?' he asked.

Hedra gazed at her reflection. 'Of course,' she replied, resisting the urge to fiddle with her hair which was looking a little windswept, 'what of it?'

Zendik tutted. 'Impatience, impatience. It will not do.'

'I implore you, sir,' Hedra said, forcing herself to smile sweetly.

In reply, he nodded sagely and looked her up and down. Her demeanour did not fool him for one moment. 'Very well,' he said, 'tell me what happens when you look into a freshwater pool?'

'You . . . you see your reflection,' she replied, feeling confused and not a little irritated by his pedantic manner. All she wanted was to find the solution to her problem and be off.

'But can you not see through the reflection?' he added. 'Can you not see beyond it to the bottom of the pool?'

Hedra thought for a moment, then nodded. 'Of course, what of it?'

183

'This looking-glass has the same attribute,' he persisted. 'You may see yourself, or look beyond your own reflection and see others, in another part of the castle perhaps – were you to install this instrument in your own bedchamber, for instance.' He paused, wondering what it would be like to spend time in her bedchamber.

It took some moments for Hedra to digest the impact of his disclosure, then she cried, 'Do you mean to say that I could observe anyone in the castle, no matter what they were doing?' It seemed too far-fetched to be true, yet if it were more than just an old man's fancy the possibilities that would be afforded her by owning such an object were beyond calculation.

'Yes, it is true. Observe.'

Zendik turned the looking-glass slightly and muttered something under his breath. In the next instant all three of them were able to see beyond the stone wall and out into the depths of the woodland beyond. And each time he muttered the same magical word, the vision shifted slightly in perspective until they had seen all the way around the outside of the tower.

Hedra was beside herself with wonder. 'That is truly amazing, sir,' she said, exhaling a breath of wonder. She turned to face him, her eyes alive and sparkling with desire, not for the old man but for the object he owned. 'I want it. I want it to be mine!'

Zendik watched her and nodded calmly, although inside the covering of his faded blue robe his heart was beating fast against his ribs. 'Then you shall have it, my lovely Lady Hedra. But of course, there must be a payment of some kind, a bargain struck.'

Despite her eagerness to own the looking-glass, she glanced at him warily. 'How much? A thousand coins, two thousand, or some gemstones perhaps?'

To her consternation he shook his head slowly. 'Money and jewels mean nothing to me,' he said. 'Whatever I want I get by means of magic – what use is currency to me?'

'Then what?' she persisted, although already in her

heart of hearts she knew and her spirit plummeted. He was old and ugly. She didn't believe she could ever countenance the thought of his hands upon her body. And yet . . .

'One brief moment of pleasure with you, my lady, and the looking-glass and all its secrets are yours for ever,' he said, tempting her.

Hedra turned to glance at Jade but the Kelf's face was impassive. 'Is that all?' she said, turning back to stare hard at Zendik. This was a business arrangement, nothing more, she told herself. The transaction would be settled in no time.

He nodded. 'I ask nothing more and nothing less.'

'Very well.'

She turned back to Jade but was relieved to see that she was already on her feet. 'I believe I should check on the horses, mistress,' she said calmly, her face betraying no emotion whatsoever.

'Yes, thank you, Jade. I shall be but a short while,' Hedra replied, making certain that Zendik understood her message. He nodded his assent and the two of them watched and waited until Jade had left the room and closed the door behind her.

The tiny 'click' of the door set Hedra's heart beating wildly and turned her legs to water, yet still she faced the sorcerer and raised an enquiring eyebrow.

At once his hands were upon her. All over her. Bony fingers reaching inside her bodice to touch her breasts. 'Take it all off,' he gasped hoarsely, starting another series of dry coughs.

With trembling fingers, she quickly undressed. In the looking-glass she could see their reflections: her body tall and strong and womanly, his stooped, old and gnarled. Fortunately he did not attempt to disrobe himself and for that she was grateful. From outside she heard the horses' whinnying and closed her eyes. His fingers probed her relentlessly; like twigs they reached into every crevice and sought out every orifice, twisting and turning until she cried out for him to take his true pleasure and have done with it.

There was no finesse in his movements as he forced her to her hands and knees and took her from behind, although deep down she marvelled at the old man's virility. It was over in a matter of short, sharp thrusts and in a moment he was back on his feet, adjusting his robe.

'I shall ride back to the castle and send someone to collect the looking-glass directly,' she said, pulling on her own clothes. The relief washed over her in a flood as he nodded his agreement.

'You will need to know the magic word,' he said, and shuffled across the room to a small writing desk. Picking up a raven's quill and dipping it into violet ink, he wrote a single word on a sheet of ivory parchment, underlining it with a flourish.

Hedra smiled and nodded her thanks. She could feel his pleasure gift trickling down her thighs and longed to be out of there. Suddenly, the room stifled her. The surrounding wood stifled her. She just wanted to be back in the familiar confines of the castle.

During the homeward ride she did not speak until they almost reached the drawbridge and then she turned to Jade and said, 'I beseech you not to speak to anyone about what transpired back there,' she said, cocking her head in the direction they had just come.

Jade glanced at her mistress and noticed, with not a little concern, how urgently her eyes pleaded and how they glistened under the veil of unshed tears. 'Of course not, mistress,' she said quietly. 'You know you can trust me, always.' She stressed the last word and was relieved when a smile touched her mistress's lips.

Upon her return Hedra sent a couple of pages to the bell-tower straightaway and, as she waited for the delivery of the looking-glass, she set about making the necessary preparations; most importantly, a request to Sir Drago.

'That does not sound like the sort of request I should

186

wish to refuse in any case, my lady,' he said when she had finished with her explanations. 'You may rest assured that I shall comply with every ounce of zeal that I possess.' His face broke into a broad smile and, for a moment, she felt tempted to let the handsome knight wipe away the memories of her earlier encounter with Zendik. But, alas, she had not the time to spare; evenfall was almost upon them. 'Be certain, you shall be well rewarded at a later date,' she said, her expression and tone of voice displaying the true meaning behind her words.

Her next stop was the bathing-chamber. It was a relief to erase the musty smell of the sorcerer from her skin and to wash away every vestige of her encounter with him. She was thankful that, as she worked, Jade made no further mention of it and she was happy that the matter would now be dropped. Now she could turn her attentions to the matter in hand.

In some ways it was fortunate that Lord Gerard was not expected back at the castle that darkfall. It would have been too frustrating to be forced to spend her time with Sir Jarl when in reality she ached to be in her lord and master's arms.

She had just dressed in a voluminous robe of sheer white fabric which had been worked into hundreds of tiny pleats and was gathered about her slender waist by a narrow belt of gold chain, when a page announced that the looking-glass had been installed in her bed-chamber. At the news, she jumped up excitedly, dislodging Jade's hands as they fixed tiny golden combs into her hair.

'This is it now, Jade,' she said. 'Victory may soon be close at hand.'

The Kelf smiled at her mistress's excitement, pleased that her earlier air of sobriety seemed to have disappeared into the mists of past time. 'Then pray be off with you, my lady,' she said. 'Sir Drago will already be in his own chamber awaiting the first sign of darkfall.'

Hedra nodded. She had told Jade the whole of her scheme. Now she just had to hope it would work.

Sir Jarl sat up in surprise as Hedra entered her bedchamber. He had been dozing upon her bed, as he had done all day and now he felt ready for a little entertainment. She looked magnificent, he thought, as she crossed the room. The gown she wore was almost virginal, yet it concealed nothing and, as she moved, a long, slender leg would appear from between the folds. The sight of those firm thighs enticed him even more and beneath his breeches he felt his interest stir vigorously.

To his immediate dismay, her arrival was followed by a trio of servants who carried platters of food and proceeded to ornament the small table with all the necessary objects for the evenfall meal: golden platters, ornately worked forks and knives, heavy, jewel-encrusted goblets and crystal flagons of ruby wine. Under the brightness of the flickering candles set in wall sconces, the table items cast their reflections upon the stark canvas of the damask cloth; pools of pink and yellow, tinted here and there with a dash of emerald and amethyst.

'Presentation counts for half the enjoyment of a good meal,' she explained when she caught his expression. 'Now please, Sir Jarl, come and be seated.'

It did not escape his attention that as she sat the front of her robe parted to the waist, revealing the ivory softness of her lower belly which contrasted so well with the dusky hue of her fleece. But she made no move to cover herself, not even while the servants were still present, and he found his eyes drawn back to the beguiling sight time and time again throughout the meal.

His fingers itched unbearably to touch her but he forced himself to concentrate on working his knife and fork, stopping every so often to pick up the heavy goblet set by his plate and swallow deeply from it. The wine intoxicated him but her presence affected him even more deeply. And, although her conversation was totally innocuous, it seemed she taunted him with this and that, hidden meanings and innuendo, the promise of delights to come, all veiled by a cloak of innocent chatter.

Presently, when they had eaten their fill and simply picked idly at sweetmeats, the conversation veered into the realms of hopes and dreams and of fantasies unfulfilled.

'Can you imagine,' she was saying, 'what a delight it would be to be a secret witness to another's pleasure-making?' She paused to sip her wine and continued immediately, knowing she had his full attention. 'I do not just refer to the fun of watching another couple, or couple of couples, as in the case of an orgy. But secret watching, the furtive thrill of discovering the private person. Do you understand what I am saying?' She laughed lightly then, deliberately disturbing the neck-line of her robe so that it too fell apart, exposing one whole breast to his view.

The pink tip mesmerised him and he licked his lips in an unconscious gesture. 'I believe I do, my lady,' he murmured, resisting the urge to tug at the front of his breeches where they had grown uncomfortably tight. 'It is a commonly beheld notion that people behave much differently when they believe themselves to be alone.'

'Quite,' she murmured mysteriously, rising to her feet.

He watched her as she crossed the bedchamber and stared at herself in the looking-glass. As she stroked the tips of her breasts, one directly and the other through the gossamer layer of her gown, she regarded herself thoughtfully, as though he were no longer there. Almost in a trance he gazed at her, his eyes glazing as they watched her every movement. He didn't remember the existence of the looking-glass but now he was grateful to it. With the benefit of its clear reflection he was able to perceive two Lady Hedras, two violet fleeces

189

and two sets of full creamy breasts. Without realising it he groaned aloud and at that moment the moon rose high and Hedra whispered the magic word.

Before the knight's amazed eyes, the vision in the looking-glass changed shape and form. Now he could no longer see her reflection but a tableau, another bedchamber where another knight rested fully clothed in black leather upon a high bed, one knee bent, the other leg straight in front of him. His arm rested on the bent knee and he appeared to be waiting for something, or someone.

'You may find this interesting,' she said to Sir Jarl needlessly. 'Why don't you join me upon the bed where we may watch in comfort?'

The knight was on his feet in an instant and lay down beside Hedra. They stretched out on their stomachs, their toes pointing towards the head of the bed, their eyes fixed to the looking-glass in front of them.

'Does this have something to do with what we were talking about, by any chance?' he said.

'Of course,' she replied. 'I never say anything without good reason.'

At that moment, their attention became diverted by the sight of the door to Sir Drago's bedchamber swinging open. The looking-glass afforded them the luxury of sound as well as vision and now Hedra heard his familiar voice speak out.

'Do not tarry, girl, enter at once.'

She heard Sir Jarl's breath catch as Bella entered the room, her tall slender figure clad in a short robe of deep violet silk that showed off her shapely thighs to best advantage. Her long, straight blonde hair was held away from her angelic face by golden combs and fell down her back like a silken shawl.

'By the mystics, that girl is beautiful!' the man beside Hedra exclaimed, as she thought he might, and she glanced sideways at him.

'There is no end to the beauty of Satyrian maidens,' she said, 'as well you may discover.'

To her amusement, the knight mumbled something under his breath. But she saw how rapt his expression had become and how deeply his chest heaved. Prepare to lose the battle, she mused to herself, for victory is soon to be mine. In a silence heavy with emotion, they continued to watch the scene unfold before them.

Sir Drago bade the girl to come closer to him and so she did, her movements hesitant although she was, by then, far from being innocent. Reaching out, he ran his large hands all over her shoulders and breasts, flattening the silk against her body as he slid his palms lower and lower. The outline of her navel was now clearly visible as Sir Drago gripped her tightly about the waist and pulled her towards him for a deep and searching kiss. As she bent forward, the hem of her dress rose up, exposing the smooth tight globes of her buttocks and the intriguing shadow between her slightly parted legs. Sir Jarl inched a little closer to the end of the bed, Hedra noticed with an inward smile, but said nothing.

His attention did not wander throughout the agonisingly drawn-out moments of Sir Drago's seduction of the lovely Bella. But, of course, Hedra realised, the Decadent Knight knew he was playing to an audience and she thanked him for his thoroughness. No portion of Bella's soft, creamy flesh went untouched, or unkissed. He unwrapped her like a gift, for the delectation of the two voyeurs, and then took her with a fierce passion that had the girl screaming and sobbing with the most intense pleasure she had ever experienced.

As she lay upon the bed in the hazy bliss of afterglow, her arms and legs thrown carelessly apart and every morsel of her reddened and pulsating flesh exposed to their view, Sir Jarl still remained motionless and wide-eyed. His breathing was heavy, Hedra noticed, and she knew it was only a matter of time before she would need to slide her own, luscious body over his and push him over the edge completely.

'I must have this enchanted object,' he sighed at last, when he too was thoroughly sated, his hardness wilting inside the tight, wet vessel between Hedra's thighs. She still gripped him tightly with her legs but now she relaxed a little and arched her back so that her breasts thrust into his face, the rosy tips nudging him into renewed wakefulness.

'Whatever you desire, sir,' she said in a low murmur, 'all you have to do is – .'

This time he did not even allow her to continue. 'Yes, yes, I know,' he groaned. 'I declare, you must also be an enchantress to make me feel so wonderful and so wretched at the same moment. Of course you have me as one of your Decadent Knights, how could I refuse you – how could I refuse all this?' He propped himself up on one arm and gave an expansive sweep with the other.

Hedra smiled. For a defeated man, he certainly looked happy, she mused. Now one was trapped within her erotic net, it was only a matter of time before the other two knights succumbed to her also. Then the whole kingdom would be saved. With the first part of her challenge successfully completed, she felt tempted to leave Sir Jarl to his slumber and yet she did not want to seem too eager to desert him. And there was the matter of the mirror. There must be a great deal else going on within the castle's bedchambers, she mused, and under her breath she repeated the magic word again and again, entertaining herself with the libidinous antics of the Watchers and Clansmen throughout the long period of darkfall.

Despite her lack of sleep, when Jade knocked timidly at the door to announce that her bath had already been drawn, Hedra was wide awake and ready to face the new challenge of the day.

Although Sir Jarl was sleeping soundly, she made sure that she and Jade were well away from the bedchamber before she imparted her news.

'It is done, Jade,' she said in an excited whisper.

192

'Zendik's mirror did the trick, Sir Jarl is now the latest Decadent Knight.'

'Oh, well done, mistress,' the Kelf said, her yellow eyes glinting with undisguised joy. 'I am sure the next two will not be as difficult to convince as he. He is a stalwart man by all accounts.'

Hedra nodded. 'Yes, that is true. So much so that I had my doubts at first but I can rejoice in the fact that from now on his steadfast character will benefit our kingdom and not King Randolph's. She stopped her musings and clapped her hands together smartly. 'Now to work with you, I want you to make me look stupendous for my next poor victim.'

Jade smiled as her mistress laughed and laughed, her body causing the bathwater to tremble in tiny waves all around her. If anyone could save their land from that infidel, King Randolph, it was Lady Hedra.

# Chapter Twelve

On Hedra's instructions, the second of King Randolph's knights was presented to her in the grandeur of the throne room. She waited for him, her pose both regal and yet subtly wanton, her booted feet placed firmly apart upon a footstool of solid silver embellished with a design of two intertwining dragon-headed serpents.

The sight of the serpents, so malevolent with their twin cold-blooded stare, was the first thing to greet the unsuspecting knight as he entered the imposing chamber and a moment later he raised his startled gaze to meet that of Lady Hedra. Suddenly, he felt himself in the grip of something he did not understand, a terrible foreboding overlaid with the white heat of pure lust.

'Come, kneel before me, my fine knight,' she said imperiously. Her lips moved beneath a tightly fitting mask of black leather that concealed the rest of her head and continued around her neck like a tight collar before flaring into a long cape of leather so fine it almost had the appearance of silk.

Shuffling forward when he meant to stride proudly, he stopped before the dais and went down on bended knee as she commanded. It did not occur to him to refuse her and now he rested one arm upon his bent knee, the other hand hovering over the hilt of his sword as he waited expectantly.

She shifted slightly in her seat, dragging his unwilling eyes up to look at her once again. On her body she wore a costume, also of black leather, that sought to conceal and yet in doing so enticed the mind to wonder at the delights that lay beneath. It covered her throat and the top part of her breasts and yet exposed the underside of each up-tilted orb. Narrow bands of leather ran across her nipples and crisscrossed her stomach where they joined a wider band that swept over her hips and covered her fleece in a deep vee that continued between her legs. When she stood up, he would see that more narrow bands of leather sliced across the white mounds of her buttocks and continued around and around her thighs to disappear into the tops of her high black boots.

Now, as he gazed up at her between her parted legs, he saw how the leather barely covered her intimate parts and that small tufts of violet hair escaped the edges. This strange sight made him wonder at the rest of her. The hood concealed her hair and most of her face, yet he could tell from the finely chiselled bone-structure and the brilliance of her eyes that she was a beautiful woman underneath the unusual garb.

'Why have you summoned me here, my lady?' he asked, grateful that he had found his voice at long last, however weak. 'What business do you have with me?'

'Business?' she said and shook her head decisively, her lips curving into a smile that touched her eyes and made them sparkle more. 'We have no business save the business of pleasure. Do you feel in the mood for a little pleasure, sir?'

Her voice was clear and dark, tinged with amusement and heavy with promise. The knight felt his knee weaken beneath the weight of his arm and had to force himself not to falter. Never had a woman inspired so much fear and excitement within him and beneath his golden breastplate he felt the insistent pulsing of his heart echoed by a quickening of his blood as it coursed through his veins.

'I am always open to the possibility, mistress,' he said, and suddenly felt himself blush.

Hedra did not miss his slip, nor had her senses remained immune to the aura that surrounded him. Her appearance and demeanour thrilled him, of that she was certain, and she silently thanked Jade for her foresight when she suggested that she wear this particular costume for her confrontation with the knight. Staring down at him, seeing his golden face turned up to her almost in supplication, she was reminded of the Chivalrous Knight whom she had chastised, and instinctively wondered how this young man would respond to the same treatment.

Kicking away the silver footstool, she rose to her feet, taking up a long leather whip in her right hand as she did so. To her amusement, the knight's eyes flickered automatically to her hand and widened when they saw the whip. He wavered slightly, she saw, and she watched his throat move as he swallowed deeply. Pacing backwards and forwards across the dais, she held his full attention, swinging the whip back and forth in perfect time with the pendulum action of her hips.

'Now enlighten me a little, my fine knight,' she said, her voice startling the hushed stillness of the chamber, 'what form does your favourite pleasure take?' She turned suddenly to face him, her legs placed boldly apart so that he had no option but to stare up at the soft leather-bound flesh between her parted thighs. 'A little punishment perhaps. The sweet kiss of the lash upon your flesh?'

Her words entered his body like a current of energy that coursed through him, ending in a stiffening beneath his breeches and before he could respond she flicked the whip lightly across his throat, just stroking the prominence of his throat apple.

196

His surprise was so great that he toppled from his already precarious position, falling flat on his back, his eyes staring wildly up at her as she towered over him like a great black demon.

Stepping down from the dais she began to walk around him, her long legs moving in a proud, stalking gait as she encircled her prey. Now and again she flicked the tip of the whip across his prone body. Of course, with his thick sueded clothing and breastplate, the sting of the lash was no more than the knowledge that it touched him and yet he felt it as keenly inside as if the leather thong sliced through his heart.

Excitement coursed through him, frissons of pleasure rushing from his solar plexus to every extremity of his body. He made no attempt to move and quaked under her piercing stare as she continued to taunt him.

'Disrobe, please,' she ordered, nudging him with the toe of her boot into a sitting position, 'take it all off.'

Hedra watched him struggling with his costume, her senses singing with the onset of triumph as she watched his trembling fingers working urgently, as though time were a rationed commodity. Little did he know that he would be forced to endure the extent of her pleasure at least until the setting of the second sun. She had nothing else to do that day after all.

Of course, she was not immune to the knight's responses; his arousal excited her to the extent that her sex burned beneath the supple leather. And the soft inside of the garment chafed at her tender flesh, arousing her even more strongly as she moved and she felt the moisture trickling away from her.

'Do not tarry now, my fine knight,' she said, murmuring more softly before resuming her circuit of him. 'I crave the sight of your body as surely as if it were a banquet set before a starving man.' She laughed lightly, the silken tones caressing the grey walls of the chamber and, as if her laughter were a command, sharp rays of light pierced the gloom through each of the thirty-six arched windows. Their brightness converged into a

197

single pool of yellow light that cloaked the naked figure of the young man who now rose to his knees before her, proud and erect.

'Is this how you would have me, mistress?' he said, cursing the voice that faltered when he wanted it to be strong.

She walked around him completely, her unfaltering gaze assessing him properly. Finally, she came to a halt before him and nodded once.

'You make a very fine sight, sir,' she said. Glancing down she saw how fiercely his hardness strained towards her and she reached down and grasped it lightly, running her fingers thoughtfully up and down the stem. 'Do you know what I want of you?' she asked, gripping him until he shook his head urgently.

'No, I know not,' he said. 'I was delivered to your castle dungeon with no instructions other than to follow my own instincts.'

Hedra smiled; King Randolph had obviously instructed all three of his knights in the same way. She had to admit, for an unscrupulous man he had shown surprising fairness in this matter.

'Very well,' she continued, gripping him harder still until she saw his mouth tighten a little, 'what I want is your pledge of allegiance to the Decadent Knights. I would ask you to renounce your duty to your king and serve a new master, Lord Gerard of Satyria. Do you think you could do that for me?' She licked her lips, glanced at his straining phallus and then looked deeply into his eyes.

'I . . . oh . . . I . . .' the knight gasped. He knew he wavered and yet she asked the impossible.

'I would be so grateful,' she said in a low murmur, her silken voice invading his uncertain mind like a powerful potion. Lowering herself to her own knees before him, she took his hardness in her mouth and tantalised him almost to the point of his zenith before withdrawing.

198

'Please,' he urged her, biting the inside of his bottom lip to stop himself from crying out.

'Perhaps you need a little more persuasion,' she said, rising to her feet once again.

Before the knight had the opportunity to collect his thoughts she walked around him and striped his buttocks with the whip, then lashed his shoulders and his back. 'How much more persuasion will it take?' she said and unfastened some tiny clips at the side of her costume so that the lower portion fell away, exposing the hunger in her own flesh. 'Would you care to pleasure me with your mouth while you think it over?' she asked, positioning herself before him.

Like a drowning man he gripped her buttocks and pulled her towards his eager mouth, his wet lips and tongue covering every inch of her burning flesh until she rocked against him in the throes of her zenith. Dropping the whip, she sank her fingers into his hair, pulling against the golden strands as wave after wave of pleasure swept over her.

As soon as the feelings began to abate she sank down to her haunches, engulfing his hardness inside the tropical chasm of her body and riding him hard until she sensed he was about to achieve his own climax.

'Oh, please, mistress,' he begged her, kneading her buttocks frantically as she withheld her body from him at that last crucial moment.

The strength in her thighs allowed her to hover over him, the tip of his phallus just brushing the entrance to her body.

'You have only to capitulate, sir,' she murmured darkly, her lips pressed directly against his ear. 'Pledge your allegiance to me and I will give my body to you freely.'

The knight was caught in a maelstrom of indecision; she could see that clearly but all at once all thoughts of him were dashed by an unexpected sight. In the doorway stood the fully armoured figure of Lord Gerard, the face she loved looking so fearsome beneath a silver ram's skull mask. She had no inkling how long he had been there, or of his thoughts and yet she felt his stillness compelled her to continue.

'Well, sir?' she said, forcing herself to continue in the same seductive tone. 'Am I about to take a Decadent Knight into my body and drive him to the heights of ecstacy or not?'

Her words tormented him beyond belief and yet he knew already that the battle was lost. He could no more refuse the opportunity to enjoy the body of this compelling young woman than swim the Tolmar Ocean with his wrists and ankles tied.

'You have me, mistress,' he said with a gasp, thrusting his hips up to meet her downward movement. 'I pledge myself to the Decadent Knights and renounce all previous allegiance.'

'Good,' she said softly, rotating her hips until she transfixed him in a vortex of pleasure, 'very, very good.'

Despite Lord Gerard's presence, she would not short-change her new conquest and continued to make pleasure with him for a good deal longer, their bodies thrashing about on the hard, red-carpeted floor until a distant gong heralded the end of the sunlight and servants began to creep about the vast chamber, lighting wall torches and candles as they went. Now the shadowed corners of the vaulted room were lit by flickering brightness and she shifted uncomfortably beneath the weight of the knight who lay, half dozing on top of her.

Lord Gerard had moved across the room to sit upon his own throne and now Hedra's eyes pleaded silently with him over the whiteness of the knight's shoulder. Pushing gently against the young man's chest, she managed to rouse him and whispered in his ear that perhaps they should seek an interlude in their pleasure-making.

In an instant he was on his feet and scrambling into his breeches, his movements becoming all the more frantic when he espied the still, seated figure of Lord Gerard.

'My lord, I did not realise,' he said, his eyes widening with fear. But Lord Gerard put up his hand and silenced the knight before ordering a Clansman to take the new recruit to his quarters to bathe and change for the evenfall banquet.

· 'It is no matter,' he said, removing the death mask and treating the knight to a warm smile. 'Now make haste. I happen to know there will be quite a few beauties present at the banquet who will be looking forward to welcoming you to our ranks.'

As soon as the knight left the chamber, Hedra let out a long sigh and stepped up to the dais. 'That is the second knight; one has already succumbed before him,' she said, moving gratefully into his outstretched arms.

'Come here, my wicked little wench,' he said, his voice caressing her like a veil of black silk, 'let me remove that hood and gaze upon your beauty.'

She knelt before him, her whole body trembling as his fingers deftly unfastened the tiny clips at the base of the throat and pulled away the hood, collar and cloak in one swift movement. If he had stripped her naked she couldn't have felt more vulnerable before him, she thought, and wondered what he truly made of her behaviour with the knight. In a hesitant voice she dared to ask him but to her relief he threw back his head and laughed, his broad thumbs simultaneously seeking to rub her nipples over the supple covering of leather.

'Oh, master,' she groaned, arching her back to offer more of herself to him, 'I have missed you so.'

'And I you,' he said thickly, 'although I'll wager your battles were just as hard fought as my own.'

'You were caught up in battle, my lord?' she replied, straightening up hastily. 'Oh, I cannot bear to think of you riding out without me – what if you were never to return?'

She cared little about the danger of showing her true feelings. To her, it would be the end of life's pleasures if he were ever to be taken from her and she wanted him to know it.

'You have much to amuse yourself with here,' he said, raising one eyebrow in an ironic gesture but she waved his words away and shook her head vehemently.

'It means nothing, master,' she said, 'none of it means anything without you. Physical gratification is one thing but I can only enjoy others when I am confident that true pleasure still awaits me at the end of the day.'

'Would that be the sort of true pleasure that involves laying across my knee?' he asked, pulling her to her feet and pushing her across his lap. 'And would that be the sort of pleasure that comes from the caress of my hand upon your naughty flesh?'

Hedra almost fainted with desire as he manipulated her. 'Yes, master,' she breathed, exhaling loudly as his leather-covered palm smacked upon her trembling buttocks, 'exactly that kind of pleasure.'

She felt the wetness trickling freely from her as her flesh warmed beneath his hand and every so often he stopped chastising her for a moment to coat her swelling clitoris with her own creamy juices. Using determined fingers he pressed her open, spreading her open further and further until she felt the cold air touch her most intimate flesh with a chilling caress that hardly dampened the heat of her arousal. She heard someone groaning and realised it was herself. She was like a creature possessed, squirming and moaning upon his lap, arching her back and spreading her thighs further and further apart.

In the next instant he picked her up and deposited her on the throne, roughly draping her careless legs over the carved arms, leaving her wide open for all to see. With an anguished groan of desire he dropped to his knees before her and took her then, thrusting deeply into her wet, open body as though he was determined to erase all that had transpired between Hedra and King Randolph's man; using his own juices and body scent to eliminate every trace.

He had thought himself hardened to the sight of others taking their pleasure before him; orgies were almost a nightly occurrence in Satyria and yet the image of his Lady Hedra gasping and moaning under the body of the new knight had almost driven him mad with wanting and an emotion that had never touched him before. So strange was it to him that he could not even give it a name and yet it made him desire her all the more if that was possible.

'Tell me your body is mine, Hedra,' he said urgently, speaking gruffly into her hair as he drove deeper and deeper inside her, 'tell me I can do with it whatever I wish.'

Hedra was surprised by his words and urged her hips up to meet him as he thrust into her, urging herself against him even though he filled her to the hilt. 'You know that is so, my lord,' she said breathlessly, diving into the blackness of her zenith. 'Be assured my body belongs to you for ever.'

When they both awoke at the rising of the first sun, Lord Gerard was surprised that Hedra immediately leapt out of bed and started to dress.

'There is no need for you to rise yet, my lady,' he said softly. 'Jade will not be along until the day has begun properly.'

She watched him buckle his belt around his waist and secure a long silver scabbard to it. 'I shall not be here when Jade comes,' she said resolutely, 'I shall be with you.'

He glanced up and looked at her in surprise. 'With me? But I am going on a good day's journey to the outer limits of the kingdom. I thought I told you that last darkfall?' he said.

Hedra nodded and began to ease a pair of golden chainmail stockings up her legs. 'You did, my lord,' she said, 'but I intend to go with you on this journey.'

'Oh, no, Hedra,' he began to shake his head, 'it is too

203

dangerous for you to ride with me. Particularly today. Where I am going is no place for a woman.'

'Huh!' she said derisively. 'No place for a woman indeed. Well, we shall see.'

'No, Hedra.' Lord Gerard gripped her by the shoulders and forced her to look at him. 'I am serious, I cannot take you with me.'

'You cannot stop me, my lord,' she said defiantly. 'If you do not take me willingly, I shall go out of my own accord and then I am likely to fall foul of danger. At least if we are together I shall be safer than if I was alone.'

Lord Gerard released her abruptly and turned to pace across the bedchamber. When he reached the far wall he swivelled around to face her. She stood defiantly, hands on hips, her body already clothed in a tight leather costume that, even with the addition of golden breastplate, arm and shoulder plates, left little to the imagination. Desperation flickered in his eyes and she knew that he knew he had lost the battle.

'Very well,' he said, his broad shoulders slumping slightly as a gesture of defeat, 'you may accompany me today. But arm yourself properly and be sure to do everything I tell you. Any arguments may end up costing one or both of us our lives.'

'Of course, whatever you say, master,' she said with a brisk nod. 'Now let us break the fast with a little light refreshment and then be on our way. I fancy a change of scenery will do me good. I still have one of King Randolph's men to deal with and perhaps this little break in routine will give me the strength I need to see his challenge through to the end.'

She was so intent on selecting a suitable sword and dagger that she missed Lord Gerard's smile. It amused him that Hedra should look upon her sexual endeavours as routine and made him wonder at her hidden depths. So far, he felt as though he had only skimmed the surface of her carnal desires. The very realisation made him long to renounce his plans for the day and spend the time in sexual exploration but he could not, sometimes affairs of the kingdom had to come before affairs of a more physical nature.

While they ate, their horses were being readied for the journey. Lord Gerard had his usual steed, a fine black stallion called Raven and for Hedra the groom prepared a dappled grey known by all the stable hands as Moonshadow. When Hedra first saw her horse it was love at first sight, for both woman and steed. She stroked her palms over the horse's neck and across its rump and held the plaited tail in her hand as though weighing it.

'It feels like a heavy skein of silken thread,' she said thoughtfully. 'What a truly beautiful beast she is.'

Lord Gerard smiled. To him a horse was simply a means of transport and yet, just occasionally, he too had felt certain soft feelings towards Raven, although he would never admit to them even under threat of death.

It pleased Hedra to note that the groom had equipped Moonshadow with a conventional saddle and, with a little help from one of the stable lads, she swung herself easily astride the broad back. Gathering up the reins, she turned her head to call to Lord Gerard who had just mounted Raven.

'Now I feel like a true Satyrian,' she said, her face wreathed in smiles, 'off to fight for king and country.'

He pursed his lips ruefully as he drew his horse alongside her and placed a restraining hand on her arm. 'No more talk of fighting, Hedra,' he said. 'Your tendency to be impetuous can be a little unnerving, even to a hardened blackguard such as myself.'

She gazed at him and saw how his deep blue eyes betrayed the slightest glimmer of amusement. 'Take heart, my lord,' she murmured, 'I have no intention of risking any harm to either of our bodies. Why, there is still so much we have yet to do with them.' Her lips curved wickedly and, with a slight dig of her heels, she urged Moonshadow away from him in the direction of the lowered drawbridge.

To begin with they took the dusty road, following the route into the nearest village. It was the first time Hedra had been in such a place since her capture by Sir Drago and the sight of the overstuffed shops and bustling streets instantly reminded her of that day. With a slight pang of nostalgia, she remembered the magnificent Gideon and their pleasure-making. If he did but know it, he had prepared her well for her life as Lady of Satyria.

'You look thoughtful, Hedra,' Lord Gerard said, drawing to a halt beside her as she watched a group of children throwing wooden hoops at a stag's antlers which were nailed to the side of a barn.

'I was just remembering something from my past,' she admitted, her voice sounding uncharacteristically soft and wistful. Then she seemed to collect her thoughts and drowned him in a brilliant smile. 'I have never been happier than I am now, my lord,' she said, 'you make me feel so alive and so well-loved.'

His eyes glinted wickedly. 'I declared, Hedra,' he said, 'if there were not so many people about and we were not on a mission, I would take the time to love you well right now.'

She shivered with delight at his words. It seemed incredible but she never stopped wanting him and the desire she felt for him burned inside her with all the intensity of a flaming torch.

In the next instant, the spell between them was broken. One of the boys playing hoopla fell on some rocky ground and started squalling loudly and Hedra and Lord Gerard flashed each other a look that sent them galloping away from village at high speed, putting as much distance between themselves and the horrible noise as possible.

Upon reaching a large expanse of forest, Lord Gerard guided them off the road and into the dense thicket. As the horses picked their way delicately through the undergrowth, he and Hedra were forced to stoop low to avoid the continual threat of overhanging branches.

Just as they reached a slight clearing, they heard a noise that turned Hedra's body to water. It was a loud roar, followed by a series of screeching cries.

'What is that?' she gasped, her eyes wide with fear.

Although he tried desperately not to show it, Lord Gerard looked equally perturbed. 'It sounds as though a group of Radies are just North of here,' he said. 'They have probably set up an encampment.'

Hedra had no idea what a Radie was and was in no particular hurry to find out. 'Shall we make our way back to the road?' she said. 'Even if it makes our journey longer, it is better that we are safe.'

To her dismay, he shook his head. 'We cannot, the only possible route is through the forest.'

'Then what are we to do?' She glanced around, panic welling up inside her. Oh, how foolish she had been to suggest that she went on this trip. If she hadn't been so hasty she could have been back at the castle, seducing King Randolph's knight.

The way her lord and master squared his shoulders so decisively sent a *frisson* of excitement coursing through her. The sensation was so powerful, it obliterated her fear at once.

'Come,' he said, urging Raven onwards into the gloomy cavern of trees that faced them, 'this is no time to doubt our courage. We make a good team, you and I.'

Hedra glowed at his words. A good team. Yes, they were certainly that and a good deal more besides.

It was easy to tell how close they were getting to the Radies' encampment: all around them lay discarded bones and carcasses of wild animals. And a tall cloud of smoke billowed above the line of trees, indicating the exact position. Presently, acrid wisps of the smoke began to invade their lungs, telling them that their enemy was not too far off.

'Could we not try to go around the encampment, my lord?' she asked, her heart starting to beat with renewed urgency behind her ribs. To her dismay, Lord Gerard shook his head.

'No, the undergrowth is too thick,' he said. 'There is no way around without firstly cutting down trees and clearing a new track.' A short distance further on he ordered her to stop and wait. 'I am going to see how many there are,' he said. 'Just wait for me here.'

As soon as she watched him disappear into the trees, she guided Moonshadow behind a clump of tall bushes, hoping that their thick red leaves would shield her from any stray Radies who might happen along. Eventually, Lord Gerard reappeared. She was relieved to see him and that he was in one piece. What was more encouraging was that he was smiling.

'I told them we come in peace,' he said, beckoning to her. Hedra couldn't help noting that the bushes obviously did not shield her as well as she thought, as he had spotted her straightaway. 'And I promised them gold and trinkets if they allow us safe passage through the forest,' he added. 'Come, follow me. I cannot wait for you to set eyes on them for they are very strange creatures indeed.'

Moonshadow carefully followed Raven, as though she picked up and echoed her mistress's hesitancy. Eventually, they came out of the trees to find themselves in a vast clearing. In the centre was a huge fire and all around the edge of the clearing were small round tents fashioned from animal hides.

Hedra stared around her. The creatures were indeed strange-looking. They were so short even the tallest would only reach her waist, she estimated, and their portly build made them look as round as they were tall. Their ears were sharply pointed and each bore a head of thick green hair, that sprouted in every direction. Try as she might, she could not distinguish the males from the females and she said as much to Sir Gerard.

'Oh,' he laughed softly, 'you really have no knowledge of these creatures have you?' She shook her head and he continued, 'They are hermaphrodites, with the pleasure parts of both sexes.'

'Really?' Despite her nervousness, she was intrigued by the description and longed to see what one of these creatures looked like naked. 'Do you think one could be persuaded to bare their body to me?' she asked and was chastened when Sir Gerard shook his head.

'I wouldn't suggest that you try asking them, Hedra,' he said, his mouth curving into a broad smile. 'I have only just secured their trust and they are a very modest race.'

'What a pity,' she murmured and followed dutifully in his wake. Despite Sir Gerard's words she still couldn't help staring hard at the Radies as he led her through the encampment. There was always the possibility that one of them should happen to be clothed in something a little more revealing than rabbit fur and moleskin.

Her expectations were soon dashed and, without any attempt by the Radies or any other strange band to delay them, they reached their destination in no time.

Hedra had not realised it but the kingdom's outer limits were bounded by a wide expanse of ocean. Its emerald-green waters sparkled under the fierce rays of the second sun, enticing her to go right up to it and thrust her hands into the foamy surf that crashed upon the orange sand. She had never seen the ocean before and was not disappointed.

Just beyond the strip of sand stood a large stone-built house. While she delighted her senses in the novelty of the ocean, Lord Gerard tethered the horses and strode up to the door of the house. Raising the knocker he let it drop and a moment later the door was opened.

'Hedra!' he called to her and she rushed to his side.

Inside the house it was not dissimilar to the castle. The walls were built of the same grey stone and were hung with a profusion of brightly coloured tapestries. The flagstones were covered with thick rugs and heavy oak furniture dominated every room the aged manservant took them through.

Eventually, they reached a staircase and Lord Gerard asked her to take a seat on a carved oak settle and wait for him while he spoke to the master of the house.

'I shall be brief,' he assured her, 'our business is merely a formality.'

Hedra waited patiently for a while but it wasn't in her nature to sit still and do nothing and presently she rose to her feet and began to wander, making a full circuit of the vast hallway and stopping every so often to peer at a particular scene on the tapestry-covered wall.

Although the pictures looked innocent from a distance, close up she realised that some of them were extremely libidinous. Naked maidens were being whipped by huge, grotesque men. Others were being sexually fondled and penetrated by satyrs and other mystical creatures. As she continued her perusal of the walls she found herself becoming uncommonly hot and was relieved when Lord Gerard appeared at the top of the staircase carrying a large book.

She watched with growing arousal as he descended the stairs and, as he reached her side, she gripped his arms and whispered that she needed him urgently.

'All in good time, Hedra,' he said, 'our journey back to the castle should not take us too long.'

She shook her head in agitation. 'I cannot wait until our return, my lord,' she said, her breath coming in short gasps. 'I must have you now.'

A smile crossed his lips and he slid an arm around her slender waist. 'Then now it shall be, my wanton maid,' he murmured darkly and led her into the nearest room, kicking the door shut behind them.

It was a storeroom of some kind but Hedra hardly noticed her surroundings. All she wanted was to wrap her fingers around her master's hardness and guide it into her hungry body. He pulled the narrow band of leather that nestled between her legs to one side and sank his fingers inside her, twisting and turning them until she began to pant loudly. Her fingers fumbled with his breeches and she was soon rewarded as his rock-hard phallus sprang into her hands.

'I want it, master,' she gasped urgently, 'I want it now.'

With little finesse, Lord Gerard turned her around and pushed her faced down across a stack of wooden crates. She felt the rough wood graze the bared portions of her flesh but cared not. The hardness she craved was already nudging the entrance to her body and she spread her legs wider and arched her back as it sank inside her. She broke several of her long nails grasping wildly at the boxes as she bucked her hips and encouraged him to take her harder and harder.

To her delight it was not over in moments but the heat spread slowly throughout her body, driving her almost to fever pitch before her climax broke and she began to sob with pleasure and relief. A moment later there came the sound of a hand clap. She felt Lord Gerard withdraw from her and then she stood up and turned around. In the open doorway stood a tall, thin man, his face so gaunt he looked like a cadaver.

# Chapter Thirteen

'*B*artolo!' Lord Gerard exclaimed as he hastily repaired his modesty. 'I do not know what to say. I have abused your hospitality badly.'

'Nonsense, my boy, nonsense,' the man said, stepping forward and smiling broadly at Hedra who returned his smile somewhat hesitantly. 'I have not witnessed such a fine display of lust in ages. I only wish that I had brought my drawing things and could have recorded it for posterity.'

At that Lord Gerard smiled. Turning to Hedra he said, 'Bartolo here is a lover of all things erotic. He is a sensualist who has the enviable ability to capture whatever he sees, or imagines, on parchment. Look here!' He picked up the book and opened it to the centre pages. 'Now is that not a delight to behold?'

Hedra leaned forward and studied the book. The pages showed a young girl with long rivulets of black hair being attended to by half a dozen handmaidens, each of them very different in appearance, yet each beautifully formed. She thought the scene breathtakingly erotic in its simplicity and said so; it was a comment which received the hearty approval of both men.

'But then my beloved Lady Hedra is also a true

sensualist,' Lord Gerard explained to Bartolo, 'and a lusty young woman as well. I don't mind admitting to you that she often saps me of my vigour.'

It had been a long time since Hedra had felt the warm blanket of embarrassment touch her cheeks but now she did and lowered her eyes in a gesture that seemed uncharacteristically humble – so much so that Sir Gerard commented immediately when he saw it. 'Do not let her demeanour fool you, Bartolo,' he said. 'She could eat a man like you for a light snack and still have the energy to wear out my entire troop of Decadent Knights.'

At that, Hedra protested. 'I do declare, my lord,' she said, 'you paint a very blackened portrait of me. Why, it was hardly any time ago that I was the picture of innocence. If I have a licentious temperament it is with all thanks due to you, as you bring out the very worst and very naughtiest in me.'

'Well said, my lady,' Bartolo interrupted before Lord Gerard had time to reply. Following them as they retraced their steps to the front lobby he added, 'Do not allow this scoundrel to have it all his own way. And please don't hesitate to visit me again. But next time, make sure you come alone, I'll wager we could spend an interesting interlude together.'

Laughing lightly, she thanked him for the compliment, whilst Sir Gerard apologised for their indiscretion once again.

'Please, hush now,' Bartolo said. 'I do not want to hear it. I only wish I were a good deal younger, then I could probably teach you a thing or two.'

By this time their steps had taken them to the front entrance and they stood for just a little while longer saying their goodbyes before Hedra and Lord Gerard stepped out of the house into the half-light of the sunset.

Riding back the way they had come, Hedra couldn't resist remarking on Bartolo and his sketches, and on Lord Gerard's relationship with him. He remained silent as she spoke, but when he did respond his words astounded her.

'Bartolo is my father,' he said, glancing down at his hands which rested lightly on the pommel of the saddle. 'The king is his half-brother. Unfortunately, they had a fierce argument one day and the king banished Bartolo from the castle. I was still only a baby at the time but my mother deserted both of us when she realised she would have to live without the riches and privileges of the royal court. Believing I did not deserve to be raised as an ordinary man, my father left me at the castle in the care of a wet-nurse. The king bore me no grudge and treated me as though I were his son. That is why he has entrusted Satyria to me.'

Throughout the surprising admission, Hedra stared at him. Her feelings ranged from pity for Bartolo and Lord Gerard, to anger at his mother and the king. Overcome by compassion, she reached out a hand and placed it upon his own. 'I shall never leave you, Gerard,' she said, her tone displaying the depth of her feelings. 'Be certain of one thing: when you took my innocence you also took my heart and here and now I pledge myself to you for all eternity.'

She truly believed it did not matter that her physical innocence had already become a vague memory by the time he chose her from all the other virgins. He and only he had opened her mind and body to its true potential. And that was what counted above all else.

By the time they reached the castle, the black cloak of darkfall had settled around their weary bodies and all they had the energy for was a light meal before falling straight away into a deep slumber that took them through to sunrise.

Hedra was the first to wake. Roused by the persistent calling of the chanticleer, she slipped from the bed and drew back the heavy velvet curtains. Far below, the courtyard was already a hive of industry. Kitchen staff were peeling vegetables and scrubbing pots and pans,

214

the fat cooks' bottoms almost encompassing the small stools on which they sat as they gutted and trussed chickens with frightening precision. And all around them other servants swept at the dust with long-handled brooms made of twigs, or polished boots, or tackled great piles of mending and laundry.

Just the mere sight of so much activity tired her and with a deep sigh, she turned away from the window and stared at the sleeping form of Lord Gerard instead. Her face softened and she went to him, placing a light kiss on his lips as he too awoke and returned her smile with every ounce of emotion he possessed. The night before, just before they had fallen asleep, he had told her that they were irrevocably linked, that there would be no possibility of her returning to Parsimonia except for short visits.

'I know that, my lord,' she had said, hastening to reassure him. 'I have no wish to return there permanently. I belong here in Satyria now. My place is beside you.'

Even as she said the words she felt the truth behind them flow through her. She was a Satyrian now, through and through. And even if something should happen to her father – perish the thought – she would not harbour any desire to return to the kingdom of her birth. It held no enchantment for her whatsoever. Only Satyria lured her and she knew beyond a shadow of a doubt that it always would.

After she had bathed and dressed and she and Lord Gerard had shared the first meal of the day, he insisted that she take her leave of him.

'I have a great deal of paperwork to deal with today,' he said, his brow furrowing deeply just at the thought. 'The castle accounts need to be put in order. I have been away so much lately that things have begun to slide in that respect. I am sure you can find something to occupy you that doesn't involve my body.' He spoke the last sentence in jest and yet he meant it. Hedra was

215

insatiable it seemed and had tried to seduce him back into their bed almost as soon as he had risen from it.

'There is that last knight of King Randolph's who still needs to be dealt with,' she muttered, her unwillingness to attend to the matter apparent in her tone and demeanour. 'I suppose I should go to see him and have done with it.'

To her annoyance, Lord Gerard simply nodded, his eyes already fixed on columns of figures. 'Yes, Hedra,' he murmured absently, 'you do whatever you think best.'

She made her way down to the dungeon, her unwilling feet almost dragging along the flagstones as she went. At the entrance to the cells she spoke to the gaoler and ordered him to take her to King Randolph's man.

'I cannot recall his name,' she said conversationally, 'although I am not sure if I was told it in the first place.'

'It is Sir Blaise whom you have come to see, if that is any help to you, my lady,' the gaoler muttered gruffly, 'and I'll warn you now, he is a stubborn fellow. He will not eat the food I bring him, nor hardly let a drop of water pass his lips.'

'Oh, is that so?' she said, her interest at once aroused for the first time that morning. 'Well, we shall see how stubborn he is in the face of my brand of persuasion, shall we not?'

As she entered the cell the knight did not even look up, nor in any way acknowledge her arrival. In the end, she shouted at him in exasperation, 'Stand when you are in my presence, knave! How dare you treat me with such vile contempt?'

At her words, the knight rose unwillingly to his feet and raised his eyes to stare challengingly at her. 'You know nothing of contempt yet, my lady,' he said in a mocking tone, 'but I'll wager you will before the setting of the second sun.'

'I'll wager you shall be beaten within an inch of your life if you continue to speak so,' responded Hedra angrily. 'How dare you, sir! Step forward at once and beg my forgiveness.'

To her consternation, he gave a wry laugh that reminded her of the call of the fascal bird, a particularly insolent creature who feared neither man nor other predatory beast.

'I'll rot in the bowels of the demon mire first,' he said. His eyes flicked over her, sending a frisson of desire coursing through her despite his effrontery.

'That may well be your fate, sir,' she replied, forcing herself to remain calm in the face of extreme provocation, 'but for now you will kneel before me.'

It surprised her that he obeyed her command; she had felt certain he would resist. And, when she looked down upon the thatch of sandy hair that covered his head and curled softly around his ears and at the nape of his neck, she suddenly saw him as an individual and not merely an unwelcome task that had to be dealt with.

'It is a fine day,' she said, relenting a little, 'let us go for a walk in the gardens. It is far too warm and bright to be cooped up inside this sullen chamber. You may rise, sir,' she added in a much softer voice. Tapping him gently on the shoulder, she stepped back a pace.

This time Sir Blaise looked properly at her and decided at that very moment to revise his opinion of her. In truth, he had been determined to dislike her and be as difficult and obstinate as he possibly could. He was a very ardent supporter of King Randolph and had been in his service since he was a young lad. He had started out as a page and went on climbing the ranks until he had been admitted to the upper echelons of the Royal Troop of Barbarous Knights – not a real name but one the knights had coined amongst themselves. Yet, despite his unwavering loyalty, it seemed the king considered him dispensable and had brought him to this place without just cause or explanation.

It had got back to him via a cheeky servant boy, who had no inkling of how to keep quiet about certain matters, that his other two compatriots, Sir Jarl and then Sir Alven, had both pledged allegiance to Satyria and to the Decadent Knights. And furthermore, the boy also let it be known that it was none other than Lady Hedra who had managed to persuade them to renounce king and country.

His first thought, of course, was that Lady Hedra must be a terrible harridan of a woman who had used vile and barbarous means to force them into submission. But, when pressed, the boy blushed redder than a beetroot and giggled fit to burst. It was only when Sir Blaise had almost lost his temper with him that he divulged that Lady Hedra was a singularly beautiful young woman and had used no threats or violence but only her physical charms to seduce the two knights into her kingdom's service.

Now, as he gazed upon her beauty – the whiteness of her skin, the sinuousness of her body and the lasciviousness that glinted in her eyes – he realised for the first time why his fellow knights had found her impossible to resist. Even though he personally did not find females particularly alluring, he had to admit that were he ever to revise his opinion, she would be the one to help him do it. Well, he thought, smiling inwardly with suppressed glee, she knows nothing of my sexual predilections; it shall be interesting to see how far she is prepared to go to seduce me into her band of knights.

Naturally, Hedra was blissfully unaware that the man before her found the squat, balding gaoler a more enticing prospect than she. And she also smiled inwardly as she took the knight's hand in her own and led him from the cell, through the maze of dank corridors and out into the brilliance of the new day.

Although she had never actually visited them before, she knew the castle grounds boasted a vast enclosure of well-tended gardens and she had paused at the kitchens on their way out to order that negus and cakes be taken out to the gazebo. After their walk, she and her companion would no doubt appreciate a little light refreshment, she thought.

As they wandered aimlessly between the borders, she and Sir Blaise talked of inconsequential matters. They remarked upon the fine weather, the beautiful flora, the heady scent and whether the prospect of rain was likely. Eventually, having exhausted 'safe' subjects, Hedra turned the conversation none too subtly to the knight himself and his reason for being incarcerated.

'I shall do you the service of saving your breath, my lady,' he said in an ironic tone. 'I am only too aware that Sir Jarl and Sir Alven have already succumbed to your, er, charms and that they have joined your band of Decadent Knights. I'll wager King Randolph will not be best pleased when he gets to hear of their desertion.'

'And I'll wager he was expecting it,' Hedra responded sharply, much to the knight's surprise.

'Do you mean to tell me he is in on this little, oh, what shall we call it, exercise?' he said, trying hard not to look too surprised by her disclosure.

'Of course, it was his idea,' she replied. Pausing to pick a rose, she raised it to her nose, smelled it and smiled at him over the soft, pink petals. 'He set me the challenge and for various reasons that I am not prepared to go into, I accepted. So far I am two-thirds of the way there.'

Despite his annoyance with both her and his king, the knight couldn't help appreciating her candour. She treated him as an equal whereas King Randolph did have an irritating tendency to talk to all his men as if they were, at best, lackeys and, at worst, the filthiest of vermin.

'And what does your Lord Gerard make of all this?' he said. 'Surely he cannot condone your methods.'

Hedra dropped the rose and laughed aloud. 'I have nothing but Lord Gerard's admiration for my handling of this difficult situation,' she said. 'If nothing else, it helps me to keep my skills well honed. I am a very versatile person but there are some things that I do better than others.' She laughed again, then fell silent as she glanced down at the rose. It was already wilting, she noticed, and therefore already on the way to metamorphosis. I too am wilting like this flower, she thought. I need new impetus or Satyria will be lost to King Randolph for ever. With a savage gesture, she ground the silken petals beneath her gold spiked heel.

After the previous day's battledress, she had thought something a little more demure would make a pleasant change. For that reason, after she had bathed and Jade had oiled and perfumed her entire body from top to toe, she had selected a diaphanous robe of sapphire silk. It fell straight from her shoulders to mid thigh, ending in a series of points. On her feet she wore long shiny boots of the same hue, the tops of which covered her knees and finished just below the jagged hem. Being such a simple costume, she had decided to adorn herself with plenty of jewellery: a gold mesh skullcap studded with sapphires, twenty or so thin gold bangles on each arm and a matching belt and necklet, also of gold and sapphires. On anyone else, the outfit would have looked far too outrageous, yet on Hedra it was perfect and just served to enhance her beauty all the more.

Sir Blaise shivered. He had a premonition that her treatment of the rose was symbolic; that, somehow, he would also find himself also being ground down and trodden underfoot. Yet, if he was honest, that was already how he felt. King Randolph was not the most understanding or accommodating of men. His temper and frequent bad moods were legendary – not just throughout the kingdom but the length and breadth of all the Fantastic Lands. He could envisage certain advantages to remaining in Satyria, not least the other Decadent Knights who were all extremely handsome fellows, so he had been told. All at once he gave himself a mental slap around the face. What was he thinking of? Had this young woman weaved a spell around him to cause him to waver so badly?

The first sun rose to its apex, casting a fierce heat down around them. Hedra and the knight simultaneously raised their faces to meet its onslaught, shielding their eyes with their hands.

'Shall we make our way to the gazebo?' she suggested, turning to him with a smile. 'We shall find shade and refreshment there.'

Sir Blaise had no argument with that idea and nodded readily. 'I must admit, I am a little thirsty,' he said.

'Tell me, sir,' she said as they resumed their walk, 'from what you know of it, is life here in Satyria that much different to the ways of your own kingdom?'

The knight shrugged his shoulders. 'To be honest with you, I do not know that much of Satyria but from what I understand I would say that you Satyrians are perhaps a little more refined than us. We are barbarians after all.'

'What about your women?' she asked. 'Are they barbarians too?'

To her surprise he nodded. 'Pretty much so,' he said, 'although there are those that are worse than others, of course. King Randolph's Bisextrix, for instance, are particularly dreadful creatures; they are enough to put a man off women for all eternity.'

He laughed then and Hedra smiled at him, pleased that she was managing to get him to relax a little at long last. He was such hard work, she had begun to think she would never get him to open up to her.

By this time they reached the gazebo, a round white wooden structure with a diameter hardly larger than a well and topped off by an ornate golden dome for a roof. She was pleased to note that the servants had done their job and the tiny table was already set with an assortment of cakes and other sweetmeats, a pewter jug of iced negus and silver plates and goblets.

She poured them each a goblet of the negus and sniffed at the wonderfully aromatic mixture of honey, water and wine. On the top floated a variety of tiny flower petals. Like confetti, their bright colours enlivened the appearance of the pale amber liquid. Sitting down on one of the white-painted wooden chairs that were grouped around the table, she sipped her drink then closed her eyes and let her head drop back.

For a moment Sir Blaise studied her in silence. He too sipped his negus from time to time and found himself suffused with an overwhelming longing to reach out and run his fingertips lightly down the length of her long white throat. Never before had he felt such an urge to touch a woman, but then never before had he met a woman quite like Lady Hedra.

She startled him by sitting up suddenly and opening her eyes wide. 'Do you find me attractive, Sir Blaise?' she asked.

Her question took him aback and he swallowed deeply. Finding himself uncharacteristically flustered he stammered his answer. 'I . . . er . . . I do not care for women as a rule.' Damn her, he had not intended to reveal his true nature!

Hedra smiled inwardly. Of course, that was it. Whether it was women's intuition, or something that had been staring her right in the face, she wasn't certain, but she had felt that there was something amiss. Now she knew what it was, she could start to work out a way to overcome it.

'Your reply leads me to suppose that you do not find me repulsive at any rate?' she said, laughing lightly. Oh, her relief was so great she felt like joining the birds overhead in a chorus.

'That is true,' he said, also laughing. 'But do not expect me to fall for your legendary charms. I am immune.'

His reply stopped her mid-thought. What did he mean 'legendary', how far had her fame spread? She had to ask him. 'Why did you refer to my charms as legendary?' she said lightly, pretending to be unconcerned.

'One of your servants is not very discreet,' he said, to

her overwhelming relief. 'He is the one who has been keeping me informed.'

'I see,' she replied thoughtfully.

She had no desire to discover who had been gossiping about her; no doubt all the servants did and who could blame them? No, all that concerned her was that information might have reached her father's ears. Whatever she did, however she chose to live her life, she did not want him to be hurt by her actions. She decided there and then that she should write to her father and explain the situation. After all, she had no way of knowing if her previous note had actually reached him or not and now she had made her decision to stay in Satyria for ever it was only right that she should advise him of her plans.

She and Sir Blaise sat for some time and talked on a more personal level. All of a sudden it seemed he had no compunction about opening up to her and freely admitted to some of his thoughts and dreams.

'I would love to meet a man who is a true match for me,' he said, accepting Hedra's offer of a second goblet of negus. 'But the men from my kingdom are so rough and uncouth, I sometimes think I was born into the wrong place at the wrong time.'

'We all feel like that from time to time,' she said. 'I never felt at home in Parsimonia. That is the land of my birth, you know?' she added, gazing at him from under long lashes as she reclined against the back of the chair, her head tipped back slightly.

He shook his head and smiled at her. 'No, I didn't know,' he said. 'You certainly do not strike me as a typical Parsimonian.'

Hedra sat up and laughed; the hot sun and the negus were beginning to get to her. She felt so relaxed and so wanton all of a sudden. What a pity the handsome knight in front of her was not amongst her choice of playthings. 'I am not a typical Parsimonian!' she exclaimed. 'That is why I had to get out as soon as I could. Why, in some ways I am grateful to your king –

without his interference I would still be residing there in a state of frustrated purity!'

Suddenly, her humorous musings were interrupted by a series of loud shouts and cries. Someone yelled, 'Stop him!' and in the next instant she saw a man running along the narrow white paths towards the gazebo. Her eyes widened in surprise. By the mystics, it was Gideon, as large at life and twice as handsome!

'Gideon, Gideon, is it really you?' she called out, jumping up from her seat and knocking it over in the process. She ran to the front of the gazebo and called to him again, 'Gideon, stop!'

He was very close to the gazebo and, when he heard the familiar voice, he stopped dead in his tracks and stared at her. 'Hedra?' he said, his face breaking into a broad smile.

'The very same,' she said, smiling in response. Holding out her hand to him she said, 'Come in here, I shall deal with them.' She inclined her head towards a band of men who had come charging through the garden after him. A couple of them were knights and as soon as they saw their Lady Hedra they stopped running.

She fixed a steely gaze on one of the knights. 'What do you think you are doing?' she said haughtily.

He glanced down, unable to meet her eyes. 'This creature has been taken prisoner, my lady,' he replied. 'Have no fear, we shall not let him harm you.'

She stared at him with a look of incredulity. 'Harm me?' she said. 'Of course he will not harm me. He is a very good friend of mine. Now be off with you. Go and find something useful to do.' She knew her manner was insulting but couldn't care less. At that moment all she felt was anger that Gideon should bave been treated badly by her own men. 'I said go!' she added forcibly, when they still hovered uncertainly.

Muttering to themselves, the men turned and made their way back through the garden. Occasionally, one of them glanced over his shoulder but Hedra stood firm, glaring at them with naked hostility. When she was certain that they were to be left alone, she turned to Gideon and smiled.

'It's been a long time,' she said softly. 'How are you?'

Without asking he poured himself a goblet of negus and gulped it down. Wiping his mouth on the back of his hand he nodded. 'Well enough,' he replied, then he glanced around before looking back at her. 'I see you have done all right for yourself.'

She let out a long breath and sat down again, indicating that Gideon should do the same. 'That day we went to the village,' she began, 'I was captured by one of the Decadent Knights and brought here. They put me in the vestal chamber and then I was picked by Sir Gerard. Afterwards, he asked me to be his Lady. It was that simple.'

Gideon studied her in silence for a moment, then to her surprise he let out a great roar of laughter. 'You, in the vestal chamber?' he cried. 'Oh, how I would have loved to see that.'

'Shh, Gideon!' She glanced around wildly, although they were all alone apart from the presence of a bewildered Sir Blaise. 'As far as everyone is concerned, I was brought here as an innocent and I would like it to stay that way if you don't mind.'

Gideon couldn't stop laughing it seemed, so eventually Hedra hit him. It was only a playful punch on the arm but he sobered immediately. 'I am sorry, Hedra,' he said, his lips still twitching, 'I suppose I should be grateful to you now for rescuing me. Of course I shall not say anything, you have my word.'

Sighing again but this time with relief, she said, 'There is no need for your gratitude. We are equal now. You saved me and now I have saved you; my debt is repaid.'

He nodded. 'Very well,' he said, adding, 'my oh my, Hedra, it is good to see you again. You look beautiful by the way, as always.'

'Flattery will get you everywhere, Gideon,' she

replied, the smile dying on her face as she noticed how serious he had become.

'Will it?' he said gruffly. Reaching forward, he pulled her to him and covered her mouth with his.

Instantly, she felt flames of desire leaping about inside her. Her pleasure parts fairly oozed with moisture and finally she was forced to push him away. 'Not here, Gideon,' she said urgently and glanced at Sir Blaise. 'Besides, I have company.'

They both turned to look at the knight who looked as though he was lost in rapture. Sir Blaise had never seen a man as handsome or as magnificently built as the one Lady Hedra called Gideon. He looked so powerful and yet treated her with a gentleness that almost made him sigh with longing.

'Sir Blaise, I would like you to meet Gideon,' she said, breaking through his reverie. 'Gideon, Sir Blaise. He is one of King Randolph's men,' she added, glancing first at the knight and then at Gideon.

It surprised her that the knight was not more forthcoming. He looked as though he had been struck by a thunderbolt and he seemed to be having difficulty finding his voice. She glanced down and noticed that he still held onto Gideon's hand. 'Sir Blaise,' she said, 'Sir Blaise, I think we should go back now.'

'Oh, um . . .' he stammered, letting go of the great paw he had been holding as though it burned him, 'of course, please forgive me, both of you.' He looked from one to the other, yet found his gaze drawn back to Gideon. Oh, my, but he was a handsome fellow. He had to find a way of being alone with him.

Hedra led the two men back through the gardens and into the castle. Without hesitating she took them up to her apartment where she rang for a servant and ordered food and wine for all of them.

'Please be seated,' she said, indicating a low sofa covered in heavy brocade in shades of red, pink and gold.

She watched with interest as the two men sat down

226

on the sofa beside each other. It was obvious to her now that Sir Blaise was thoroughly taken with Gideon, although Gideon seemed blissfully unaware of the fact. As she watched the two of them chatting amiably, a thought began to take shape in her mind which, at first, she dismissed as totally out of the question. But, as they ate and drank and became more relaxed with each other, she found herself realising that the fates had sent her an opportunity which she could not afford to let slip through her fingers, not if she was to save Satyria.

# Chapter Fourteen

$C$opious amounts of wine mellowed them all and gradually they began to unwind properly. Feeling particularly hedonistic, Hedra slipped off her high boots and asked Gideon if he would massage her feet as she reclined on a sofa opposite him and Sir Blaise – a task which he accepted readily. Throughout the meal their conversation had become more and more relaxed and now she steered it into more intimate waters, making certain that the content succeeded in arousing all three of them, as she recounted tales of Satyrian orgies and other erotic escapades that Lord Gerard had originally entertained her with in the privacy of his bedchamber.

As her words drifted around their heads, Sir Blaise found himself still unable to take his eyes off Gideon. And, as soon as the wonderful creature had taken Lady Hedra's feet between his huge hands, the knight had felt his stomach constrict painfully with longing. There was nothing he desired more right at that moment than to feel those great paws running over his own body, smoothing it and massaging it in exactly the same way as they handled each delicate portion of those tiny feet.

His was a longing that Hedra's acute senses didn't miss and couldn't ignore. She could see the naked desire reflected in his eyes and an aura of wanting seemed to hang around him like a cloak. She knew she would have to make the most of this opportunity, yet had no idea how to broach the subject. What she really needed was to get Gideon alone and, when Sir Blaise happened to fall into a light doze – lulled by the warmth of the fire and the potency of the wine – she seized the opportunity without hesitation.

'Come and sit next to me, Gideon,' she said, patting the seat beside her and wriggling seductively. 'Let us take advantage of this momentary solitude. I am sure there is something we can think of to do to pass the time.'

Noticing the way her lips curved invitingly and her breasts seemed to thrust against the transparent material, he wasted no time and only glanced briefly at the gently snoring form of the knight before rising to his feet and sitting down beside her. His bulk made the seat dip slightly, tipping her eager body into his waiting arms. For a moment or two he simply held her, stroking his hands with familiarity over her shoulders and down her back. He closed his eyes, simply delighting in the re-acquainting himself with her physical geography until she pressed her body against him hard and claimed his mouth with her own. In an instant, it was though time and their clothing simply fell away.

'Oh, how I have longed to hold you like this again, Hedra,' Gideon said hoarsely, his face buried in the enticing softness of her breasts, his strong tongue flicking at one of her nipples. 'I care not that you are promised to another, I want to take you over and over.'

She shivered with delight at his actions and his words. 'Do not be disquieted about my personal arrangements,' she said, anxious to reassure him. 'Lord Gerard is most understanding of my needs. We do not attempt to bind each other, far from it. Be certain, you and I may take our pleasure together as often as we wish and without fear of reprisal.'

Gideon groaned. She was like a dream come true and so were the things she said. To have found a woman

like her in the first place was wonderful. Now, to have
found her again only to discover that she wanted him
as much as he wanted her was beyond belief. It all
seemed so perfect and so simple, yet something in his
inner senses disquieted him, as though he suspected
there was a price to be paid for so much pleasure.

Their need of each other was so great that he took her
almost straightaway. As he knelt on the floor in front of
her, her thighs parted for him readily, displaying all the
charms she had to offer. The rosy folds of her love lips,
the pouting wetness of her sex and the prominent nub
of her pleasure bud all cried out for him to touch them.

'Yes, oh yes, Gideon,' she urged, grinding her body
against his fingers as he plundered the musky depths
of her body and rubbed gently at her pleasure bud,
'take me now, I cannot wait to feel you inside me again.'

He leaned over her to kiss her and, as he did so, she
reached down between their bodies to wrap her fingers
around his phallus. With a fierce surge of pleasure she
was reminded how large he was and pulled her knees
back until they almost grazed her breasts, her breathless
voice urging him yet again to take her.

The instant he lunged forward and felt her tight body
enfold him he cried aloud, waking the dozing knight.
Gideon did not notice what had happened, he was too
intent on the sensation of Hedra's body underneath
him and all around him. In truth, if a tornado had
ripped through the chamber right at that moment he
would not have paid it any heed. He was already too
deeply ensconced in the dark morass of pleasure.

Hedra heard Sir Blaise cough slightly and sensed his
embarrassed movements upon the seat opposite. As
her eyes flickered open she caught his gaze and held it
for a moment until his line of vision dropped deliberately to the sight of Gideon's powerful buttocks clenching and unclenching as he thrust inside her. With little
difficulty she managed to convey her thoughts to him,
underlining them with a slight nod of her head as
though giving him permission to seek his own pleasure.

230

He rose without hesitation and sank to his knees behind Gideon, but then his courage seemed to desert him and he hesitated for a moment. Eventually, with one tremulous hand, he reached out and stroked his fingertips down the length of Gideon's spine, feeling encouraged to explore further as the other man seemed not to notice his attentions.

The knight could not have known that he was fooling himself by his tentative gestures. Gideon had read the content of his mind, and Hedra's, and was well prepared from the outset for the events which were now unfolding; she had apparently forgotten about his gift and thought that she could manipulate him. But he wanted to be used by her; he couldn't think of anything more exciting.

Hedra couldn't see what Sir Blaise was doing but she could sense, by the change in Gideon's movements, that her lover was feeling something. What she couldn't be sure about was whether he would spurn Sir Blaise, or acquiesce. They were thoughts that had little time to ferment. Her arousal was mounting by degrees, a luscious warmth spreading through her that was spiked with a myriad piquant sensations. On the outside, her arms went around Gideon's shoulders pulling him closer to her, her legs doing likewise. While on the inside she gripped him harder and harder too, milking him of his pleasure gift.

Through the haze of lust that engulfed him as he took Hedra, Gideon became aware of an unfamiliar touch upon his flesh. Tentative, questing fingers touched and stroked him and his first impulse was to protest. He knew only too well who it must be and yet he couldn't deny the added frisson of excitement that came from knowing a third party had chosen to become involved in their pleasure-making. If he had the option, he would have preferred a second woman but Sir Blaise's touch was not unpleasant by any means and his body reacted to it as it would to a maiden's caress. And, just as his pleasure began to peak, he felt the knight's fingers invade the cleft between his buttocks and all was lost. With a loud groan his climax overtook him and the added sensations drove him over the precipice of pleasure.

He did not withdraw from Hedra. His stamina was such that he remained hard inside her even though he had spilt his juice and he continued to thrust gently as she ground her body underneath him. The fingers that had caressed him so hesitantly became bolder, opening him wider and investigating the most secret part of his body with more determination. Gasping from the unaccustomed pleasure, Gideon continued to please his mistress and yet now he felt a different hardness touch him, nudging ever so gently until he relaxed and took the knight inside him fully.

The three of them rocked together in perfect harmony. Hedra felt Gideon's renewed interest and took her pleasure from it, feeling the sensitive flesh around her clitoris being tugged and stimulated by his movements. And Gideon felt a strange fullness that he had never experienced before. It is not unpleasant, he thought, and in the next instant the thrusts became more determined and he felt a powerful heat assail him, his body feeling as though it might explode at any moment.

For Sir Blaise, the pleasure he took in Gideon's body was indescribable. Of course, men's bodies were no mystery to him and yet this great beast of a man was physical perfection beyond his wildest dreams. Every part of him felt so large and so firm, although his body also seemed to cede readily. It was as though Gideon's flesh had been laying dormant for a good long while simply waiting until he awakened it with light kisses and caresses.

All too quickly he felt himself begin the ultimate ride into the dark cavern of desire. Oh, how wonderful it was to be enfolded so warmly and gripped so tightly. He could hardly restrain himself, his own phallus throbbing with an urgency he was sure he had never felt before with any other man. Let the fates hold them both in the grip of eternal pleasure, he thought, it could not be enough for him to love this man but once and once alone.

A little while later all three of them fell apart like petals from a dying flower. Their passions and energy were spent for the time being and all each of them wanted to do was sprawl before the warmth of the fire and bask in the hazy afterglow of pleasure. Gideon lay face down with his head upon Hedra's breast and she toyed with his mane of hair, her fingers lazily entwining with the silken strands. Glancing sideways, she noticed that Sir Blaise looked similarly replete. A smile touched his lips as he lay on his back, one hand behind his head, the other resting protectively on Gideon's buttocks.

She wondered if this was the right time to speak and yet she knew there would never be a better one.

'Sir Blaise,' she said softly, her voice hardly more than a low murmur.

He turned his head to look at her, his expression dreamy. 'I know what you want to ask me, my lady,' he said, 'and the answer is yes.' She felt her heart leap inside her chest with joy as he continued, 'I would never have thought it possible that I could willingly renounce my king and country for the service of another but that is the case. I have never felt such happiness or such rightness of feeling as I experienced here today. You have my unconditional allegiance, mistress. I pledge myself to you and to your kingdom for the rest of my days.'

Blinking back a tear at his eloquent speech, Hedra smiled at him. 'You do not know what this means to me, what it will mean to all Satyrians,' she said. 'You are truly a heroic man, sir. Make no mistake about that.'

To her surprise he shook his head. 'I would say this man here is the true hero,' he said, glancing at Gideon and caressing his back lightly. 'If it were not for the way he gave his body so willingly I would have been as intractable as the ocean's tides.'

They talked for a little while then gradually drifted off into a light slumber. Hedra was the first to rouse herself and when she did she decided to leave the two men alone for a while and enjoy a luxurious soak in the bathtub.

Jade, naturally, was overjoyed when her mistress told her the good news. Although her expression immediately sobered as a thought occurred to her.

'What is it, Jade?' Hedra said, looking concerned. 'You look as though a shadow has crossed your soul.'

'Indeed it has, mistress, in a way,' she said. Picking up a long sponge she began to soap Hedra's shoulders thoroughly. 'I suddenly wondered at King Randolph's reaction when he gets word of this.' She added, 'I dare say he will be beside himself with rage. I am certain he did not intend that any good should come of his challenge. He expected you to fail.'

Hedra nodded. 'I realise that too, Jade,' she said, sighing deeply, 'but what can I do? He set me a challenge and I met it head on. I just hope that he is an honourable rogue.'

Despite her concern, Jade laughed. 'An honourable rogue,' she said. 'That is like saying there could be such a thing as a cool-tempered dragon.'

'And who might that be?'

A voice sounded in the doorway making them both jump. Jade and Hedra glanced around and saw that it was Lord Gerard. Immediately, Hedra's face lit up and she urged him to come closer.

'Is your work all finished for the day, my lord?' she asked softly, hope radiating in her eyes.

He nodded. 'Indeed it is and I might ask the same of you,' he said, smiling down at her.

To Jade's surprise he winked broadly and waved her away. Dropping to his haunches beside the bathtub he picked up the sponge and started to wash Hedra himself, sliding the foamy sponge over her shoulders and down her arms. Groaning with pleasure she lay back in the tub and arched her back, encouraging him to soap her breasts over and over, stimulating her circulation until they glistened pinkly and the nipples had hardened into tight little buds.

'Oh, that feels so, so good, master,' she said in a breathy voice, 'and you will be so pleased to hear my news.'

He stopped washing her at once, much to her chagrin. 'What news?' he said.

'The best possible kind,' she replied, laughing lightly. 'Jade and I were just discussing it. It seems our friend, King Randolph, appears to have lost his challenge. His third and last knight succumbed to me this very day. You now have three new Decadent Knights to join your troops.'

She smiled broadly as Lord Gerard threw back his head and laughed aloud. 'By the mystics, Hedra, you are a wonderful woman!' he cried. Thrusting his leather-clad arms into the foamy water he scooped her up in his arms and carried her to his bedchamber.

'I want to know everything,' he said, dropping her onto the bed and spreading her legs wide.

As he began to pleasure her, he insisted that she tell him every last detail and as soon as she was finished he spanked her soundly for her 'bad' behaviour.

'I'll swear, Hedra,' he said, entering her for a second time, 'you are without equal.'

'And so are you, my lord,' she said softly, pulling him down until his lips touched hers, 'and so are you.'

Later, when she had been well and truly satisfied by her lord and master and was dressed in a costume that comprised little more than clusters of long, black leather claws tipped with golden talons that wound about her flesh and gripped it, she summoned Gideon to the throne room for a private consultation before the banquet commenced.

'You will stay for the revelling, won't you?' she said, stroking his long mane of hair as he sat at her feet. 'If it were not for you, Satyria would not have been saved this day.'

Gideon smiled at her modesty. 'It is you we all have to thank, my lady,' he said softly. 'You are the one who took up King Randolph's challenge and met it so wonderfully. From what I hear, his three knights adore and revere you and that goes for the rest of the inhabitants of Satyria by all accounts. You are not only the people's heroine, you are their saviour.'

For the first time in a long while, Hedra found her cheeks suffused by warmth and dropped her gaze in embarrassment. 'I do not seek that kind of adulation,' she said softly. 'I merely did my duty, nothing more.'

'And that is what makes you so special, dear Hedra,' he said, reaching up with one great hand and cupping her chin gently. 'You are totally without vanity.'

She coughed lightly and urged him to cease with his flattery. Instead she asked after Vanora. 'How is she – do you still have her in your safekeeping?'

To her relief, Gideon nodded. 'Of course, she is something you hold dear. How could you ever doubt that I would guard her with my life?' he said.

'Then if you do not mind, I shall send a stable-hand to collect her,' she said. 'I have missed her greatly and ordinary horses are no substitute for a unicorn.'

'I realise that,' he said, smiling, 'but why not come and collect her yourself – you could spend the darkfall with me and ride back the following day?'

Feeling a *frisson* of excitement course through her, Hedra clapped her hands in delight. 'What a perfectly wonderful idea,' she said and then leaned forward and lowered her voice to a conspiratorial tone. 'I do believe, Gideon, that we may find ourselves enjoying each other on quite a regular basis. I am certain that in future I shall often have pressing business that takes me within the vicinity of your cottage.'

He smiled broadly at her audacity and her lusty

nature. 'You are a wanton hussy, Hedra,' he said, and added, 'please promise me you will never change.'

'Not as long as I have breath in my body,' she replied, stroking her hands over her breasts and down her torso as she inhaled deeply, then exhaled with obvious satisfaction.

Gideon was smiling as he shook his head in wonder at her attitude and her behaviour. There would never be another woman like Hedra, he thought, and he felt privileged to know her.

At that moment they were disturbed by the loud summoning to the evenfall banquet. It was to be a night of feasting and of revelling. The royal court, and indeed all the land, had a lot to celebrate that day. Despite her 'duties', Hedra had still found the time to give special instructions for the forthcoming celebration and delighted in the prospect of witnessing the expression on everyone's faces, Clansmen, Watchers and Decadent Knights alike, as they filed into the great banqueting hall.

Everyone without exception had been invited to the feast, entailing the use of four long tables set at right angles to each other so that they formed a square. On Hedra's instructions each table was covered with heavy damask cloths in a deep purple and set with the finest jewel-encrusted gold platters, cutlery and goblets which would, in itself, be a breathtaking display. But she had further amusement up her sleeve and had given special instructions, which she was pleased to see had been followed to the letter.

Along the length of each table lay four girls, the prettiest young maidens that ever graced the royal court apart, perhaps, from Hedra herself and the lovely Bella who had since become the permanent companion of Sir Drago. It was not enough that each one of the girls was comely in her own right. To the servants' great amusement and titillation, Hedra had ordered that the girls be decorated with tasty morsels of food: their stomachs piled high with sweetmeats, their breasts garlanded with berries and other soft fruits, and their fleeces concealed by bunches of sweet, juicy grapes.

That would delight one half of the court, she reasoned, but there were still the others to be considered and so she had arranged for the most handsome young men from the local towns and villages to be brought to the castle. Once there they had been bathed and then their hard, muscular bodies gilded and set upon plinths and columns strategically placed around the banqueting hall as living statues.

She laughed aloud with delight when she entered the banqueting hall and surveyed the scene. 'I knew they would make a fine display,' she said, walking slowly around the huge square of tables and checking everything was as it should be, 'you have done well.' She directed her compliments at the kitchen staff who had prepared the whole feast, knowing that in the kitchens great platters of roasted meats and vegetables awaited the diners.

It was with a feeling of great pride and pleasure that she walked back into the throne room and took her rightful place beside Lord Gerard who now awaited her. He was looking a little more rested than when she had last seen him and as handsome as ever in his usual top to toe garb of black leather.

'The banquet awaits, my lord,' she said, murmuring to him under her voice before announcing it more loudly to the gathered throng of courtiers who were still waiting for their Lord and Lady before they entered the banqueting room.

He stood up and offered her his arm in a gallant gesture that she accepted readily and with a smile that was uncharacteristically demure. Glancing down at her, he noticed how her long eyelashes cast shadows over her cheeks, the modest demeanour belied by her outrageous costume – a study in pure eroticism.

'Why is it my hunger always seems to desert me when I am with you, Hedra?' he murmured darkly as they walked together, leading a group of Watchers and

Clansmen into the banqueting hall. 'My thoughts of food always seem to vanish whenever I set eyes on you. They suddenly seem so inconsequential in the face of such wanton beauty.'

Just as she was about to say something witty in reply they reached the doorway and her thoughts were silenced by a gasp of surprise that initially burst from Lord Gerard's lips and echoed throughout the gathered throng as they stared in amazement at the exquisite banqueting scene.

'I do not need to ask if this is your work, Hedra,' he said.

She nodded. 'I thought it might entertain you, master,' she said, 'and we have due cause to celebrate in a special way.'

'We do indeed,' he concurred.

As they all took their places, the compliments circulated the room in a constant ripple of high and low voices. She had expected some response, of course, but even in her wildest imaginings had not anticipated that so many people would fête her ingenuity. There was not a single bad remark to be made it seemed and for that she was grateful. At last, she felt as though she had truly earned her place as Lady of Satyria.

'You are a funny little thing, Hedra,' Lord Gerard said fondly, when she voiced her thoughts to him. 'You did not need to "earn" anything. I chose you, that is enough.'

'Oh, no,' she said, shaking her head. 'Someone once taught me that respect is not a birthright, it must be earned.' She cast a glance down the table to her left where Gideon had taken a seat between two very lovely Watchers who, it seemed from the expression on their faces, could hardly believe their good fortune.

Lord Gerard reached across the table, plucked a ripe cherry from the nipple of the young maiden in front of them and popped it in Hedra's mouth. She held his fingers between her lips as he did so, sucking the juice from them suggestively and was about to say something

239

else to him when a loud cacophony of sound just outside the banqueting hall made everyone turn their heads to stare at the open doorway.

A moment later the expected but nevertheless unwelcome spectre of King Randolph appeared. He paused in the open doorway for a moment, waiting for the gasps of surprise and horror to subside, and then marched up to the head of the tables where Lady Hedra and Lord Gerard sat.

At the sight of him, Hedra opened her mouth in surprise, releasing Lord Gerard's fingers. 'King Randolph,' she said with a coolness that her lord and master was tempted to applaud, 'I have been expecting you, although a little prior warning would not have gone amiss. We are in the middle of a banquet as you can see.' She waved her hand around and spoke in a falsely airy tone, adding, 'but as you are here, perhaps you and your "men" would care to join us.' She glared hard at his Bisextrix who shielded him either side, her words deliberately insulting.

To her chagrin, King Randolph merely threw back his head and laughed. 'I'll swear you are one of the most entertaining women I have ever met,' he said, wiping his eyes with the back of his hand. 'How could I possibly refuse such a charming invitation?'

Feeling insulted and yet at the same time intrigued by his careless attitude, she stared at him openmouthed. He stood with his powerful legs astride, his hands on hips, his great body clothed in light-brown sueded leather trimmed with the fur of the white wolf. The fur trim was almost indistinguishable from the whiteness of his hair and beard and once again she found herself wondering how someone could be so handsome and yet so loathsome at the same time.

She hated the way he made her feel. It disquieted her. Lord Gerard was her lord and master, as well as her lover for all eternity and yet this . . . this . . . she couldn't even think of words that adequately described him as the word *man* would hardly suffice, set her senses reeling in a way that she couldn't control. She hated him for it and despised herself.

'You must already know I have met your challenge and won, my liege,' she said, 'or you would not be here.'

He nodded but did not smile. 'That is true. I have to hand it to you, wench, I did not expect to be standing next to the victor. It is usually I who wins any contest.'

'I suspected that much,' Hedra said sagely, nodding her head as a servant offered to pour more wine for all of them, 'but it is just something you will have to come to terms with I am afraid.' She smiled sweetly and was gratified to note that a flicker of annoyance crossed his implacable expression for just a moment.

Ignoring the king's agitation, she struck a gong that stood beside her, as the signal to the kitchen staff to bring forth the food. Gasps of pleasure and approval swept the room and, when she glanced back in his direction, she realised that King Randolph was staring at her. For a moment she wavered, unsure whether to glare or smile, and in the end she pursed her lips slightly and nodded her head just once.

At that moment a servant boy stepped forth; he was holding a chair and wondering whether the king would really be staying to dine or not. He was relieved when his mistress told him to move the gong and place the chair beside her instead. Then she asked him to bring two more chairs for the Bisextrix.

King Randolph sat down heavily beside her, discarding his fur cloak and handing it casually to another servant who hovered close to them in case he was needed. 'I thank you for your hospitality, my lady,' he said, nodding his acceptance as other servants rushed forth with platters of food and began to pile his plate high. 'We have travelled a good distance and are famished.'

She glanced at him deliberately. His stalwart frame hardly looked as though it was starved of nourishment.

Laughing lightly, she said so, to which he also laughed in reply.

'You have no care what you say to anyone, do you, my lady?' he said. 'Although I'll wager, if it hasn't already, such a trait will land you in trouble one of these fine days.'

Deciding his reproving comment did not merit a reply she simply picked up a leg of duckling from her plate and bit into it, enjoying the constrasting textures of the crunchy skin and succulent meat beneath.

As if this were a signal, all the courtiers began to eat and chatter amongst themselves. Under such convivial circumstances it was not difficult for everyone to relax, even though King Randolph was in their presence. And he made no attempt to prove difficult or spoil their fun in any way. Instead, he turned his own attention to the food which he ate heartily and complimented extravagantly.

Despite her earlier unease, Hedra found that she was actually starting to enjoy his company. His conversation – although crude at times and with certain references to acts of barbarism that made her wince – was entertaining, and she was surprised to find herself laughing along with some of the remarks he made.

Throughout the meal, Lord Gerard remained strangely subdued. Although he spoke with some of the knights and courtiers nearest to him, he couldn't help stopping every so often to listen into the conversation between Hedra and the King. He sensed a growing comradeship between them that unsettled him. And he was further discomfited to notice that, from time to time, King Randolph would touch Hedra: placing a hand lightly upon her arm, or shoulder, or moving a stray tendril of her hair away from her face as they talked. He didn't like it and felt tempted to tell her so but he knew that she would not thank him and he would also risk angering the king who had already proclaimed his acceptance of the Peace Accord that had been drawn up.

Gradually the diners began to push their plates away, declaring that although it was the best food they had ever tasted, they had eaten their fill. And they began to call for the entertainment to start. Of course, there were the usual troops of acrobats, musicians and singers but on this occasion there was also a group of eight dancers, four male and four female, who delighted the courtiers by performing dances of an increasingly erotic nature, the finale being an orgiastic scene that had everyone reaching urgently for the people nearest to them.

'Well, I must say,' King Randolph remarked, looking around at the copulating bodies in frank amazement, 'you certainly know how to keep your subjects happy.' He directed his comment at Sir Gerard but he declined the praise.

'This is all Hedra's work,' he said modestly. 'It seems there is no limit to her imagination, or sensuality.' He put his arm protectively around her shoulders and smiled at her.

She returned his smile openly and then glanced at the king whose face bore a strange expression that she had not seen before.

'What would I have to do to win your favours?' he asked her, leaning forward suddenly. 'How many caskets of jewels would it take?'

Lord Gerard cut in before she had a chance to answer him, although in truth she had been rendered speechless by his unexpected question.

'There will be no talk of that nature here, my liege,' he said in a carefully controlled voice. 'Hedra is not in the habit of doling out her favours to every scoundrel who happens along.'

Ignoring the insult, King Randolph merely laughed and switched his attention back to Hedra. 'I asked you a question, my lady,' he said more softly. 'How much?'

This time she managed to find her voice, although it was with some difficulty as a tight knot seemed to be turning her stomach inside out and a similar one blocked her throat. 'I am already perfectly happy; no amount of wealth could entice me.'

Pausing for only a moment, the king leant even closer to her so that his hot breath caressed her naked breasts, forcing her to look back at him. Lowering his voice even further he growled, 'If I cannot buy what I want, I generally steal it. Make no mistake, my dear Lady Hedra, I shall have you sooner or later. When you least expect it, I shall come back here and take you, with or without your consent.'

Lord Gerard was on his feet in an instant and so was King Randolph. With only the stunned figure of Hedra separating them the two men faced each other, spitting fire and flames like angry dragons.

'Please . . . do not fight over me,' she said faintly but the men ignored her. 'I said stop!' she cried, jumping to her feet.

In that instant, an ominous hush fell over the room and some of the Decadent Knights reached for their swords but Lord Gerard instructed everyone to calm down and go back to what they were doing.

'I think we should complete our business away from here, King Randolph,' he said firmly. 'Let us sign the Peace Accord and have done with it.' He took a scroll from the nervous hands of a servant who had been standing patiently behind his chair throughout the entire banquet, just waiting for this moment.

To everyone's relief the king nodded and the two men walked stiffly towards the door to the ante-chamber accompanied by two Decadent Knights and the king's Bisextrix.

'I do not want you to come, Hedra,' Lord Gerard said as she automatically started to follow them. His voice was firm but soft as he added, 'Please, wait for me here or in my apartment.'

As soon as the door closed behind them, the whole room seemed to come back to life but for Hedra the party was over. Pausing only to speak briefly with one of the servants she bade goodnight to the gathering and made her way to Lord Gerard's bedchamber.

It was quite some time later when the door opened and he entered, looking uncommonly tired and dejected.

'Is the deed done, my lord?' she said, sitting up suddenly so that the sheet fell away from her naked body and pooled around her waist.

Despite his weariness, Lord Gerard smiled warmly. The sight of Hedra never ceased to restore his spirits and fill him with renewed optimism. 'It is,' he said, nodding. 'The Peace Accord between our kingdoms is now signed. Although King Randolph was not best pleased about the outcome, he made no bones about it.'

Laughing lightly she reached out her arms to him. 'Then come here and let me sooth you, master,' she said seductively. 'It is over now. Let us not refer to such matters again lest they spoil our fun.' Her eyes twinkled with barely disguised mischief.

'By the mystics, Hedra,' he said, stripping off his clothes with one hand as he cupped her chin with the other, 'you are the most incorrigible woman I have ever met.'

She threw back the covers and spread her legs invitingly. 'Do you not mean insatiable, master?' she said softly.

He watched as her hands dipped between her parted thighs and she opened herself up to him completely, her fingers delicately parting fold upon fold of her luscious flesh until he fancied he could almost see right inside her.

Just for a moment he found himself paralysed, transfixed by the very sight of her wanton body and by the depths of his feelings. Outside the castle he could hear the sound of the drawbridge being raised and imagined he could hear retreating hoof beats. King Randolph was gone from their lives and peace restored. But for how long, he wondered? That loathsome man had never been known to make a threat that he did not keep and, even as they signed the Peace Accord, he had made it crystal clear how much he wanted Hedra for his own and repeated his threat.

As long as I have breath in my body I shall not let him take her, Lord Gerard vowed silently, climbing onto the high bed and sliding his naked body alongside hers. All at once she wrapped herself around him, holding him tightly and pressing her hot flesh against him as she panted with desire. Her obvious excitement for him made him groan aloud and he allowed his hands to roam her willing flesh, losing himself in the silky texture of her skin. It was a constant delight to him the way she moaned and squirmed under his touch and the way she caressed him.

'Let us make our pleasure, master,' she said, guiding him inside her, 'let us enjoy the most exquisite indulgence now and for the rest of our lives.'

He did not disappoint her, his hardness sinking into her perfumed warmth with a sense of relief that came from wanting her so much. As he thrust gently he gazed down at her. The fire that burned warmly in the grate cast a rosy glow over her pale flesh and turned her violet hair to a rainbow that fanned out across the pillow. Her lips were ruby red and parted slightly, the soft pink tip of her tongue just appearing between pearly teeth. And her grey eyes grew even more dusky as her passion mounted.

She smiled dreamily. Urgent feelings were beginning to overtake her, driving away all ability to speak but she clutched at him with her hands and thighs and inner body so that he could be certain she felt the impact of his words. There was so much she wanted to tell him, so many words of sensuality and desire she harboured inside her still and yet it was not the moment to speak further. Her hips bucked beneath him, drawing out every ounce of pleasure, the power of her zenith spasming around him.

'You are so beautiful, Hedra,' he said softly, bending his head so that his mouth moved tantalisingly against her ear, 'so, so beautiful.' And then he shuddered and spilt his pleasure gift inside her.

Some time later, Hedra and Lord Gerard began to rediscover each other yet again, with such wonder and passion it was as though they had never come together before. And by this time, the whole castle was heaving and groaning under the onslaught of unrestrained eroticism released by all its inhabitants without exception – from courtiers to servants both old and young.

Shadowy rooms and corners played host to lust, the thick stone walls absorbing a thousand gasps and moans of voluptuousness. And further afield, throughout the kingdom known as Satyria, men and women succumed to every one of their carnal desires with vigorous abandon and took their pleasure in one another – white thighs parting, hard phalluses thrusting, and tight buttocks clenching, or reddening under a smacking palm.

It was true that Satyria was, perhaps, not the most moral of all the Fantastic Lands. But all the subjects there were true to themselves and to their desires. And therein, they believed, lay the secret to happiness for all eternity.

Hedra was happy and believed she had everything she wanted. Yet on the odd occasion, usually when she was without the company of Lord Gerard, she felt a little wistful. Part of her had been lost forever; the protected, innocent part. And from time to time she allowed her mind to dwell on her childhood and to wonder how her father fared.

She had heard from travelling minstrels that he was well and that the plague had not touched him. And, thanks to her agreement with King Randolph, Parsimonia was now spared from any further threat and its people were apparently returning home in droves. A tiny part of her envied them. Her birthplace seemed very distant and not just in the physical sense. If she was being honest with herself, she would admit that Satyria was sometimes a little too good to be true and she longed for the chance to speak with her father face to face again. It would be a relief to be someone's little girl once more and take a rest from being the fearless, whip-wielding lady of Satyria.

Although she longed for it to happen, when the news came that her father was on his way to the castle and, indeed, was only half a sun away, Hedra flew into an immediate panic and began to dread his arrival. Her first task was to give the servants their instructions. Then she summoned Jade to her bedchamber and immediately began to vent all her concerns upon the tiny Kelf.

'What am I going to do, Jade?' Hedra asked, flinging costume after costume onto the bed. 'There is nothing here that protects my modesty even in the slightest. My father will take one look at me and fall into breathless repose.' She held up a black pigskin corset in one hand and a costume comprised of only a few leather bands in the other. 'In Parsimonia, even the horses wear more adornment than this,' she concluded.

Jade smothered a smile and spoke in a calm, placating tone. 'I have already anticipated such a dilemma and have sent a servant to borrow a gown from one of the Watchers. You have no need to distress yourself, Mistress.'

Hedra stared at her attendant for a moment and then relaxed visibly. Her tense shoulders suddenly dropped and the frown was instantly erased from her face. 'What would I do without you, Jade?' she said softly.

Jade merely smiled serenely as always and suggested a relaxing bath and massage, to which Hedra readily agreed. And it was just a short while later that a servant lad appeared with a voluminous gown in his arms; the heavy jewel-encrusted velvet almost too heavy for his slight frame to bear.

Hedra was still relaxing in the deep marble tub when he arrived, and she urged him to come closer.

'Hold up the gown and let me see it properly,' she commanded.

Trying to hide his nervousness at being so close to his beloved Lady Hedra in such intimate surroundings, the servant stepped forward and, with the help of Jade, held the gown up between them for his mistress to see. He blushed deeply as she sat up straighter in the bath and leaned over the edge to view the rich amethyst velvet robe that was styled modestly around the bodice and fell to the floor in generous folds.

As she leaned forward, Hedra felt her naked breasts flatten against the cold marble tiling. Glancing away from the dress to the servant boy's face, she noticed how wide his eyes were and how they could not help straying to her wet body. A wicked smile touched her lips.

'Jade, would you take the dress and check it for any imperfections and then press and perfume it before I put it on?' she asked.

The Kelf nodded instantly. 'Of course, Mistress,' she said, 'but do not hurry your bath. There is ample time.'

Hedra smiled. 'Oh, I had no intention of hurrying,' she murmured.

As Jade turned to leave, so did the servant, but Hedra called out to him.

'Stay, boy,' she commanded. And then, in a softer voice, added, 'You look a little hot and bothered. Why not indulge yourself in a refreshing bath? I do not mind.' She smiled, reclined in the bath and stretched voluptuously, spreading her legs.

The boy hesitated for only a moment while the door closed behind Jade, before taking full advantage of the rare privilege of being left all alone with his mistress.

Hedra was seated on her throne, looking as regal and as calm as possible as she awaited her father's arrival. The servant boy had been just what she needed to provide a welcome diversion from her concerns, and had not done too badly servicing her ever-hungry body, either. She was still smiling at the recollection when Lord Gerard arrived.

'You look like the cat that has just ripped a field mouse from ear to ear,' he joked, kissing her lightly on the cheek before taking his rightful place beside her on his own throne.

'My Lord, you are so disgusting,' she said, her lips forming a slight moue. 'I believe the correct term is "the cat that got the cream".'

He grinned wickedly and stretched his long, leather-clad legs out in front of him. 'I prefer my version,' he replied.

She was prevented from making any further observations by the sound of a slight commotion just outside the throne room. In the next instant, the tall wooden doors were flung open by two Clansmen and Hedra felt her stomach clench in anticipation of the first sight of her father after such a long separation. A moment later, her heart surged. He looked no different to when she had last seen him. Except, perhaps, he now seemed a good deal happier.

'Father!' she cried.

Forgetting all her good intentions to appear grown up and regal, she was on her feet in a flash and running into his outstetched arms. His soft white beard caressed her cheek as they held each other tightly, their salty tears mingling.

'My liege, it is good to meet you,' Gerard said, his voice soft but firm enough to interrupt the reunion.

Hedra released her father and took his hand instead to lead him up to the throne where Lord Gerard was seated.

'May I present Lord Gerard of Satyria,' she said, smiling firstly at her father and then at her lord and master. 'Lord Gerard, permit me to introduce my father, King Hector of Parsimonia.'

The two men inclined their heads in a semi-bow to each other and then shook hands.

'I wish I could say that my daughter has told me a lot

about you, Lord Gerard,' King Hector said. 'It seems odd to meet you now, after you are both already wedded.'

'Oh, but we are not – ' Hedra began, but Gerard interrupted her smoothly.

'You can be certain, my liege, that Hedra has not stopped singing your praises from the moment she arrived at the castle,' Lord Gerard said. 'But here is not the right place to talk.' He rose to his feet and offered his arm to Hedra. 'Come; a banquet is prepared. Let us make our proper acquaintance over a good meal and seal our friendship with a goblet or two of wine.'

'You talk like a king yourself, my lord,' King Hector joked, much to Hedra's amazement. 'I would be honoured to dine with you.'

Hedra glanced from one man to the other and slipped a hand through each proffered arm. Had she ever dreamed that one day she would walk between her father and her lover and feel so well loved by both? she mused, with an inward sigh of happiness. No, she had not. But what bliss the reality was. What perfect and utter bliss.

## NO LADY
Saskia Hope

30-year-old Kate dumps her boyfriend, walks out of her job and sets off in search of sexual adventure. Set against the rugged terrain of the Pyrenees, the love-making is as rough as the landscape.

ISBN 0 352 32857 6

## WEB OF DESIRE
Sophie Danson

High-flying executive Marcie is gradually drawn away from the normality of her married life. Strange messages begin to appear on her computer, summoning her to sinister and fetishistic sexual liaisons.

ISBN 0 352 32856 8

## BLUE HOTEL
Cherri Pickford

Hotelier Ramon can't understand why best-selling author Floy Pennington has come to stay at his quiet hotel. Her exhibitionist tendencies are driving him crazy, as are her increasingly wanton encounters with the hotel's other guests.

ISBN 0 352 32858 4

## CASSANDRA'S CONFLICT
Fredrica Alleyn

Behind the respectable facade of a house in present-day Hampstead lies a world of decadent indulgence and darkly bizarre eroticism. A sternly attractive Baron and his beautiful but cruel wife are playing games with the young Cassandra.

ISBN 0 352 32859 2

## THE CAPTIVE FLESH
Cleo Cordell

Marietta and Claudine, French aristocrats saved from pirates, learn that their invitation to stay at the opulent Algerian mansion of their rescuer, Kasim, requires something in return; their complete surrender to the ecstasy of pleasure in pain.

ISBN 0 352 32872 X

## PLEASURE HUNT
### Sophie Danson

Sexual adventurer Olympia Deschamps is determined to become a member of the Légion D'Amour – the most exclusive society of French libertines.

ISBN 0 352 32880 0

## BLACK ORCHID
### Roxanne Carr

The Black Orchid is a women's health club which provides a specialised service for its high-powered clients; women who don't have the time to spend building complex relationships, but who enjoy the pleasures of the flesh.

ISBN 0 352 32888 6

## ODALISQUE
### Fleur Reynolds

A tale of family intrigue and depravity set against the glittering backdrop of the designer set. This facade of respectability conceals a reality of bitter rivalry and unnatural love.

ISBN 0 352 32887 8

## OUTLAW LOVER
### Saskia Hope

Fee Cambridge lives in an upper level deluxe pleasuredome of technologically advanced comfort. Bored with her predictable husband and pampered lifestyle, Fee ventures into the wild side of town, finding an outlaw who becomes her lover.

ISBN 0 352 32909 2

## THE SENSES BEJEWELLED
### Cleo Cordell

Willing captives Marietta and Claudine are settling into life at Kasim's harem. But 18th century Algeria can be a hostile place. When the women are kidnapped by Kasim's sworn enemy, they face indignities that will test the boundaries of erotic experience. This is the sequel to *The Captive Flesh*.

ISBN 0 352 32904 1

## GEMINI HEAT
### Portia Da Costa

As the metropolis sizzles in freak early summer temperatures, twin sisters Deana and Delia find themselves cooking up a heatwave of their own. Jackson de Guile, master of power dynamics and wealthy connoisseur of fine things, draws them both into a web of luxuriously decadent debauchery.

ISBN 0 352 32912 2

## VIRTUOSO
### Katrina Vincenzi

Mika and Serena, darlings of classical music's jet-set, inhabit a world of secluded passion. The reason? Since Mika's tragic accident which put a stop to his meteoric rise to fame as a solo violinist, he cannot face the world, and together they lead a decadent, reclusive existence.

ISBN 0 352 32907 6

## MOON OF DESIRE
### Sophie Danson

When Soraya Chilton is posted to the ancient and mysterious city of Ragzburg on a mission for the Foreign Office, strange things begin to happen to her. Wild, sexual urges overwhelm her at the coming of each full moon.

ISBN 0 352 32911 4

## FIONA'S FATE
### Fredrica Alleyn

When Fiona Sheldon is kidnapped by the infamous Trimarchi brothers, along with her friend Bethany, she finds herself acting in ways her husband Duncan would be shocked by. Alessandro Trimarchi makes full use of this opportunity to discover the true extent of Fiona's suppressed, but powerful, sexuality.

ISBN 0 352 32913 0

## HANDMAIDEN OF PALMYRA
### Fleur Reynolds

3rd century Palmyra: a lush oasis in the Syrian desert. The beautiful and fiercely independent Samoya takes her place in the temple of Antioch as an apprentice priestess. Decadent bachelor Prince Alif has other plans for her and sends his scheming sister to bring her to his Bacchanalian wedding feast.

ISBN 0 352 32919 X

## OUTLAW FANTASY
### Saskia Hope

On the outer reaches of the 21st century metropolis the Amazenes are on the prowl; fierce warrior women who have some unfinished business with Fee Cambridge's pirate lover. This is the sequel to *Outlaw Lover*.

ISBN 0 352 32920 3

## THE SILKEN CAGE
### Sophie Danson

When university lecturer Maria Treharne inherits her aunt's mansion in Cornwall, she finds herself the subject of strange and unexpected attention. Using the craft of goddess worship and sexual magnetism, Maria finds allies and foes in this savage and beautiful landscape.

ISBN 0 352 32928 9

## RIVER OF SECRETS
### Saskia Hope & Georgia Angelis

Intrepid female reporter Sydney Johnson takes over someone else's assignment up the Amazon river. Sydney soon realises this mission to find a lost Inca city has a hidden agenda. Everyone is behaving so strangely, so sexually, and the tropical humidity is reaching fever pitch.

ISBN 0 352 32925 4

## VELVET CLAWS
### Cleo Cordell

It's the 19th century; a time of exploration and discovery and young, spirited Gwendoline Farnshawe is determined not to be left behind in the parlour when the handsome and celebrated anthropologist, Jonathan Kimberton, is planning his latest expedition to Africa.

ISBN 0 352 32926 2

## THE GIFT OF SHAME
### Sarah Hope-Walker

Helen is a woman with extreme fantasies. When she meets Jeffrey – a cultured wealthy stranger – at a party, they soon become partners in obsession. Now nothing is impossible for her, no fantasy beyond his imagination or their mutual exploration.

ISBN 0 352 32935 1

## SUMMER OF ENLIGHTENMENT
### Cheryl Mildenhall

Karin's new-found freedom is getting her into all sorts of trouble. The enigmatic Nicolai has been showing interest in her since their chance meeting in a cafe. But he's the husband of a valued friend and is trying to embroil her in the sexual tension he thrives on.

ISBN 0 352 32937 8

## A BOUQUET OF BLACK ORCHIDS
### Roxanne Carr

The exclusive Black Orchid health spa has provided Maggie with a new social life and a new career, where giving and receiving pleasure of the most sophisticated nature takes top priority. But her loyalty to the club is being tested by the presence of Tourell; a powerful man who makes her an offer she finds difficult to refuse.

ISBN 0 352 32939 4

## JULIET RISING
### Cleo Cordell

At Madame Nicol's exclusive but strict 18th-century academy for young ladies, the bright and wilful Juliet is learning the art of courting the affections of young noblemen.

ISBN 0 352 32938 6

## DEBORAH'S DISCOVERY
### Fredrica Alleyn

Deborah Woods is trying to change her life. Having just ended her long-term relationship and handed in her notice at work, she is ready for a little adventure. Meeting American oil magnate John Pavin III throws her world into even more confusion as he invites her to stay at his luxurious renovated castle in Scotland. But what looked like being a romantic holiday soon turns into a test of sexual bravery.

ISBN 0 352 32945 9

## THE TUTOR
### Portia Da Costa

Like minded libertines reap the rewards of their desire in this story of the sexual initiation of a beautiful young man. Rosalind Howard takes a post as personal librarian to a husband and wife, both unashamed sensualists keen to engage her into their decadent scenarios.

ISBN 0 352 32946 7

## THE HOUSE IN NEW ORLEANS
### Fleur Reynolds

When she inherits her family home in the fashionable Garden district of New Orleans, Ottilie Duvier discovers it has been leased to the notorious Helmut von Straffen; a debauched German count famous for his decadent Mardi Gras parties. Determined to oust him from the property, she soon realises that not all dangerous animals live in the swamp!

ISBN 0 352 32951 3

## ELENA'S CONQUEST
### Lisette Allen

It's summer – 1070AD – and the gentle Elena is gathering herbs in the garden of the convent where she leads a peaceful, but uneventful, life. When Norman soldiers besiege the convent, they take Elena captive and present her to the dark and masterful Lord Aimery to satisfy his savage desire for Saxon women.

ISBN 0 352 32950 5

## CASSANDRA'S CHATEAU
### Fredrica Alleyn

Cassandra has been living with the dominant and perverse Baron von Ritter for eighteen months when their already bizarre relationship takes an unexpected turn. The arrival of a naive female visitor at the chateau provides the Baron with a new opportunity to indulge his fancy for playing darkly erotic games with strangers.

ISBN 0 352 32955 6

## WICKED WORK
### Pamela Kyle

At twenty-eight, Suzie Carlton is at the height of her journalistic career. She has status, money and power. What she doesn't have is a masterful partner who will allow her to realise the true extent of her fantasies. How will she reconcile the demands of her job with her sexual needs?

ISBN 0 352 32958 0

# DREAM LOVER
## Katrina Vincenzi

Icily controlled Gemma is a dedicated film producer, immersed in her latest production – a darkly Gothic vampire movie. But after a visit to Brittany, where she encounters a mystery lover, a disquieting feeling continues to haunt her. Compelled to discover the identity of the man who ravished her, she becomes entangled in a mystifying erotic odyssey.

ISBN 0 352 32956 4

# PATH OF THE TIGER
## Cleo Cordell

India, in the early days of the Raj. Amy Spencer is looking for an excuse to rebel against the stuffy morals of the British army wives. Luckily, a new friend introduces her to places where other women dare not venture – where Tantric mysteries and the Kama Sutra come alive. Soon she becomes besotted by Ravinder, the exquisitely handsome son of the Maharaja, and finds the pathway to absolute pleasure.

ISBN 0 352 32959 9

# BELLA'S BLADE
## Georgia Angelis

Bella is a fearless, good-looking young woman with an eye for handsome highwaymen and a taste for finery. It's the seventeenth century and Charles II's Merrie England is in full swing. Finding herself to be the object of royal affections, Bella has to choose between living a life of predictable luxury at court or following her desire to sail the high seas – where a certain dashing young captain is waiting for her.

ISBN 0 352 32965 3

# THE DEVIL AND THE DEEP BLUE SEA
## Cheryl Mildenhall

A secluded country house in Norfolk is the setting for this contemporary story of one woman's summer of sexual exploration. Renting a holiday home with her girlfriends, the recently graduated Hillary is pleased to discover that the owner of the country estate is the most fanciable man in the locale. But soon she meets Haldane, the beautifully proportioned Norwegian sailor. Attracted by the allure of two very different men, Hillary is faced with a difficult decision.

ISBN 0 352 32966 1

## WESTERN STAR
### Roxanne Carr

Maribel Harker is heading west, and she's sure grown up since the last wagon train moved out to California. Dan Cutter is the frontiersman that Maribel's father has appointed to take care of his wilful daughter. She is determined to seduce him – he is determined not to give into temptation. Thrown together in a wild and unpredictable landscape, passions are destined to run high!

ISBN 0 352 32969 6

## A PRIVATE COLLECTION
### Sarah Fisher

Behind an overgrown garden by the sea, a crumbling mansion harbours a tantalising secret: a remarkable collection of priceless erotica belonging to a fading society beauty and her inscrutable chauffeur. When writer Francesca Leeman is commissioned to catalogue the collection, she finds herself becoming embroiled in a three-way game of voyeurism and mystery.

ISBN 0 352 32970 X

## NICOLE'S REVENGE
### Lisette Allen

Set against the turmoil of the French Revolution, opera star Nicole Chabrier faces a life of uncertainty now that angry hordes are venting their wrath on the aristocracy. Rescued by a handsome stranger and taken to a deserted palace, Nicole and her insatiable lover, Jacques, seek a reversal of their fortune using charm, sexual magnetism and revenge!

ISBN 0 352 32984 X

## UNFINISHED BUSINESS
### Sarah Hope-Walker

As a financial analyst for a top London bank, Joanne's life is about being in control. But privately, her submissive self cries out to be explored. She has tried to quell her strange desires, but they insist on haunting her. There is only one place where she can realise her desire to be dominated: the *Salon de Fantasie*, run by her enigmatic Parisian friend, Chantal. Soon, the complexities of Joanne's sexuality begin to take over the rest of her life.

ISBN 0 352 32983 1

# CRIMSON BUCCANEER
## Cleo Cordell

Fiery noblewoman Carlotta Mendoza is cheated out of her inheritance by the corrupt officials of Imperial Spain. But help is at hand in the form of a rugged young buccaneer who introduces her to a life of piracy and sexual adventure. Carlotta is determined to make her enemies squirm with shame as she takes her revenge.

ISBN 0 352 32987 4

# LA BASQUAISE
## Angel Strand

The scene is 1920s Biarritz. Oruela is a modern young woman who desires the company of artists, intellectuals and hedonists. Jean is her seemingly devoted lover who will help her to realise her wildest dreams. But when she is accused of murdering her cruel father, Oruela's life is thrown into turmoil. Bizarre characters play games of sexual blackmail against a background of decadence.

ISBN 0 352 329888 2

# THE LURE OF SATYRIA
## Cheryl Mildenhall

Satyria is a mythical land of debauchery and excess: a place where virtuous maidens dare not venture. When Princess Hedra's castle is threatened with invasion, she takes refuge in this land and finds plenty of virile suitors willing to make her feel welcome. When she is captured by the leather-clad King of Satyria, her lascivious talents are really put to the test.

ISBN 0 352 32994 7

# THE DEVIL INSIDE
## Portia Da Costa

One morning, the usually conventional Alexa Lavelle wakes up with a dramatically increased libido and the gift of psychic sexual intuition. In order to satisfy strange new desires, she finds herself drawn to an exclusive clinic where an enigmatic female doctor introduces her to some very interesting people. A world of bizarre fetishism and erotic indulgence is about to unfold.

ISBN 0 352 32993 9

BLACK
*lace*

## WE NEED YOUR HELP . . .
*to plan the future of women's erotic fiction –*

### – and no stamp required!

Yours are the only opinions that matter.

Black Lace is the first series of books devoted to erotic fiction by women for women.

We intend to keep providing the best-written, sexiest books you can buy. And we'd appreciate your help and valued opinion of the books so far. Tell us what you want to read.

---

# THE BLACK LACE QUESTIONNAIRE

## SECTION ONE: ABOUT YOU

1.1 Sex (*we presume you are female, but so as not to discriminate*)
Are you?

Male ☐
Female ☐

1.2 Age

under 21 ☐ 21–30 ☐
31–40 ☐ 41–50 ☐
51–60 ☐ over 60 ☐

1.3 At what age did you leave full-time education?

still in education ☐ 16 or younger ☐
17–19 ☐ 20 or older ☐

1 4 Occupation _____

1.5 Annual household income

    under £10,000 ☐     £10–£20,000 ☐
    £20–£30,000 ☐     £30–£40,000 ☐
    over £40,000 ☐

1.6 We are perfectly happy for you to remain anonymous;
    but if you would like to receive information on other
    publications available, please insert your name and
    address

    _____

    _____

    _____

    _____

# SECTION TWO: ABOUT BUYING BLACK LACE BOOKS

2.1 How did you acquire this copy of *The Lure of Satyria*?

    I bought it myself ☐     My partner bought it ☐
    I borrowed/found it ☐

2.2 How did you find out about Black Lace books?

    I saw them in a shop ☐
    I saw them advertised in a magazine ☐
    I saw the London Underground posters ☐
    I read about them in _____
    Other _____

2.3 Please tick the following statements you agree with:

    I would be less embarrassed about buying Black
    Lace books if the cover pictures were less explicit ☐
    I think that in general the pictures on Black
    Lace books are about right ☐
    I think Black Lace cover pictures should be as
    explicit as possible ☐

2.4 Would you read a Black Lace book in a public place – on
    a train for instance?

    Yes ☐     No ☐

## SECTION THREE: ABOUT THIS BLACK LACE BOOK

3.1 Do you think the sex content in this book is:
    Too much ☐    About right ☐
    Not enough ☐

3.2 Do you think the writing style in this book is:
    Too unreal/escapist ☐    About right ☐
    Too down to earth ☐

3.3 Do you think the story in this book is:
    Too complicated ☐    About right ☐
    Too boring/simple ☐

3.4 Do you think the cover of this book is:
    Too explicit ☐    About right ☐
    Not explicit enough ☐

Here's a space for any other comments:

## SECTION FOUR: ABOUT OTHER BLACK LACE BOOKS

4.1 How many Black Lace books have you read? ☐

4.2 If more than one, which one did you prefer?

4.3 Why?

# SECTION FIVE: ABOUT YOUR IDEAL EROTIC NOVEL

We want to publish the books you want to read – so this is your chance to tell us exactly what your ideal erotic novel would be like.

5.1 Using a scale of 1 to 5 (1 = no interest at all, 5 = your ideal), please rate the following possible settings for an erotic novel:

Medieval/barbarian/sword 'n' sorcery ☐
Renaissance/Elizabethan/Restoration ☐
Victorian/Edwardian ☐
1920s & 1930s – the Jazz Age ☐
Present day ☐
Future/Science Fiction ☐

5.2 Using the same scale of 1 to 5, please rate the following themes you may find in an erotic novel:

Submissive male/dominant female ☐
Submissive female/dominant male ☐
Lesbianism ☐
Bondage/fetishism ☐
Romantic love ☐
Experimental sex e.g. anal/watersports/sex toys ☐
Gay male sex ☐
Group sex ☐

Using the same scale of 1 to 5, please rate the following styles in which an erotic novel could be written:

Realistic, down to earth, set in real life ☐
Escapist fantasy, but just about believable ☐
Completely unreal, impressionistic, dreamlike ☐

5.3 Would you prefer your ideal erotic novel to be written from the viewpoint of the main male characters or the main female characters?

Male ☐        Female ☐
Both ☐

5.4 What would your ideal Black Lace heroine be like? Tick as many as you like:

| | | | |
|---|---|---|---|
| Dominant | ☐ | Glamorous | ☐ |
| Extroverted | ☐ | Contemporary | ☐ |
| Independent | ☐ | Bisexual | ☐ |
| Adventurous | ☐ | Naive | ☐ |
| Intellectual | ☐ | Introverted | ☐ |
| Professional | ☐ | Kinky | ☐ |
| Submissive | ☐ | Anything else? | ☐ |
| Ordinary | ☐ | _____ | |

5.5 What would your ideal male lead character be like? Again, tick as many as you like:

| | | | |
|---|---|---|---|
| Rugged | ☐ | | |
| Athletic | ☐ | Caring | ☐ |
| Sophisticated | ☐ | Cruel | ☐ |
| Retiring | ☐ | Debonair | ☐ |
| Outdoor-type | ☐ | Naive | ☐ |
| Executive-type | ☐ | Intellectual | ☐ |
| Ordinary | ☐ | Professional | ☐ |
| Kinky | ☐ | Romantic | ☐ |
| Hunky | ☐ | | |
| Sexually dominant | ☐ | Anything else? | ☐ |
| Sexually submissive | ☐ | _____ | |

5.6 Is there one particular setting or subject matter that your ideal erotic novel would contain?

_____

## SECTION SIX: LAST WORDS

6.1 What do you like best about Black Lace books?

_____

6.2 What do you most dislike about Black Lace books?

_____

6.3 In what way, if any, would you like to change Black Lace covers?

_____

## 6.4 Here's a space for any other comments:

_____
_____
_____
_____
_____

_Thank you for completing this questionnaire. Now tear it out of the book – carefully! – put it in an envelope and send it to:_

**Black Lace**
**FREEPOST**
**London**
**W10 5BR**

_No stamp is required if you are resident in the U.K._